Praise for the Culin

Fortune Cookie

"The mystery's personal this time as Sadie confronts painful memories and makes a surprising discovery in her quest for answers. **A story chock-full of humor and tenderness**—and of course plenty of yummy food. Sadie Hoffmiller is the real San Francisco treat!"

—Jennifer Moore, author of *Becoming Lady Lockwood*

Rocky Road

"Another fabulous installment of the Sadie Hoffmiller series. **The further I got into the story, the more complex it became** . . . definitely a rocky road of a plot!"

—Heather Moore, author of *Heart of the Ocean* and the Timeless Romance anthologies

Baked Alaska

"Sadie is a well-loved character with plenty of genuine issues which add depth to her personality. I love that **Josi's books are clean and well-rounded with a bit of humor, plenty of mystery, and nail-biting suspense.**"

—Rachelle Christensen, author of *Diamond Rings Are Deadly Things*, *Wrong Number*, and *Caller ID*

Tres Leches Cupcakes

"Kilpack is a capable writer whose works have grown and taken on a life of their own. *Tres Leches Cupcakes* is an amusing and captivating addition to her creative compilations."

—Mike Whitmer, *Deseret News*

Banana Split

"In *Banana Split*, Josi Kilpack has turned a character that we've come to love as an overzealous snoop and given her the breath of someone real so we can love her even more. **This is a story with an ocean's depth's worth of awesome!**"

—Julie Wright, author of *Spell Check*

Pumpkin Roll

"*Pumpkin Roll* is different from the other books in the series, and while the others have their tense moments, **this had me downright nervous and spooked.** During the climax, I kept shaking my head, saying, 'No way this is happening.' Five out of five stars for this one. I could not stop reading."

—Rachel Holt, www.ldswomensbookreview.com

Blackberry Crumble

"**Josi Kilpack is an absolute master** at leading you to believe you have everything figured out, only to have the rug pulled out from under you with the turn of a page. *Blackberry Crumble* is a delightful mystery with wonderful characters and a white-knuckle ending that'll leave you begging for more."

—Gregg Luke, author of *Blink of an Eye*

Key Lime Pie

"I had a great time following the ever-delightful Sadie as she ate and sleuthed her way through **nerve-racking twists and turns and nail-biting suspense.**"

—Melanie Jacobsen, author of *The List* and *Not My Type*

Devil's Food Cake

"Josi Kilpack whips up **another tasty mystery where startling twists and delightful humor mix** in a confection as delicious as Sadie Hoffmiller's devil's food cake."

> —Stephanie Black, four-time winner of the Whitney Award for Mystery/Suspense

English Trifle

"**English Trifle is a delightful combo of mystery and gourmet cooking,** highly recommended."

> —Midwest Review Journal

Lemon Tart

"**The novel has a bit of everything. It's a mystery, a cookbook, a low-key romance and a dead-on depiction of life.** . . . That may sound like a hodgepodge. It's not. It works. Kilpack blends it all together and cooks it up until it has the taste of, well . . . of a tangy lemon tart."

> —Jerry Johnston, Deseret News

"**Lemon Tart is an enjoyable mystery** with a well-hidden culprit and an unlikely heroine in Sadie Hoffmiller. Kilpack endows Sadie with logical hidden talents that come in handy at just the right moment."

> —Shelley Glodowski, Midwest Book Review

THE SADIE HOFFMILLER CULINARY MYSTERIES

Lemon Tart

English Trifle

Devil's Food Cake

Key Lime Pie

Blackberry Crumble

Pumpkin Roll

Banana Split

Tres Leches Cupcakes

Baked Alaska

Rocky Road

Fortune Cookie

Wedding Cake

The Candy Cane Caper recipes

Download a free PDF of all the recipes in this book at josiskilpack.com

A COZY CULINARY MYSTERY

THE CANDY CANE CAPER

JOSI S. KILPACK

A MYSTERY WITH RECIPES

SHADOW
MOUNTAIN

Visit us at shadowmountain.com

Library of Congress Cataloging-in-Publication Data

Names: Kilpack, Josi S., author. | Kilpack, Josi S. Culinary mystery.
Title: The candy cane caper / Josi S. Kilpack.
Description: Salt Lake City, Utah : Shadow Mountain, [2019]
Identifiers: LCCN 2019014115 | ISBN 9781629726014 (paperbound)
Subjects: LCSH: Hoffmiller, Sadie—Fiction. | Cooks—Fiction. | Fort Collins (Colo.),
    setting. | LCGFT: Detective and mystery fiction. | Novels.
Classification: LCC PS3611.I45276 C36 2019 | DDC 813/.6—dc23
LC record available at https://lccn.loc.gov/2019014115

Printed in the United States of America
Lake Book Manufacturing, Inc., Melrose Park, IL

10   9   8   7   6   5   4   3   2   1

To all the readers who asked,
"Will you ever write another Sadie book?"
This story would not exist if not for you.

CHAPTER 1

γ

"It takes an awful lot of work to get ready for the most wonderful day of the year, Pete, but it doesn't take much to destroy it." Sadie paused long enough to take a breath, but quick enough to keep Pete from speaking. "One drunk uncle or forgotten gift or inconvenient storm could be the difference between a 'Happy Holiday' and a Rankin and Bass movie."

Pete laughed through the phone while Sadie scowled at the threatening clouds hanging low over Fort Collins, Colorado, where she and Pete had lived for five years of wedded bliss. Pete was in Phoenix today, though—seventy-two degrees, thank you very much.

"Haven't you been dreaming of a white Christmas, Sadie?" Pete teased.

"Not eighteen inches of white Christmas in twenty-four hours! What if the storm shuts down the airport and no one can get here? What if there is black ice on the roads?" Pete's son, Jared, and his family were driving up from New Mexico. Shawn and Maggie were flying in from Sacramento, and Breanna's family was flying all the way from London. Pete's two daughters lived in town; at least she didn't have to worry about them.

"Sadie," Pete said in his patient-husband tone. "Everyone will get there in time, I promise."

Sadie sat up straighter in her car, sufficiently triggered by the patronizing comment. "I'm supposed to trust a promise like that? You promised you'd be home today and look how that's turned out."

"I said I *hoped* to be home tonight," Pete corrected. "I *promised* to be home for Christmas Eve."

"Which is—" She checked her watch—4:18 p.m. "Thirty-one hours and forty-two minutes away."

"But Christmas Eve lasts for twenty-four hours, so I have fifty-five hours and forty-two minutes before you can accuse me of breaking my word."

Technically he was right, but the disappointment of him having to extend the cold case investigation that had taken him to Arizona for a few days amplified Sadie's holiday-induced anxieties that having all of their children and grandchildren together would not end up as holly jolly as she'd expected. Pete's daughter had generously offered her home for the Christmas party on December 26, which was perfect because Pete and Sadie's condo would have been terribly cramped.

Sadie had volunteered to be in charge of the food: holiday favorites from both sides of the family, which had sounded fun back in October. However, the pressure to get everything just right so that both families felt comfortable and included was growing in intensity as the big day grew closer. Just that morning, Pete's daughter Michelle had emailed Sadie a copy of a cake recipe her mom had made every year when they'd been young—Cunningham Candy Cane Cake. What if Sadie didn't make it as well as Pete's late wife had? What if his children interpreted her failure as a dismissal of an important part of their past?

The anxiety spiral tightened.

"What if you get delayed again, Pete? What if I don't make the Candy Cane Cake as well as Pat did?" She didn't wait for him to answer. "What if the clams don't come in for the cioppino? What if the grandkids hate the marshmallow guns we got them? What if one of the littler grandkids chokes on a marshmallow? It's the first time everyone has been together since the wedding, which was, well, a disaster."

For most people, a "wedding disaster" would be having the buttercream frosting melt on the cake or burgundy tablecloths instead of Christmas Red. For Pete and Sadie's wedding, it had meant explosions, shoot-outs, psychopaths, and one gravely injured minister. Pastor Donald, thankfully, had made a full recovery and was back in Garrison, preaching fiery sermons about miracles, guardian angels, and the power of adversity in each person's personal development throughout their lives. After five years, there were even parts of that day guests could laugh about.

Some guests.

Not often, though.

Pete spoke. "A wise woman once told me that allowing negativity to cloud your focus can influence the event itself through unconscious choices that then lead to additional conflicts."

That "wise woman" was Sadie herself. She was always talking to him about energy and mindfulness, but the negative energy of a difficult cold case or an argument with the guy who let his dog run loose in the neighborhood was not the same as twenty-some-odd people whose last encounter with each other had been a traumatic experience.

Sadie had been having honest-to-goodness nightmares about this blended holiday celebration three nights in a row, now—pretty much since Pete had left town. Anxiety-ridden dreams had led to poor sleep, which made the stress worse during her overscheduled days, which led to more tension, which led to additional anxiety-ridden dreams and . . .

"The guys are here," Pete said, his voice sounding more professional. "I've got to go, but I promise that everyone will be there for the family party on the twenty-sixth, and Christmas Eve will find me where the love-light gleams."

Sadie couldn't help but smile. "What is love-light, anyway?"

Pete laughed. "I have no idea, but we'll figure it out. Together. In two more days, okay?"

Sadie wanted to pout and cry, but she'd better not, what with Santa Claus coming to town and all. She was already risking her status of being on the "nice list" by being such a big whiner about Pete's case.

"I'll literally be counting the hours. What time is your flight to Denver on Tuesday?"

"I'm not sure yet, but I'll let you know as soon as I know."

And just like that the spiral started all over again. What if everyone showed up but Pete wasn't there? Talk about awkward. "You're not sure? Pete, there aren't a lot of last-minute seats available to pick up on Christmas Eve."

"The department figures all that out, but I'll be home. I

promise. Try to find something to distract yourself, okay? How's the book coming?"

"I turned it in on Friday," Sadie said, a little hurt he didn't remember.

Since retiring from investigations, Sadie had converted her experiences into storylines for culinary mystery novels. The last one had been a bear to write, so it had been a relief to send it off to her wonderful editor right before Christmas. She would start on her next story in January sometime. The space between one book and the next was golden, time she could use to catch up with friends and deep clean her house and travel with Pete since his work was flexible, too. This time, however, she'd only felt more stressed due to the holiday demands.

"That's right," Pete said. "Then if not a book, try to find something else to take your mind off your stress—that shouldn't be too difficult this time of year. I'm really sorry I can't be there to help."

Sadie heard the voices of Pete's partners grow louder in the background. Their time was up.

Sadie said goodbye and then tapped her phone on the steering wheel, gazing through the windshield to the entrance of Nicholas House, a care facility with hospice services. Sadie's friend Mary had moved in there a few months ago, and Sadie had been visiting several times a week since. She felt her anxieties settle into a gentle walk instead of dashing through the snow as they had been.

Mary Hallmark had been the first neighbor to introduce herself when Pete and Sadie had moved to Fort Collins. Since then, Mary had become a dear friend in addition to being the best across-the-street-neighbor anyone could wish for in a new town. Mary had been eighty-nine years old back then and as spunky and independent as anyone could hope to be at her age. She'd helped find Sadie volunteer opportunities, which had led to meeting people and feeling at home. Mary had also tried to teach Sadie how to quilt, though Sadie didn't have much of a knack for it.

Mary's age had started catching up to her a few years ago, however, and her blurred vision that had troubled her so much on the last quilt turned out to be macular degeneration, which progressed quickly, limiting her precious independence until she was all but confined to her home. Luckily, her great-granddaughter, Joy, had moved in to care for her, which had allowed Mary to stay in her home a while longer.

Then, last spring, Mary had been diagnosed with stage three pancreatic cancer. She'd felt that treating it at her age was ridiculous and instead spent the summer putting her affairs in order and giving away most of what she'd spent a lifetime collecting. In September, she put her remaining heirlooms and gifts for her family into storage, sold her home, and moved into Nicholas House with the last few pieces of her own furniture. Mary comforted the people who loved her with the reminder that she'd lived a good life and was ready to step into the next one. It was difficult to feel sorry for her when she did not feel sorry for herself.

Each person in her circle—which had been growing smaller for years as friends and family preceded her passing—had come to accept her decision. Nicholas House had been an excellent choice. The food was first-rate, and families were encouraged to dine with their loved ones; they could even stay overnight on occasion. Joy had done so several times during the first couple of weeks, helping both her and Mary ease into the change.

Mary's doctors had told her she'd be lucky to make it three

months without treatment. Mary had also stopped her blood-pressure medication and the statin she'd been taking to manage her cholesterol. The only medications she took now were for pain management, and only sparingly. No one thought she would make it to see the leaves change colors. Or Halloween. Or Thanksgiving. And now Christmas.

With each holiday that approached, Mary had been reluctant to expect she'd be there to enjoy it, which was why she hadn't called Sadie until yesterday to ask if Sadie would help her set up her Christmas tree. Sadie had been encouraging her to do that very thing for the last week and was committed to do everything she possibly could to make Mary's last Christmas as wonderful as possible. She had fetched Mary's Christmas ornaments from Mary's storage unit yesterday afternoon, and now that the church Christmas program and social was over, she could give Mary and her tree her full attention. For a couple of hours anyway. Helping a dear friend prepare for Christmas would be the perfect distraction from her silly anxieties.

"Time to forget yourself and do some good," Sadie said out loud as she turned off the car's engine. She'd kept it running during her conversation with Pete in order to keep the heat on. The temperature dropped as soon as the engine went still. It might be seventy-two degrees in Arizona, but in Fort Collins, it was a bracing twenty-six. Sadie adjusted her red-and-white-striped scarf tighter around her neck and slid her phone into the pocket of her puffy red coat before opening her door.

Holy nutcracker, but it was cold outside!

She hurried to the back of the car and popped the hatchback. Two green plastic tubs labeled "Christmas Ornaments" waited alongside a basket filled with ten individual plastic containers of cookies for Mary to give to the staff.

Sadie placed the basket of cookies on top of one of the tubs and lifted it from the car—it wasn't heavy. The thought of seeing Mary and decorating her tree brought Sadie the peace she had been searching for. *This* was exactly where she needed to be right now, and Pete would be back by Christmas Eve. He'd promised.

It was Christmastime, she reminded herself, and nothing terrible would happen so long as Sadie kept her wits about her and made a conscious effort to focus on the positives.

CHAPTER 2

Hee-haw, Mary," Sadie called out as she pushed the door open with her backside while carrying one of the tubs. She and Mary had adopted the greeting years ago after a Jimmy Stewart movie marathon. It was particularly appropriate right now.

Mary raised her head from where she seemed to have been asleep in her overstuffed recliner. She was sleeping more and had trouble with her breathing now and then, but thankfully wasn't in much pain.

"Hee-haw, Sadie," Mary answered sleepily, turning her head in Sadie's direction.

Sadie knew Mary could only see light and shapes, and mostly in her peripheral vision, so she rarely faced anyone straight on anymore. Joy had put grippy tape in varying widths along the floor to make trails Mary could follow in her stocking feet—the thickest line was for the bathroom, with narrower widths for the dresser, the bed, and the door to her room. Mary remained fiercely independent despite her limitations, and Joy did what she could to help her stay that way.

"The ornaments were exactly where your inventory sheet said

they would be," Sadie said. West side of the storage unit, third stack, top two green totes. Everything had been lined up, laid out, and labeled like tin soldiers in there. The names of whoever that particular tub was meant for after Mary was gone had been written on each one. Seeing a tub with her and Pete's name on it had brought a surprised lump to Sadie's throat, but the temptation to take a peek had lasted only a moment. Sadie wasn't going to become the sort of person who peeked after a lifetime of patience and poise.

A four-foot, white-flocked tree waited in the corner of Mary's room farthest from the door. Two crisscrossed boards screwed into the base of the tree kept it upright. With Christmas only three days away there was no need for a watering stand. Sadie was glad the flocking hadn't covered the scent of pine—Christmas just wasn't Christmas without that smell.

Sadie put the first tub of ornaments—plus the basket of cookies— beside the tree and went out for the other tote she'd left in the hall. "I'm so glad Joy found a flocked tree," Sadie said as she set the second tote beside the first.

"She had to go to three different lots to find one, if you can believe it," Mary said with a disappointed click of her tongue. "Flocked trees used to be all the rage. Bless Joy's heart for not giving up."

Flocked trees hadn't been the rage for nearly fifty years, but one of the benefits of aging was that you earned the right to honor the fads and fashions from any decade you'd lived through. Sadie herself still had a VCR and would never feel the pressure to purchase a pair of low-rise jeans.

Sadie brushed the dust from her hands, though not much dust had gathered in the months since the tubs had been put into storage. "I can only hope to have a granddaughter as wonderful as Joy one day."

Sadie did, however, have two wonderful grandsons who melted her heart like marshmallows in cocoa when she Skyped with them every Sunday, and sometimes during the week when she missed them too much. Breanna's boys, William Everet IV, and Phillip Neil, were three and one respectively.

The family lived at Southgate, Liam's family estate in Devonshire, England, for nine months of the year and then came to Fort Collins once Parliament closed in mid-summer. It was still strange to think of Liam as the Earl of Garnett, a title he'd inherited after his father had passed away after many years of poor health.

To keep their American ties strong and satisfy Breanna's need for a normal life at least some of the time, they had purchased a modest cabin outside of Fort Collins where they lived for a few months each year. During those months, Liam grew a beard and Breanna wore flip-flops. They ate fish they caught themselves and made homemade jam when the peaches were on. Best of all, Sadie got to feel like a real grandmother. Sadie managed the cabin as a vacation rental when they were in England, even though they had no need of the additional income.

Shawn and his wife, Maggie, had been trying to start a family. Sadie and her late husband, Neil, had been childless for several years before adopting Breanna and Shawn, so she knew not to express her wish for more grandchildren, and a granddaughter especially, out loud.

"Every grandmother should be so lucky as to have a granddaughter like Joy," Mary said wistfully, bringing Sadie's thoughts back to the present.

Joy was actually Mary's great-granddaughter through Mary's oldest son, Charles, Joy's grandpa. She was twenty-five years old but hadn't transitioned very well into adulthood after graduating from high school. She and Mary had become close after Mary learned to text. Close enough that Mary felt comfortable inviting Joy to move in with her a couple of years ago, and Joy felt comfortable enough to say yes. They had been the perfect team in the two years since then—Mary helping Joy learn independence while Joy helped Mary hold on to hers. When Mary had sold the house, Joy had moved into an off-campus apartment.

"She and Frank will be coming over for dinner tonight with Frank's daughter, the little dear. They're going to sneak me in some sushi."

Frank was Joy's boyfriend of the last few months—something Sadie hadn't expected to happen so fast for Joy, who had never been very social. Sadie hadn't met Frank, but Mary thought he was wonderful.

"The rascals." Sadie shrugged out of her coat and scarf, hanging them on the hat tree that had once graced the foyer of Mary's house. The walnut dresser, side table, and vanity had all been part of Mary's original bedroom set, and she'd brought two of her dining room chairs along with her late husband's overstuffed and threadbare recliner. Sadie had kept Neil's chair for years after he died too, so she understood Mary's reasons to bring the item that looked out of place with the other pieces. Mary couldn't see the incongruence anyway.

"I have the cookies for the staff." Sadie moved the basket of cookies to the dresser top, then brought one container back to Mary. "I brought some for you, too."

Mary's face brightened. Sadie put the gingerbread-men-printed container into Mary's hands. She put the container in her lap and then popped off the lid before feeling around the top of the cookies and selecting one. Holding the star-shaped cookie in one hand, she traced the top edge and sides, covering her fingers with powdered sugar. "They turned out perfect," Mary said in a reverent tone.

"You haven't even tasted one," Sadie said, laughing, but was gratified to know that Mary was pleased with the shape. Snow Flurries consisted of two very thin, star-shaped cookies held together with a dollop of raspberry jam. The top cookie was turned so its points filled the space between the points of the bottom cookie and the jam could peek through. Sprinkling powdered sugar on top finished the confection, and the tangy jam perfectly complimented the flaky, almond-flavored cookie without being too sweet.

Mary took a delicate bite, chewing contemplatively. When she finished swallowing, she turned her face in Sadie's direction, her smile as bright as the Christmas star the cookies symbolized. "As I said, Sadie—perfect. You are an angel."

"I prefer Christmas elf," Sadie clarified. She started the CD player on Mary's dresser, and Bing Crosby's voice floated out of the device. Music was essential to the perfect Christmas experience. Sadie adjusted the volume so it wouldn't get in the way of conversation, however.

Mary enjoyed the rest of the cookie with a satisfied smile that did Sadie's heart good. Mary had made this recipe for her neighbors at Christmas for more than sixty years, and Sadie counted it an honor to have made them on her behalf this year. She had already taken some to the neighbors, who had been so gracious and touched by the gesture. Most of them had said they would come to thank Mary in person, which had been Sadie's intent.

Mary declined a second cookie, and Sadie put the container on the nightstand and helped clean up the powdered sugar that had gotten all over Mary's hands and nightgown.

"So," Sadie said after Mary handed back the wet washcloth. "Are we ready to decorate this tree?"

"Ho, ho, ho," someone sang from the doorway.

Sadie turned to see Mary's daughter, Ivy, stride into the room. She wore snug, high-heeled boots that reached her knees. Her long, lean legs were clad in designer jeans and topped with a lovely raspberry-colored trench coat tied around her slim waist. A shopping bag swung at Ivy's side, making her look like an actress in a Christmas commercial for the local mall. Ivy was a few years older than Sadie, but looked ten years younger due to her long, blonde hair, athletic figure, and wrinkle-free face. She worked for a medical spa and received discounted treatments in order to be able to recommend procedures to the clients.

Sadie, however, looked like the fifty-nine-ish, retired school-teacher she was. She'd stopped coloring her hair nearly six years earlier, and her color was now a soft gray with some lighter streaks that gave it texture. Her hairstylist had given her what she called "a long, short cut," which meant that Sadie could curl it or spike it or wear it smooth, according to her preference, from one day to the next.

Sadie had made peace with her wide hips and exercised for the health and social benefits rather than her waistline. Being comfortable in her own skin didn't save her from feeling like a frump in Ivy's company, however, and the Christmas sweater she'd chosen that morning with a sunglasses-wearing penguin on the front suddenly felt silly.

"Oh, hi, Sadie," Ivy said, attempting a smile. The smile didn't quite reach her eyes—a hazard of holiday Botox treatments.

"Hi," Sadie said. "Great to see you."

They both visited Mary regularly but not often at the same time.

Ivy crossed to the bed and began unpacking the shopping bag on top of the duvet. "So, Mom, I found the socks you wanted, and then I found *this*." She unfurled a robe, and even though Sadie was too far away to read a price tag, she could tell it was expensive. The green fabric looked thick, but moved like silk as Ivy laid it over Mary's lap.

Mary touched the robe lightly at first, then rubbed the fabric between her fingers.

"It's a robe," Ivy said proudly. "Don't you just love it?"

"I told you I didn't want any more clothes, dear. Just the socks." Mary did her best to fold the robe before holding it out to her daughter.

Ivy didn't take it back. "But, Mom, didn't you feel how soft it was? And it's the most beautiful shade of green—emerald, with just a hint of sheen to it. It really plays up the jewel tone. It's perfect for Christmas." Ivy looked past Mary to Sadie, lifting her microbladed eyebrows as best she could. "Tell her how beautiful it is, Sadie."

"It *is* beautiful," Sadie said, busying herself with putting the containers of cookies in alphabetical order along the top of Mary's dresser based on the name tag attached to each one. If she looked busy maybe she wouldn't be drawn into their argument. Ivy had only moved back to Fort Collins a year earlier, and since then,

Sadie had experienced her fill of bickering arguments that Mary and Ivy accepted as conversation. Ivy hadn't visited much until Mary was at Nicholas House. Sadie sensed she was trying to put more effort into her relationship with her mother. Ivy had chosen not to have children, and Sadie wondered if that decision made it that much harder to lose her own mother now.

"I have a robe that's perfectly fine, Ivy. Please return this one."

The Botox couldn't hide the look of disappointment on Ivy's face as she took the robe, then stared at it in her hands. "Mom, it's just a robe. It's comfortable and pretty, and I want you—"

"Ivy, dear, after spending months going through a life's worth of *things*, I don't want anything more than what I need, and I don't need another robe."

Sadie changed her mind and decided to put the cookies in *reverse* alphabetical order instead. Xander probably never got the first of anything. Merry Christmas to Xander.

Mary held out her hands. "Can I see the socks, please?"

There were thirty definitions of the word "see" in the English language, and though Sadie considered breaking in to offer this fascinating bit of trivia, she chose not to. Better to let this exchange work itself through.

With a tight jaw, Ivy picked up the three pairs of socks from the bed and placed them in her mother's hands.

Mary inspected them with her fingers, then handed one pair back to Ivy. "I only need the two."

"It was buy two, get one free," Ivy said with a clip of irritation.

Mary's retort was equally clipped. "Then you can keep the third one. I only need the two."

Luckily, Mary couldn't see the way Ivy tried to unsuccessfully wrinkle her nose. She looked at the socks as though they were a dead rodent. "What do I want fuzzy socks with nonslip tread on the bottom for?"

"Then take the third pair back to the store," Mary said, shaking the offending pair still in her hand. "I only want two pair."

"Fine," Ivy said, snatching back the socks. Sadie saw her blinking fast, however, as the anger turned into an emotion that did not show in her tone of voice.

"A third pair might be nice, Mary," Sadie said, failing at her commitment not to get involved. She stepped toward Mary and put a hand on her shoulder, causing Mary to turn her head in Sadie's direction. "You never know what might happen to socks in the laundry. Maybe keep the third pair, just in case. Ivy went to all the trouble to get them, and it didn't cost anything extra."

Mary frowned as she considered Sadie's suggestion, then relaxed her expression after a few moments. "All right. Ivy, would you put all three pair in the top, right drawer, please?"

"Sure," Ivy said, though she sounded petulant.

Sadie moved out of Ivy's way and gave her an encouraging smile when she passed, which Ivy returned with a weaker, sadder version.

"I better return this robe and finish my shopping," Ivy said after she'd put the socks away. "Can I do anything for you when I come by tomorrow, Mom? Perhaps paint your nails?"

"Joy did my nails last night," Mary said, holding out her hand. The nails were painted bright red with little snowman decals on both ring fingers.

Ivy looked at them sadly. Sadie had never heard Ivy express jealousy of Mary's closeness with Joy, but now she wondered if it was getting more difficult for Ivy. Maybe that was behind Ivy putting in additional effort.

Mary continued, "How about bringing some peppermint ice cream? No more skipping dessert for me."

"I can do that," Ivy said, though her tone was still sad. "If you think of anything else I can do, give me a call." She walked to Mary's chair, and they exchanged their usual kisses on the cheek that had always seemed more habitual than affectionate. Ivy met Sadie's eyes briefly as she turned toward the door, and Sadie's heart went out to her.

Snow Flurries

½ cup butter or margarine, softened
½ cup shortening
1 cup sugar
2 large eggs
1 tablespoon grated lemon zest
1 teaspoon vanilla extract
½ teaspoon almond extract
3½ cups all-purpose flour
½ teaspoon baking powder
½ teaspoon salt
⅓ cup seedless raspberry jam
1 cup sifted powdered sugar

In a large bowl, beat butter and shortening with an electric mixer on medium speed until soft and creamy. Gradually add sugar, beating well. Add eggs, lemon zest, and extracts, mixing well. In a separate bowl, combine flour, baking powder, and salt. Gradually add to butter mixture, mixing well. Cover and chill 1 hour.

Divide dough in half, storing one portion in refrigerator. Roll remaining portion to ⅛-inch thickness on a lightly floured surface. Cut with a 2½-inch star-shaped cookie cutter and place on ungreased cookie sheets. Bake at 375 degrees F. for 7 to 8 minutes, or until lightly browned. Cool 2 minutes on cookie sheets. Move to wire racks to cool. Repeat with remaining dough.

Just before serving, spread center of half of cookies with about ¼ teaspoon raspberry jam. Place a second cookie on top, alternating points of stars on top and bottom cookies. Sprinkle generously with powdered sugar.

Makes approximately 3 dozen sandwich cookies.

CHAPTER 3

When the tapping of Ivy's heels down the hall had disappeared, Sadie turned to Mary. "I think you hurt her feelings."

Mary waved her hand dismissively. "She's always been a poor sport when she doesn't get her way. She'll be fine."

"I know the two of you have never been close, but—"

"Really, Sadie, don't worry about it." There was a tone of finality in her voice that Sadie chose to ignore. Now that she'd decided to address the relationship between Mary and Ivy, she wasn't going to duck out.

"I think Ivy is making an effort to improve things between the two of you, Mary."

"How? By buying me something I don't want, don't need, and told her not to buy? See, it's a matter of values between us, Sadie." Mary put a self-righteous hand on her chest. "I have always valued people whereas Ivy values things. It's always been that way."

"Well, that explains why she bought you that robe, then, doesn't it? I think gifts communicate to Ivy that she is loved, and she's trying to show that love to you in the same way."

Mary shook her head before Sadie even finished. "She just likes an excuse to shop."

"Then why didn't she buy something for herself? She's come to visit almost every day since you moved here, Mary. I think this is really hard for her."

Mary leaned back in her recliner, resting her hands in her lap with her eyes toward the floor. A shimmery lock of white hair fell out of her chignon, the same style she'd worn every day since she had been in her fifties. Even without her eyesight, Mary could achieve the style with practiced movements, though Joy or the staff sometimes had to help smooth it out when she finished. When her hair was down, it reached halfway down her back in thin locks that looked like spun glass. Mary brushed the stray lock of hair back into place, where it obediently stayed.

"I love Ivy, Sadie, she's my daughter, but we've never gotten along very well. I spent decades trying to make things better with her while she slapped my hand away each and every time. Finally, I had to accept her agency to choose what she wanted from me—which wasn't much. When she moved back to Fort Collins after her divorce last year, I thought it could be a chance for us to develop a healthy relationship, but it wasn't. She wouldn't help me pack up the house or even come see if there was anything she wanted from it. She didn't help me list the house or find a facility to move into. That she suddenly wants a relationship now is almost offensive after how many times I have tried and she's snubbed the attempt." Mary let out a breath and shrugged. "Doral always got along better with her than I did. At least I had a good relationship with the boys, which helped ease the sting of her rejection—that's what it was, you know." Doral, as well as Mary's "boys" were gone now too. Ivy was the only close family Mary had left, aside from Joy. The grandchildren and great-grandchildren who had come through Mary's sons lived out of state and didn't visit often.

"I can understand the frustration of not having your efforts accepted," Sadie said, her tone conciliatory as she thought about her sister, Wendy, and the relationship she'd tried to build with her for so many years. One person in a relationship could only do so much, and yet just because Sadie's relationship had never been sorted out with Wendy didn't mean that every difficult family connection was beyond repair.

Sadie sat on the edge of Mary's neatly made bed, which was covered with a handmade quilt Mary had made years earlier along with matching pillow shams. It wasn't one of her best—those had been set aside for family members—but it was lovely all the same. Sadie wondered if Mary had set aside a quilt for Ivy. She hoped so.

"Not to be indelicate, Mary, but Ivy will be the one left to carry the burden of your broken relationship. Once you're gone, she won't have any family left—no children, no parents, no brothers. I think you should try to repair things before it's too late—or at least recognize and acknowledge the effort she's making."

Mary was quiet for several seconds, then said, "'First go and be reconciled to them; then come and offer your gift.' Is that what you're saying?"

"It's the perfect time of year to reconcile and prepare for a fresh start," Sadie said by way of agreeing with Mary's humble response. "And it's not just for Ivy's sake. No one knows exactly what awaits us in the next life, but I believe it is infinitely easier to heal our relationships on this side of the veil. I think Ivy is trying to find a way to improve things. Maybe with both of you trying, you can make it better than it's ever been for the time you have left."

Mary nodded slowly. "I'll think on that, Sadie. Thank you for your insight. I've never felt that Ivy cares much about our relationship, but she *has* been more attentive and that deserves some recognition."

"And," Sadie said, making sure there was enough lightness in her voice to make an appropriate segue, "making some improvements between the two of you will add to that happy feeling nothing in the world can buy."

Mary laughed. "It may just become one of the wonderful things we'll remember all through our lives."

She laughed, too, grateful that Mary's illness hadn't taken away her quick wit and sharp memory. Sadie clapped her hands in order to change the subject even more dramatically. "So, where do we begin with this tree?"

Mary sat up in her chair and wriggled forward on the cushion like a little girl excited to teach her friends how to play her favorite game. "If you'll put the tubs in front of me, I can reach in and lift the ornaments out, then hand them to you to be hung on the tree. Will that work? Oh, but I always put the candy canes on last; they're in three separate boxes in one of the tubs."

"Sure thing," Sadie said. "Let's trim up this tree with Christmas stuff!" she sang the line from the original Grinch Christmas special. "I do hope you have some bingle balls and whofoo fluff in these tubs."

"Oh, most certainly," Mary said with a grin as she gestured grandly toward the tubs. "Right next to the bizilbix and wums."

CHAPTER 4

W hite lights on white wire were at the top of one of the tubs along with a red tree skirt that Sadie used to cover the unsightly tree stand. Nat King Cole—who Mary had actually seen perform once—came up on the CD player, and Sadie and Mary sang along while Sadie wrapped the lights around each branch. It was a small tree, so it didn't take long. When Sadie announced the tree ready for ornaments, Mary leaned forward in her chair and felt through the contents of the tub with both reverence and childlike excitement. She lifted a silvery-blue glass ornament in the shape of a teardrop. She cradled the ornament in the palm of one hand and ran her fingers lightly over the entire surface while looking straight ahead. Johnny Mathis crooned in the background as a new song started.

"This is the blue teardrop, isn't it?" Mary asked.

"Yes," Sadie said, impressed. "I guess you know these ornaments pretty well."

"All my life." Mary held out the teardrop to Sadie by the little silver hook.

The ornament was heavier than Sadie expected, and she tapped it with her fingernail. "Is this real glass? It's stunning," Sadie said as she turned to hang it on one of the fluff-covered branches.

The teardrop looked as though it was only a moment away from dropping from the branch and pooling on the floor in a silvery-blue puddle. Mary always had the same sort of tree—white with these pastel ornaments. She also had some other ornaments shaped like people and animals and a bunch of glass candy canes. The ornaments didn't really match each other in color or style, yet they managed to look just right on Mary's tree. Sadie was humbled by the opportunity to help create it one last time.

"Have you really had these ornaments since you were a child, Mary?"

Mary bent over and began rustling through the paper for another bulb. "My father brought the entire collection home from France after World War I a few years before I was born."

World War I?

Mary removed another bulb from the tub and began inspecting it with her fingers.

"This is the green artichoke," Mary said with confidence, holding it out.

"Yes." Sadie held it a bit longer than she had the teardrop, looking at it closely. "Your dad brought them home from France?" she repeated as she hung the artichoke, bending the hook over the branch to make sure it held, and then going back to secure the blue teardrop the same way.

Mary unwrapped a pink grape cluster from within several layers of white tissue paper. She let the tissue fall on the floor beside the chair as she ran her fingers over every bulbous curve as though it were the face of a child. "The Vergo factory was outside Nancy,

France, by then, and Papa used to tease us that the ornaments were still hot from the ovens when Mother opened the box he'd brought all the way across the Atlantic. Blown glass, you know. The silver sheen comes from the mercury or bismuth that was mixed into the glass. Are these the pink grapes or the green ones?"

"Um, pink," Sadie said as Mary handed them over. "These aren't original kugel ornaments, are they?"

Sadie had seen an episode of *Antiques Roadshow* about vintage ornaments a couple of years ago and was pretty sure they'd said the production of tree-weight kugels—*kugel* being the German word for *bulb*—had centered in Nancy, France, by the early 1900s. She'd remembered the name because of her favorite cousin, Nancy. But no one would store *actual* kugels in a plastic tub in a storage unit in Fort Collins, Colorado. These must be one of the millions of replicas that had been made after the popularity of the originals. Sadie looked closely at the pink grapes she held and weighed the ornament in her hand. So heavy.

"You know your collectables," Mary said, sounding impressed while Sadie's heart sank an inch in her chest. "See how the brass caps are stamped with VG1721? The caps were put on when the glass was still hot so they fused together. Between that and the stamp, it's pretty easy to spot the difference between the Vergo pieces and the knockoffs."

Sadie ran her finger over the small embossed cap set at the top of the cluster of grapes itself rather than on the neck as was common of typical Christmas bulbs bought for $2.99 a pack and easily replaced. VG1721 was easy to read, stamped into the brass, and there were tiny ripples and bubbles in the surface that further confirmed the origin.

Mary continued, a nostalgic smile on her age-worn face. "Papa brought thirty-six of them back for Mother, as well as twenty-two Dresdens he got from Germany somehow—he never did tell how he managed that. The Dresdens must be in the other tub with the candy canes. Those are Kentlees that Papa got here in the US after the war. They're my favorites. Mercury glass, you know. Oh, and the tinsel must be in the other box too—the individual strand kind; I don't go for those tinsel ropes. I always feel like that stuff should be roped between posts at the movie theater or something."

When Sadie found her ability to speak, she tried to keep her tone calm while she hung the pink grapes. "Um, so, to be clear, you own original kugels *and* Dresdens?"

On the antiques show Sadie had seen, a woman who had brought in a dozen kugel ornaments learned they were worth almost eight thousand dollars. The expert had then explained that one of the few vintage ornaments worth more than the kugels were Dresdens, pressed three-dimensional cardboard ornaments from Germany that came in a variety of shapes and were hand-painted with exquisite detail. Dresdens were extremely rare due to the natural breakdown over time of both the paint and the cardboard. Mary couldn't possibly own *twenty-two* of them, could she?

Sadie didn't know anything about Kentlee candy canes, but if they were nearly a century old, they had to be valuable, too.

"They're lovely, aren't they?" Mary fished out another priceless heirloom she'd chosen to store in a Walmart tote and wrap in dollar-store tissue paper for protection. They should be packed in sculpted foam and kept in a metal, fireproof box. Possibly in a bank vault. If a dozen kugels were worth eight grand, twenty-two were worth . . . nearly sixteen thousand dollars! Sadie was glad Mary couldn't see her shocked expression.

"My parents gave the candy canes to me when Doral and I married. I've never had a Christmas tree without them. They gave me the other ornaments when they sold the big house. Do you really like them, Sadie? Ivy thinks they're old-fashioned and gaudy. She tells me every year to try something new."

"They are absolutely gorgeous," Sadie said. "Um, I believe they're also quite valuable. Are you sure it's safe to have them here?" In an unsecured room. Of a blind woman. In a care facility where dozens of people came and went every day.

"Safe?" Mary said with a laugh, her fingers roving over a perfect orb of silvery orange. Hadn't the antiques show said orange kugels were extremely rare? Could Sadie find the episode on Netflix to refresh her memory? Maybe Hulu.

Mary sighed nostalgically before continuing. "I haven't missed my sight as much as I do right now. I would love to see these one last time. It's because of these ornaments that I get a white tree every year—it better showcases their colors, don't you think?" She didn't give Sadie a chance to answer before she spoke again, an excited tremor to her words. "Would you mind finding the candy canes for me? I'm too excited to wait."

Sadie opened the other plastic tub and lifted out a package of strand tinsel and then a large Swedish cookie tin with a masking tape label that said "Dresdens" on the top in brown magic marker—unbelievable. Sadie set aside the tin and turned her attention to the three vintage cardboard boxes at the bottom of the tub.

She opened the first box and looked over the six glass canes, each about eight inches long of varying colored stripes twisted with the traditional white—one blue, one yellow, two green, and two red. The white stripe had turned to silver, and some of it was flecked with black where the mercury on the inside of the curved tube had flaked away, reminding Sadie of antique mirrors.

"Do you see a red-and-white one with a chip out of the bottom?" Mary asked eagerly.

Sadie set the first box aside and opened the next, where she found the candy cane Mary wanted.

"Here it is." Sadie carefully lifted the ornament from the fitted holds of its cardboard home. The glass was strong but not much bigger around than a pencil. At the end of the staff was the chip, a missing triangle of glass all but invisible unless someone were looking for it. Each candy cane had its own secure place in the box, and Sadie wished the kugels and Dresdens had similar packaging. She handed the red-and-silver cane to Mary, who put the orange bulb she'd been holding in her lap, took the candy cane, and then leaned back in her chair, running her fingers over the crook and down the shaft. She grinned as her fingers delicately felt around the chip.

"When I was two years old, Mother found me under the tree, licking this particular ornament and frustrated that it didn't taste like the candy ones we'd gotten from church. When she tried to take it from me, I pulled away, and the candy cane hit the windowpane, chipping the end." She chuckled with nostalgia. "Apparently, that was when I said 'Mine' for the first time, and my mother laughed and laughed. She always called them Mary's candy canes after that and would give me a candy one after the tree was trimmed every year if I promised to wait to take the glass ones off the tree until after Christmas was over."

Sadie felt a lump in her throat and wished she had a candy

cane to give Mary when they finished decorating *this* tree. "That's a lovely story, Mary."

Mary handed the candy cane to Sadie. "Hang that one as high as you can on the tree so I know right where it is. We'll do the other ones when we finish with the bulbs and Dresdens."

Sadie did as she was instructed, then took the orange bulb from Mary and placed it on the back of the tree. She told herself it was to keep the colors on the tree balanced, but she was also hiding it in case she was right that orange was more valuable than the others. They continued to chat about Christmas memories as Mary fished out ornaments and Sadie hung them. Sadie's concerns about the safety of these ornaments continued to pop like corn in a hot kettle. Finally, she couldn't keep the lid on any longer.

"I saw an episode of the *Antiques Roadshow* about vintage ornaments a couple of years ago, and I think that thirty-six kugels and twenty-two Dresdens could be—"

"There aren't thirty-six and twenty-two anymore," Mary cut in. "Two kugels, a Dresden, and a candy cane have been broken over the years."

Sadie nearly choked on the dollar signs. "That's terrible," she finally said.

"My brother tried to float the Dresden boat in the bathtub, and it turned to mush. He had a sore behind for days after the lickin' Papa gave him. Four years ago, I dropped one of the kugels when I was taking down the tree." She shook her head. "So help me, but I cried over that."

"I would have cried, too," Sadie offered with sincere solidarity.

"The Dresdens have to be handled very carefully. I only hold them from the hooks, and no one is allowed to touch them."

"That's a good rule," Sadie agreed. "What about the other kugel and the candy cane that you don't have anymore?"

"Well, those were no accident." She shifted slightly in her chair and her tone hardened. "When Ivy was fourteen, she threw one of the kugels at her brother during an argument. The next year, she snapped one of the candy canes in half when I wouldn't let her go out with an eighteen-year-old boy who drove a motorcycle." Mary closed her eyes and took a deep breath. "I cried over those too, after the screaming stopped."

Sadie imagined a younger Mary tackling a teenaged Ivy to the ground and holding her in a headlock. "That's awful," she said when she could speak again. It was silly to think those ornaments could have a bearing on Mary and Ivy's current relationship, but it definitely reflected that things had never been easy between them.

"It really was," Mary agreed, withdrawing another ornament she quickly identified as the green grapes.

Sadie carefully hung the grapes and then turned back to Mary, who held a turquoise pine cone in her lap, going over every bump and groove with her fingers. It was instantly Sadie's favorite—the color was reminiscent of Caribbean seas while the shape reminded her of the Rocky Mountains she loved. Fort Collins was only thirty minutes away from the Rocky Mountain National Park, and she and Pete loved to visit when they could. Hiking was hard on Pete's knee, due to the injury sustained during the shoot-out at their wedding, but that didn't prevent long drives and romantic picnics.

Sadie looked from the ornament to Mary. Maybe Mary didn't know what these ornaments were worth. If she did, she'd surely think twice before putting them on her tree where they would be so vulnerable.

"Um, if I'm not mistaken," Sadie said carefully, kneeling down next to the tub, "these ornaments could be worth a lot of money."

"Forty-six thousand dollars," Mary said, causing Sadie's eyes to pop and her mouth go dry. "The candy canes aren't worth as much as the others," Mary continued. "There are a lot more Kentlee candy canes in America since they were manufactured here, after all. But I was still pleased with the bid." Mary sifted through the first tub while Sadie stared.

Had Mary really said forty-six *thousand* dollars?

CHAPTER 5

A *thunk* sounded at the bottom of the tub as something slipped out of its wrapping, and Sadie's stomach fell as though in a too-fast elevator. Mary leaned over the tub to retrieve the item, unconcerned. "Jedidiah from Marley's Antiques came out to evaluate several items last summer—my mother's silverware and some antique furniture none of the family wanted, things like that. I sold him a few pieces, and he made me that offer for my ornament collection, but I think we could get more off eBay if they were sold individually."

Sadie blinked. "You're going to sell them?"

"Well, not me. Joy."

Sadie sank back on her heels even though her knees were aching something terrible. Fifty-nine-ish-year-old women were not meant to kneel for long periods of time. "Joy is going to sell them?"

Mary ran her fingers over the pine cone. "She doesn't know that yet, nor how valuable they are—no one does." A sneaky smile appeared on her lips and brightened her face. "Except you, Sadie, and I'm only telling you because I need your help, or, well, Joy will need your help."

The news made Sadie feel more nervous than special. "My help?"

"I've had these set aside for Joy since this summer along with a letter explaining my intentions, but now that I'm putting them on the tree, I think I want to give them to Joy after Christmas Eve Mass on Tuesday." Her smile fell slightly. "I wish I could see her face when she realizes what these will mean for her future."

Sadie put up a hand—this was all happening too fast—but then Mary couldn't see the gesture so Sadie added words. "Wait, you expect Joy to sell these ornaments after you've given them to her as a gift?"

"I won't be here to enjoy the ornaments next year, Sadie, and you can't take sentiment to the bank or to heaven."

"You just told me you've had these ornaments on every Christmas tree you've ever had. Well, the candy canes at least."

"Exactly. On *my* Christmas trees. Just because they mean more than money to me doesn't mean they should mean the same for Joy."

Mary put the pine cone in her lap and reached her hand toward Sadie.

Sadie had to finagle her legs out from under her in order to get close enough to take Mary's hand, her red fingernails flashing in the light from the window.

"Things are things and stuff is stuff, Sadie. I've told you that before."

"Yes, you have."

Even before Mary had started packing up her things, her home was crisp and clutter-free. There had been minimal photographs and artwork on the white walls. Mary preferred gifts of food to things she had to display. Ivy had shipped her a Blendtec blender for Mother's Day a few years ago. Mary had used it once—hated the resulting green smoothie—and put it back in the box as though it was the appliance's fault, rather than a poor recipe. Sadie had seen the box in the storage unit with a sticker that said "For Ivy."

"Your father brought some of these ornaments from Europe nearly a hundred years ago, and you've kept them all this time. They are not just stuff."

Mary laughed, a trilling sound that barely softened Sadie's discomfort. "Yes, they are, Sadie. Valuable *stuff*, sentimental *stuff*, but *stuff* all the same. Someone else who is searching for a collection like this will enjoy them for years to come, but Joy doesn't need old-fashioned ornaments. She needs a future, and these ornaments can help her with that." She squeezed Sadie's hand and then clasped it with her other hand.

Sadie stared at the pine cone in Mary's lap and tried not to imagine it rolling onto the ground and shattering into a million pieces.

"If I can't convince Joy of my sincere desire for her to sell these, I want you to promise me that you'll help explain things to her. Maybe she'll want to keep one or two, that's fine, but . . . it's time for her to live a life of her own, which she can have if she sells these ornaments."

Sadie wasn't sure she understood Mary's determination. Joy was already living her own life. Two years ago, when Joy had first come to Fort Collins, she hadn't been to college, and she didn't know how to cook, or clean, or even converse very easily. She'd had a data-entry job back when she'd lived in Bakersfield and spent most of her money on video games, which is what she did with all her free time.

Since moving in with Mary, Joy had learned a lot; taking care of someone else tended to do that for anyone. She'd learned how to clean, do laundry, reconcile a bank account, and bake bread, among other things. When Joy had moved out, Sadie had worried that the girl would be overwhelmed by the changes, but Joy had done really well for herself. She worked full-time in the management office at the mall, went to school part-time, and visited Mary every single day. Sadie wasn't sure she understood Mary's level of concern for Joy's future.

Mary continued before Sadie could verbalize her thoughts. "Joy brought so much sunshine into my life these last years, Sadie, and she helped me live independently for far longer than I could have done otherwise. I just . . . Well, I love that child and want to help her work toward a solid future. These ornaments are the only thing I have left that can really do that. She can pay for the rest of her schooling, maybe put a little down on a house, or even a condominium like yours. I just want to give her a jump-start, to make up for the time she's missed taking care of me."

How could anyone argue with an explanation like that?

The retirement plans Mary and Doral had invested in hadn't counted on Doral being sick for five years or Mary living into her nineties. Mary had taken a reverse mortgage on her home to pay Doral's medical bills his life insurance hadn't covered after he died, and without Social Security, Mary would have been forced to leave her home a long time ago. When Mary had moved to Nicholas House, she'd told Sadie that she could afford to stay for six months before they'd have to put her on the curb. That would never happen of course, friends and family would help if she really did run out of money, but the material point was that Mary would not be leaving much of an inheritance.

"I intend these ornaments to help Joy find a more stable future than she might have otherwise," Mary continued. "But she'll need help to see it that way, and while I'm excited to give them to her in person, I'm a little concerned that Ivy might be upset. Not because of the ornaments—she doesn't care for them, like I said—but their value is more than what I'm leaving for Ivy. Will you help Joy understand what these ornaments are meant to be and make sure no one interferes?"

"I'll do my best," Sadie said. "But you'll tell her their value and your intentions when you give them to her, won't you?" The idea of trying to convince Joy to sell these heirlooms after Mary was gone made Sadie's stomach feel like she'd eaten an entire box of chocolates in one sitting.

Mary nodded. "Of course, but I imagine it might be difficult for her to part with them when the time comes. I have other items set aside for her that she can keep for sentimental reasons. These ornaments should be seen as an investment."

"I'll be there if she needs my help," Sadie said, then paused for a breath. "But I worry about displaying the ornaments here in your room. What if something happens to them? They could get broken or even stolen if someone found out what they were worth." Sadie glanced at the open door to Mary's room, realizing that anyone could have overheard their conversation. She turned back to Mary and lowered her voice as a new angle for her argument came to mind. "Wouldn't it be terrible if something happened to them before Joy has a chance to benefit from your generosity?"

Mary let go of Sadie's hand and made a shooing motion in the general direction of the tree. "They look like fusty, old bric-a-brac to anyone else, and it'll only be for a few days. I'll ask Joy to help me take them off the tree after Mass so that I can wrap them one more time. Jedidiah will treat Joy fairly if she decides to sell to him, but make sure she at least thinks about eBay." Mary lifted the turquoise pine cone from her lap and held it out to Sadie.

Sadie bit her lip to keep from continuing the argument. Despite the magic of the season brought on by snow, brightly colored trimmings, and the peace of Christ's hope renewed in the hearts of men, larceny and petty thefts rose thirty percent during December, a statistic that emphasized the foolishness of hanging almost fifty thousand dollars on a Christmas tree in a blind woman's room where the majority of staff members were underpaid and overworked.

"Will you at least let me put up a sign asking people not touch the ornaments?"

"Oh, that's an excellent idea," Mary said, nodding. "My mother had a firm rule that once the ornaments are on the tree, they do not come off again until we're putting everything away. I've lived by it, too, and even though it's only for a few days, it would be good to have an extra measure of safety."

"And what about a barrier of some kind?" Sadie said, looking around the room. The tree was set at the foot of Mary's twin bed, so it wasn't in a traffic area, thank goodness. And though the door opened toward it, there were a few feet between the swing of the door and the tree itself. "Maybe I could rope it off with tinsel ropes and . . . the legs of the quilt frame you gave me." The quilt frame was natural wood and had aged into a lovely golden color. They were the perfect height and would look rather pretty in the room.

"Maybe a silver tinsel rope wouldn't be too bad. Gold will clash with the ornaments, though. I can't agree to gold."

"Silver, of course." The kugels were silvery, and gold *would* look all wrong.

"That would be fine if it makes you feel better," Mary said.

"It does."

"Very well, then."

The sign and the tinsel rope would prevent accidental tampering, but nothing of the criminal variety. Should she talk to someone about her concerns? Ivy would be the logical person as she was next of kin, but Mary didn't want Ivy involved. Sadie could go to Jackie, the director of nursing who Sadie had known for years from the community health fair, but wouldn't they just go to Ivy with their concerns? Telling anyone would also alert them to the value of the ornaments, which might go unnoticed otherwise.

What would it take to set up an alarm system and camera to guard the Christmas tree for the next forty-eight hours? Maybe Sadie would look into that after her book group's Christmas dinner party tonight. She'd been looking forward to the party—she was taking her "Red and Green Salad" for the dinner, and a bath set in her favorite scent for the gift exchange—but now she wished she could stay here and keep an eye on the tree. There simply was no time for a stakeout, though. And Mary wasn't worried, so maybe Sadie was building this into something more than it was, the same way she was worrying about the combined family Christmas to the point of having nightmares.

"Oh, isn't Christmas wonderful, Sadie?" Mary leaned forward to retrieve another ornament from the box. "It's such a season of miracles, don't you think?"

Red and Green Salad

2 bunches fresh raw broccoli, cut into bite-sized pieces
1 cup sunflower seeds
½ cup chopped red onion (optional)
1 cup dried cranberries or pomegranate seeds
1 cup grated Swiss or mozzarella cheese
1 pound bacon, cooked crisp, cooled, drained, and chopped

Mix all ingredients together in large mixing bowl.

Dressing

1 cup mayonnaise
1 tablespoon red wine vinegar
1 tablespoon sugar

In a small bowl, mix all ingredients together with wire whisk and pour over vegetable mixture, stirring to coat thoroughly. Add salt and pepper to taste.

CHAPTER 6

Sadie was late to the book group Christmas dinner party because she'd had to go to two different stores looking for silver rope tinsel, and then get the quilting frame legs from the storage closet at the back of the garage, and then print out a sign that read "Please do not touch Mary's tree. Merry Christmas."

Luckily, Mary was in the common area chatting with some other residents when Sadie arrived to set up the protective measures, which allowed Sadie to be in and out quicker than she would have been if she'd also visited with Mary. She felt bad about not visiting, though.

When Sadie made her Red and Green Salad during the summer, she used dried cranberries, which she switched out for pomegranate seeds for the holidays. Everyone at the dinner loved it, and Sadie promised the recipe to three different women who asked for it. Danyelle, the evening's hostess, made the most delectable slow-cooked ham; Sadie had then begged for *that* recipe. She would make it a few times before deciding if it deserved to be in her Little Black Recipe Book, but if it turned out for her the way it had turned out for Danyelle, it was a shoo-in. She'd been planning to do a ham for the family party on the twenty-sixth, but she liked Danyelle's recipe better than her own—a rare occurrence. The pineapple and orange juice helped tenderize the meat, though she might add a little sriracha to boost the flavors. Not that it wasn't excellent as it was.

Sadie woke up early Monday morning—Christmas Adam, as she jokingly called it—to a news report that the winter storm she'd been watching was gaining power to the east. Forecasters were predicting record snowfall—twenty-four inches in that many hours—and issuing driving precautions that made Sadie's throat constrict. She texted Pete before even getting out of bed—should they cancel the party? Move it back? Would next year be better?

He calmly talked her down, reminding her that they had smart kids who wouldn't take unnecessary chances, but to make sure she had batteries in the flashlights and extra food in the cupboards, just in case. Two years earlier, they'd been homebound for three days after an ice storm, though only out of power for about four hours. Talking—well, texting—with him helped put her at ease, and by the time she got out of bed, she was ready to tackle the to-do list she'd made the night before.

Christmas events with her community and friends were finished, and people seemed to be turning their attention to their own families and home celebrations—the best part of the season.

Sadie started her own family holiday preparations by making the layers for the Cunningham Candy Cane Cake—not too tricky, though she weighed the cake layers on her kitchen scale rather than eyeballing them to make sure everything was even. She also whipped up the yellow cake she would use for Americanized English Trifle from the Hoffmiller side of the family. She made the trifle puddings while the cakes baked, and then assembled the soup-in-a-jar gifts she'd be giving to the ladies in her yoga class later that morning. While the cakes were cooling, she decorated the jars with cute cards that said "Wishing You a Souper Merry Christmas" and tied each one with a bow before loading them into a box.

Then she reviewed what else she needed to do—neighbor gifts were a high priority—and made a grocery list that included extra of everything in case they got snowed in. The only relief from the stress of having to go to the grocery store this close to Christmas was that she would not be there on Christmas Eve—that was enough to turn anyone into Ebenezer Scrooge.

Once the lists were made—one of recipes left to make, one for recipes left to assemble, and one of groceries needed to complete the items from the first two lists—Sadie changed into her yoga clothes, loaded the jars of soup mix into her car, and headed out the door for her 11:00 Silver Sneaker Yoga class. It'd be the last one she'd attend this week since the studio would be closed on Christmas Day and then she'd have family in town for a few days afterward.

She hadn't had a nightmare about the family party last night, though she *had* dreamed she'd been chasing a reindeer that had a dozen of Mary's kugels hanging from its antlers. The moon boots Sadie had been wearing in the dream were super heavy, making it even harder to chase after the reindeer.

When Sadie was waiting to pull out of the parking area of her complex, she noticed something different about Mary's house on the other side of the street. Hanging on the eves were Christmas lights that had not been there yesterday—Sadie would have noticed.

Sadie wasn't sure yet how she felt about the people who had bought Mary's house. The sale had happened so fast that Sadie hadn't had time to prepare for it, and then Mary hadn't seemed to know anything about the new owners. In the three months since the sale, Sadie had watched work crews come in and out and furniture be delivered. Twice, she had left treats with notes on the door in hopes that it would start a conversation with her new neighbors. The treats disappeared, but the people never reciprocated.

Despite the activity, it didn't seem like anyone actually lived there—it was always dark at night—and Sadie worried that the work being done on the interior would erase the charm of Mary's 1950s Craftsman—built-in shelves in the living room, steps up to the dining room, a chute that sent clothes from the upstairs to the downstairs laundry room. None of that was Sadie's business, she knew that, but to her, the house was part of Mary, and she didn't like knowing that it might change to the point where it no longer reflected her.

When she'd complained to Pete, he'd suggested that it was because she had wanted them to have bought the house, but that wasn't it. They didn't need that much space, though it would be nice when family came to visit. She just didn't want to see it changed, that was all. She'd miss Mary. And she'd miss Mary's house, which had been such a haven for her in a new town with a new marriage and a new life to build. It was symbolic, she'd explained to Pete. He'd smiled, but remained unconvinced.

Sadie looked at the lights another moment and made the decision to take a neighbor Christmas gift over later tonight, just in case. People wouldn't put lights on a house they weren't going to live in, right?

Decision made, she pulled onto the street and headed for yoga.

The yoga class was refreshing after having been on her feet all morning, and so good for her bone health. The teacher had given them all Santa hats to wear, which fell off a dozen times before they all threw them to the side. After class, though, they put them back on and took a dozen photos that would make the rounds on Facebook. After sharing hugs and giving each of the ladies one of her soup mixes, Sadie headed to the grocery store, pumping herself up with some "Jingle Bell Rock" played extra loud on the stereo as she drove beneath the gray sky. The forecast said the snow wasn't due until Christmas Eve night, but it looked as though the sky could crack open at any time and unleash its mayhem.

The store was packed, and tempers were fragile, but Sadie managed to find everything she needed plus plenty of snacks for the grandkids and life-sustaining items like tuna and granola in case the storm got out of hand. Soup and chili were already getting low on the shelves, making Sadie grateful for Pete's advice to stock up.

Sadie had just finished loading the groceries into the back of her car when her phone rang from inside her purse on the front seat. She practically dove through the driver's door, praying that it wasn't one of the kids saying that, due to the weather reports, they weren't coming after all. She would feel personally responsible if this combined Christmas celebration fell apart now. She saw that the call was Joy, and her heart leaped in her chest for a different reason as she answered.

"Hi, Joy." Sadie hurried to get settled in the front seat and pull the door closed against the cold. "Is Mary okay?"

"Grandma's fine," Joy said.

Sadie exhaled and relaxed against the seat, her eyes falling closed in relief while the rest of her shivered in the cold. "Oh, thank goodness." Sadie started the car, double-checking to make sure the seat heater was on. "I was going to stop by and see her this afternoon. How's she doing today?"

"She doesn't have her usual energy," Joy said. "And she's already had a breathing treatment this morning."

"Oh, shoot, should I come sooner?" Mary's bad days were usually set from the very start, and everyone would worry it was the beginning of the end. That Christmas was only two days away and Mary had just barely accepted that she would be here to enjoy the holiday made it that much more upsetting for her to have a bad day now. "Sometimes company helps restore her energy."

"Fiona will be here around 2:30, but, um, I actually called you about something else. I thought you might be the best person to talk to since you helped Grandma decorate the tree and everything."

Sadie's breath caught in her throat as the disturbing dream about the kugel-hijacking reindeer came to mind. "Did something happen with the tree?"

Sadie imagined the tree being knocked over despite her protective tinsel rope, all the kugels and candy canes breaking in the process. Or a fire alarm triggering the fire suppression system that would drench the tree and destroy the Dresdens before you could say "Look at Frosty go."

"Not the tree. Grandma's ornaments. Some of them are missing."

Every muscle in Sadie's body tightened, then adrenaline rushed through her as she put the car in gear and pushed her to-do list completely out of her mind. "I'll be there in four minutes."

Christmas Ham

1 spiral pre-cooked, pre-sliced ham on the bone, about 5 pounds*
1 (20-ounce) can crushed pineapple, undrained
1 ¼ cup orange juice
2 teaspoons mustard

Spray 6-quart slow cooker with nonstick cooking spray, turn to low.

Cut up spiral-sliced ham into individual portions. (For the end that isn't sliced, cut into chunks.) Open pineapple can, but do not drain liquid. Add mustard to can of pineapple and mix well with a spoon.

Add ½ cup pineapple to the bottom of the slow cooker then layer ham and pineapple until all the ham is in the slow cooker. Pour orange juice over ham-and-pineapple layers. Cook on high for 2 to 3 hours.

Remove ham from slow cooker, layer on a platter, and serve.

*Adjust amounts of ingredients based on the size of your ham.

CHAPTER 7

J oy was waiting outside of Mary's room, and her expression softened
in relief when she saw Sadie. She tucked her hair nervously behind
both ears as Sadie crossed the final few feet. Joy was wearing straight-
leg jeans and an oversized CSU sweatshirt with tennis shoes. She was
pretty, with soft features and big eyes, but Sadie had the impression
that she didn't want anyone to notice her most of the time.

"Thank you so much for coming," Joy said, worry in her voice.

"Of course," Sadie said. "Tell me exactly what happened."

Joy's thick eyebrows came together. "I don't know what happened, that's why I called you."

"I mean, tell me how you noticed the ornaments were gone,
when you noticed they were gone, and what you've said about it to
anyone."

"I haven't said anything to anyone but you."

"Good," Sadie said, nodding. "How did you discover the missing ornaments?"

"I got here about half an hour ago—at 1:45," Joy said, her voice
anxious. "I asked Mary about lunch and how she'd slept while I
straightened up the room like I always do. Then I noticed that

something just didn't look . . . right with the tree. Like . . ." She scrunched up her face, looking at the ceiling as though searching for the right words. She met Sadie's eyes again after a few moments. "Like, it wasn't as full, if that makes sense."

Sadie knew exactly what she meant. She had hung nearly seventy ornaments on a four-foot tree, which was easily half the size of the trees Mary had put up in her living room in the past, creating a very crowded tree. She waved Joy to continue.

"So, I counted them. There are only twenty-nine of the bulb kind and seventeen of the cardboard kind."

Sadie closed her eyes in hopes of hiding the horror she felt. It was all she could do not to say "I told you so!" even though that had nothing to do with Joy. When she opened her eyes to meet the worried gaze of Mary's granddaughter, she felt capable of regular speech.

"You're sure?"

Joy nodded. "I counted them three times before I called you."

"Did you tell Mary?"

"No," Joy said, shaking her head. "She'll be so upset. Her father brought them back from World War I before Grandma was even born." Her eyes got glassy. "Who would take them?"

"An equally important question might be, who *could* take them." Sadie looked past Joy. "I'd like to take a look at the tree. I'll just tell Mary I'm stopping in to say hi."

Joy moved out of the way, and Sadie led the way into the room. Mary was listening to an audio recording of *A Christmas Carol*, and Joy crossed to the dresser to pause the CD.

"Hee-haw, Mary," Sadie said.

Mary straightened in her chair and smiled broadly, but her

movements seemed slower than usual, evidence of her lack of energy. "Hee-haw, Sadie. I wasn't expecting you this morning, was I?"

"I wanted to come by and wish you a Merry Christmas," Sadie said, bending over Mary's chair to give her a hug. As soon as she straightened, she looked toward the tree, easily seeing what Joy had noticed. The tree was still brimming with ornaments, but not quite as much. "How was your night, Mary?"

"Excellent. I slept like a hibernating bear." She turned toward Joy. "Would you mind getting me a Diet Coke, Joy?"

"I'll go see if they've restocked the vending machine," Joy said.

"Thank you, dear," Mary said.

Joy shared a look with Sadie before stepping out of the room.

"So, what are your plans for the rest of the day, Mary? Joy said Fiona is coming over."

"She's knitting scarves for all her grandkids according to their Hogwarts houses, which was determined from some online quiz. She still has five to finish before tomorrow—can you believe that? She says she isn't leaving until they are done, but I told her I'd get sick of her if she stayed that long." Mary smiled when she said it, and Sadie laughed at the joke.

Fiona was Mary's oldest friend—literally—and yet she was almost ten years younger than Mary. At eighty-five years old, Fiona still lived in her own home, traveled, gardened, quilted, and, apparently, knitted. She would often spend time with Mary when she had something to do like organizing photos, making invitations, or some other handwork that was always better to do with company. They had quilted together for years, but these days, Fiona never brought blocks to work on. She knew it was too painful to Mary, who missed the skill she'd spent so many years perfecting.

"I think Fiona's company sounds like a perfect Christmas present," Sadie said.

"She's also bringing me some of her homemade caramels. That's the real reason I'm letting her come."

"You are terrible," Sadie said with a laugh, knowing Mary was just warming up for the banter she and Fiona would exchange throughout the visit.

Mary told Sadie about the Christmas Eve party the facility was hosting for residents and staff. Several of the residents were going home with family members following the party, but Mary had declined Ivy's offer to do the same. She was comfortable in her room, where she could find her way around and ask for help from people trained to know how to assist her. Sadie was relieved Mary was staying at Nicholas House, considering how frequently Mary needed the breathing treatments these days.

While they chatted, Sadie moved close enough to the tree to inspect the ornaments. Sure enough, there were five kugels and five Dresdens . . . and one candy cane missing. Joy hadn't mentioned that. And not just any candy cane. The one missing was the one with the chip out of the bottom—Mary's favorite.

Sadie's head spun, and it took all she had to keep her tone light and conversational as she tried to determine which specified ornaments were missing. Joy came back with a Diet Coke and Fiona.

"Gracious, Mary, you look terrible. Would it kill you to put on a little lipstick?" Fiona marched into the room and deposited her bag of yarn on the floor by the bed so she could take off her coat.

"Oh, Fiona," Mary said with a disappointed sigh. "You came, after all? Well, at least I can't see your ugly mug. There are perks to being blind, you know."

Fiona laughed as she settled into the dining chair set next to Mary's recliner and put her knitting bag between her feet. "Just for that, I'm not going to tell you where the smudge is on your face. You're going to have to find it yourself."

Usually, Sadie loved to stay and listen to the two of them go at it—eventually the banter would level off into normal conversation—but today she was eager to get out of the room.

"I've got that Diet Coke," Joy said, popping the top and finding a straw in the drawer of Mary's nightstand. She adjusted the bedside table to the right height so Mary could reach the can.

"I'll see you later, Mary," Sadie said. "Please try to keep Fiona out of trouble."

Mary sighed dramatically. "I've been trying to do that for fifty years, and it hasn't done a lick of good."

Once back in the hall, Sadie leaned her forehead against the wall until the nausea passed.

Someone had stolen Mary's ornaments.

Mary would be devastated.

Sadie felt the sharp knife of regret twist. She should have acted on her instincts last night and insisted Mary not put the ornaments on the tree. She could have put them back in the tub without Mary noticing, or talked to Jackie, who could have told Mary she wasn't allowed to have such valuable things in her room, or even gone to Ivy, who would have started a fight with Mary but probably won if Sadie had sided with her. Why hadn't Sadie stayed overnight and kept watch herself?

The feelings swirled and twisted, and then Sadie took a deep breath and felt dusty yet familiar tumblers clicking into place inside her mind as she swapped out her self-reproach with a target more deserving of her anger—whoever took the ornaments. The thief hadn't just stolen something from Mary, he'd stolen something from a woman who was dying of cancer. He'd stolen the memories that were tied to those ornaments. He'd stolen from Joy and from Nicholas House, too.

Joy came out of Mary's room and closed the door.

"See what I mean?" Joy asked.

Sadie pulled herself upright and got to work. She was an investigator now, and Joy was her first interview. "You counted them today when you noticed the tree looked different. Did Mary tell you how many there were of each, or had you counted them yourself before now?"

"Both. Grandma told me the story about them last night, and about the ones that had been broken over the years. I counted them with Star last night."

"Star?"

"My boyfriend's daughter. We brought sushi for dinner, and Grandma told us about how my great-great-grandfather had brought the ornaments from Europe. I'd never heard that part of the story. And Star's working on her numbers so I used the ornaments for a counting lesson."

"What time was that?" Sadie asked, wishing she had a notebook so she could start sketching out a timeline. Mary had mentioned yesterday that Joy and Frank were bringing her sushi that night, so at least Sadie could count that as confirmation of Joy's story.

Joy scrunched up her face a moment. "It was after I got off work at five o'clock, so maybe a little before six? Grandma said I'd just missed you."

"I left at 5:30," Sadie confirmed. "What time did you leave?"

"A singing group had come in, so we stayed to listen with Grandma in the common room. It was probably 7:30 before we left." She considered for a moment. "Yeah, 7:38, because when we got back in the car, I commented that I had to be to work in fourteen hours and twenty-two minutes, and then I helped Star count the hours on our way to the Everbrights' house. She slept over at their house since Frank worked late last night and early today." She looked at her watch and frowned. "I work at 3:30 today, so I need to leave here by three."

Sadie checked her watch; it was 2:22. She nodded. She'd have to speed things along. "The ornaments likely disappeared between 7:00 last night and 1:30 this afternoon, then."

"We were here until 7:30 last night," Joy reminded her.

"But you weren't in Mary's room the whole time. Someone could have come in while you were watching the performance."

"Oh, yeah." Joy looked back toward Mary's room and frowned. "This is awful."

"Of the missing Dresdens, I know the woman in the rocking chair, the knight, and the rabbit are gone, but I'm not sure about the other two."

"The star is missing," Joy said. "I'm not sure of the last one, but I can probably figure it out. I've helped Grandma with her tree the last couple of years."

"From the kugels, it's the green artichoke, blue teardrop, pink grapes, yellow gourd, and the teal pine cone," Sadie remarked after reviewing the list again in her mind. "All different colors."

"Does that matter?" Joy asked.

"I don't know," Sadie said. "The chipped candy cane is gone, too."

"Mary's Candy Cane?" Joy said, her eyes wide.

"Another red-and-white candy cane was put in its place," Sadie said. "I'd hung the chipped one myself because Mary wanted it near the top. I looked to see if it was somewhere else on the tree, but it wasn't."

Joy wrapped her arms around her stomach and started blinking back tears again. "I don't know how to tell Grandma."

"We don't tell her," Sadie said before she'd fully explored the options. Once the words were out, however, she knew it was the right step for now.

"We don't?" Joy repeated, sounding unsure.

Sadie took hold of the girl's upper arms and looked her in the eye. "We don't tell her unless we absolutely have to, which I hope never happens. She can't see them, and she told me she has a firm rule that the ornaments are not to be moved until they are being put away. We're going to find those ornaments before that happens, Joy."

"But . . . how? And why would someone take them?"

Sadie let go of Joy's arms, deciding to tell some of the truth but not all of it. "Christmas is a time of desperation for some people. Money is tight, and opportunities to make a little extra can be a big temptation."

Joy's eyes widened. "You think someone would take them to sell?"

Sadie thought that was pretty obvious, but not everyone had the investigative gifts she had honed over the years. "I think so, yes. The ornaments are antiques."

Tears filled Joy's eyes again. "Oh, yeah, I guess they would be, huh? Why would someone do such a thing to Grandma?"

"Greed," Sadie said, revealing the underbelly of most crime. The root of all evil was not money, as most people liked to say. Greed could be fueled by addiction or fear or jealousy, but in Sadie's experience, at the heart of most assaults on justice was wanting more than what was your share. "We're going to figure out who did this, and then we're going to get those ornaments back on your grandmother's tree before she knows they're missing."

"But, how are we going to find them?"

Sadie's mind immediately made a list of what had to be done in order to find Mary's ornaments. It had been years since she'd sunk her teeth into a case, but the tingle of excitement was banked by the reminder of what was at stake. Mary had survived against all odds to celebrate one last Christmas with the people she loved. Someone had stolen her most prized possessions, a beautiful remnant of her past that was marked to bless her dear granddaughter with a beautiful future.

"We'll find them by questioning every possible person who could have taken them," Sadie confirmed, feeling commitment take hold in her chest. She stared at Joy. "I need your word that you won't talk to anyone about this without me, okay? Whoever took these ornaments tried to hide the crime, which means we don't want them to know we're onto them."

Still looking like a reindeer caught in the headlights, Joy nodded. "I won't talk about it to anybody. What can I do to help?"

CHAPTER 8

B *less this girl,* Sadie thought. "To start, I'd like you to find out who came to see Mary between your visit last night and the discovery you made today."

"How do I do that?" Her voice was shaking, just a little.

"Just have a normal conversation with Mary about who came to visit after you left yesterday and this morning, which staff members have been working the floor, that sort of thing. It's not too much time to cover so hopefully it won't be difficult to get a full accounting of people I can then talk to."

"Oh, okay," Joy said, nodding. "I could, uh, write it down. Make a list! And I can figure out which other Dresden is missing."

Sadie smiled. "Great idea. In the meantime, I'll see what I can find out about who came and went at the facility during that time." As a partially secured facility, visitors to Nicholas House were required to sign in through a computer program that buzzed them in. It wasn't a perfect system: Once, Sadie had slid in before the door closed behind someone else because she was holding a basket of fruit she'd brought for the staff, and twice, an exiting visitor had held the door open for her before she'd finished signing in.

An account of everyone who had visited the facility from the sign-in program might not be complete, but every investigation started with getting the obvious things out of the way. Would Jackie let her access that information? Sadie's established relationship with Jackie through their community work would hopefully help.

Sadie looked at her watch and noticed she was still dressed for yoga—black leggings, UGG boots, and her oversized Pentatonix Christmas hoodie she'd bought at the concert she and Pete had attended three years ago in Salt Lake City. Sadie sighed. It was one thing to go grocery shopping in this outfit after her yoga class—everyone would be so frantic about their own shopping no one would notice her—but there were serious limitations to what she could do as part of an investigation when she looked like a bum.

Joy was watching her expectantly, and Sadie pushed aside her vanity for the sake of finalizing their plan. "You talk to Mary about who came to see her, Joy, that's very important. I'm going to see if I can get some information from Jackie."

"Okay." Joy looked terrified.

Sadie forced a reassuring smile. "We'll find them. There are always clues when a crime is committed. We'll find those clues and follow the trail until we get those ornaments back."

Joy nodded, but it wasn't confident. Sadie understood that feeling too well. They were on a deadline. Not only did she need those ornaments back where they belonged before Mary discovered the theft, she had to find a way to protect the remaining ornaments.

"Do you know how long Fiona is planning to stay?"

"She asked Mary if she could join her for dinner, so I think she's planning to be here for a while."

Sadie could work with that, and she had Fiona's number if she needed to ask her to stay a little longer. "What time is Mass tomorrow?"

"We're going at two o'clock, but Grandma wants to be there around one in order to get a good seat."

"And Mass lasts an hour?"

"Usually a little longer for Christmas Mass."

That meant Sadie had approximately twenty-four hours to find Mary's ornaments. The price of failure was an unacceptable cost.

Soup in a Jar

Mix
1½ cups of lentils, at least two colors, divided
¼ cup dehydrated onions
1 teaspoon salt
1 teaspoon black pepper
½ cup dried carrots (optional, use an additional ½ cup of lentils instead)
¼ cup brown sugar
1 bay leaf

Layer items in a pint-sized canning jar in the following order from bottom up:
- ½ cup lentils
- dehydrated onion
- ½ cup lentils
- salt and pepper
- dried carrots (or ½ cup lentils)
- brown sugar
- ½ cup lentils (or more to top of jar)
- bay leaf

Put lid on tight.

Soup

1 pound hamburger*
1 (46-ounce) can tomato juice
3 cups water
1 cup celery, chopped
1 cup carrots, chopped (optional if using dehydrated carrots in mix)
"Soup in a jar" mix
1 teaspoon Worcestershire sauce
Salt and pepper to taste
Chili powder, curry, or other spices, to taste

Brown hamburger, drain if desired. Add tomato juice, water, vegetables, and "soup in a jar" mix. Mix well. Bring to a boil, then simmer 3 hours.

Season with Worcestershire sauce and salt and pepper. Serve with sour cream and cheese, if desired.

*Can use 1 pound diced chicken in place of hamburger.

CHAPTER 9

S adie straightened the waistband of her sweatshirt as she headed toward the nurses' station to talk to Jackie. She was counting on the fact that, as a friend, Jackie wouldn't hold yoga clothes against her—plus, the sweatshirt was still Christmassy. She also hoped Jackie wouldn't be too protective of the information Sadie was requesting.

The front doors of Nicholas House opened into a beautiful foyer, set with leather couches in front of a stone fireplace that, this time of year, was always on. Tucked to one side was a door that remained locked at all times, separating the foyer from the facility itself. Passing through the locked door required a sign-in code; each resident had their own that they gave out at their discretion. Visitors without a code could use an intercom system to contact the nurses' station and be buzzed in.

Once through the secure door, the rest of the facility was laid out with spacious hallways. The residents' rooms were set around the exterior of the building so that each room had a window. The hallway created a circle as it looped around the center rooms of the facility that included the nurses' station—right at the front—public restrooms, executive offices, a dining room, an activity room, and a laundry room. The nurses' station consisted of an open countertop area that looked more like a reception desk than the control center of the building.

Sadie headed toward the nurses' station because that was the best place to find a staff member. She smiled politely at another resident, Rachel Haskins, and her daughter, Melissa, walking arm in arm down the hall. They didn't look like diabolical thieves, but Sadie couldn't count anyone out this early in the game and made a note that both of them were here around the same time that Joy discovered the missing ornaments. She'd know soon enough if Melissa had also been here last night, a much more likely window of opportunity.

Jackie wasn't at the nurses' station, but Carol was. She was one of the Certified Nursing Assistants—called aides—and though Sadie hadn't ever talked to Carol, she'd seen her around the facility. Carol was reading a letter so intently that she didn't notice when Sadie stopped on the other side of the chest-high countertop.

There was a computer on a rolling table with a locked cabinet in front that Sadie knew was the medication cart. The computer monitored the access, and the cart could be wheeled around the facility as needed. On the back wall was the "On Staff" whiteboard with spaces to fill in which nurses and nurse's aides were working at any given time. Today, *Nadine* was written into the nurse's spot in red dry-erase marker, and *Molly* and *Carol* were written in green dry-erase as the day's aides.

Sadie coughed discreetly, and Carol startled to her feet, pushing the rolling chair back so quickly it hit the wall underneath the whiteboard. Carol refolded her letter and tucked it into one of the front pockets of her scrubs before dropping both arms to her side.

"Sorry," Carol said, overly alert now.

Sadie's eyes lingered on the top of the paper poking up from the woman's pocket for only a moment before she met the woman's anxious expression. "No worries, I didn't mean to sneak up on you."

"Oh, you didn't sneak up on me." She tried to give Sadie a reassuring smile but was obviously embarrassed by her reaction. Or paranoid. "I was just, um, distracted."

Sadie took in every detail of this woman for the notes she would be making as soon as she had her hands on a notebook. And a pen. Preferably one of the gel roller kinds that wrote dark and smooth but didn't seep through the other side of the paper. Size .07mm. Black. "I was looking for Jackie."

"She's running some errands."

Carol tucked an errant lock of frizzy red hair behind her ear. Sadie guessed she was in her mid-forties, trim, with nice skin and chocolate-brown eyes that complemented the woman's bright hair in ways the burgundy-colored scrubs did not. Another shade of burgundy might work, but this one had too much . . . red in it, probably. Nurses wore navy blue, which would be a much better option for Carol.

"Darn," Sadie said, looking toward Jackie's office door at the back of the nurses' station. "Any idea when she'll be back?"

"No, sorry. Can I help you with something?"

Sadie didn't even consider telling her about the ornaments, that needed to stay on the down-low. She was only willing to talk to Jackie about it because she needed her help with determining who had access. How much she would tell Jackie was still up in the air. They were friends, and Jackie had worked here at Nicholas House for twelve years, but Sadie couldn't risk her telling anyone else. It could give the thief time to come up with a story or, worse, destroy evidence, which, in this case, was the ornaments themselves.

"I'm Sadie Cunningham, a friend of Mary Hallmark, and yes, maybe you could help me. I was wondering who worked last night."

"Is there a problem?"

"No, I'm just curious."

"Why?"

"Um, is it private information?"

"Not necessarily, but if there's something we need to discuss with the staff, it's better for the management to handle it than for family members or, in your case, friends."

Sadie did have something to discuss with the staff, but not in the way Carol thought, and why was she taking such a position of power anyway? She was an aide, not even a nurse who would be in charge when Jackie wasn't around. Rather than try to sweet-talk her way into getting the information, Sadie dropped the smile and decided to try the direct approach.

"Mary couldn't remember who worked last night, and I said I would ask."

Carol hesitated, and Sadie could almost see her trying to determine if there was some reason *not* to tell Mary who her caregivers had been. When Carol relaxed just a titch, Sadie knew she'd won. "Harry was the nurse last night, and Shep was the aide, with Molly as float."

"Float?"

"An extra aide who works from five to nine."

"Oh, I see. And who would have worked until the seven o'clock change? That's when the shifts change over, right? You guys work twelve hours?"

"Mary wants to know that, too?" Carol asked.

Sadie held her eyes. "Yes." She knew how much Mary paid each month, and it certainly earned her this kind of information. Never mind that Mary wasn't really asking. Even Santa would understand Sadie's reason for the teeny-tiny lie.

"Okay, well, Bella was the nurse yesterday, and Jose and I were the aides. What's this about?"

Why was she so paranoid? And demanding? It wasn't like Sadie was asking how much each staff member owed on their credit cards or if they'd ever parked illegally in front of a fire hydrant. "Thank you," Sadie said, smiling stiffly. "I'll let Mary know. Could I also leave a message for Jackie?"

A muted ding sounded from somewhere within the nurses' station. Sadie looked around for the source of the sound—maybe a cell phone—then noticed Carol fumbling in her pocket—not the same pocket where she had hidden the letter.

She pulled out a small, black device that looked like an old-fashioned pager. "That's a patient's call light, I've got to go."

Outside of each resident's room was a lantern-type sconce that lit up when a resident pushed the button each of them wore like a pendant around his or her neck. Carol fumbled through some things on the counter and then handed Sadie a pad of message slips—the pink kind that secretaries sometimes used. Very old-school, but Sadie was glad to have something to write on—a record. "Go ahead and write your message, I'll give it to Jackie when she gets back."

Sadie was standing in the doorway of the nurses' station, blocking Carol's exit. She moved as though to step out of the way but went the same direction as Carol, then went the other way when Carol did too—the awkward dance of two people seemingly trying to get out of one another's way and choosing badly. Or choosing well, depending on the intention. Finally, Sadie turned sideways so that the flustered aide could move past her, necessitating they brush against each other. Pinching the corner of the letter from the wide pocket of Carol's loose-fitting scrub top was easy, and Sadie allowed herself a moment of triumph as Carol hurried down the hall, stopping at the door just past Mary's. Carol knocked softly and let herself in.

Sadie looked around to make sure no one was watching her. Rachel and Melissa had already crossed to the other side of the building. Assured no one was there to tattle, Sadie stepped into the nurses' station far enough to be out of view of anyone who might be coming down either hallway. She flipped the letter open and scanned the return address—Department of Regulatory Agencies—before moving her attention to the letter's contents. It was addressed to Carol Benson, care of Nicholas House, and talked about some kind of assessment? No, it was a *report* on an assessment. No, it was the *request* for confirmation of an assessment report. Sadie moved on to the next paragraph, her lips moving as she read key words and phrases.

Reinstatement of *nursing* license—Carol was a nurse? Or had been a nurse, anyway.

Compliant with terms of probation.

Final administrative approval required.

If confirmation of assessment by supervisor was received by January 7, the license would be reinstated on January 15 with no further restrictions.

Footsteps in the hall pulled Sadie's attention away from the letter. She quickly folded it and held it at her side while deciding what to do next. There might be time for her to cross the station and slip out the doorway on the opposite side, but she'd rather get more information from whoever was coming, which could be one of the staff members.

If it was Carol, however, Sadie didn't want to be caught holding her letter. She flicked the paper under the counter, hoping that, when discovered, it would seem as though it had fallen out of Carol's pocket. Sadie adopted a more casual position as she leaned against the wall at the back of the nurses' station, put her hands behind her back, and began humming "O Christmas Tree."

A moment later, Carol turned into the nurses' station and right into Sadie. Sadie exaggerated the impact, grabbing at Carol's arm as though for balance, and, she hoped, creating a scenario in which the letter could have fallen from Carol's pocket in this moment.

"Oh, I'm so sorry," Sadie said as she stumbled sideways, taking Carol with her a couple of steps. Sadie took hold of the back of a chair to steady herself.

"What are you doing here?" the flustered aide said as she pulled her arm out of Sadie's grip. "Visitors aren't allowed in the nurses' station."

"I was just waiting for Jackie," Sadie said innocently. She hoped. She quickly moved to the visitor's side of the counter. "I'm so sorry, I didn't mean to upset you. Are you alright?"

Overstating Carol's reaction would take attention off Sadie being somewhere she wasn't supposed to be. Carol's eyebrows pulled together. "What?"

"You seem upset. Did I hurt you?"

"No, you didn't hurt me," Carol said sharply.

"Oh, good. Is everything else okay?"

"Everything's fine." Her hand went to her pocket and froze when it didn't feel the letter. She looked down and pulled both pockets open, which Sadie took as her cue to exit immediately. Except she'd forgotten to fill out the message slip. She pulled the pad still on the counter toward her, took one of the pens topped with artificial poinsettias from a jar filled with beans—cute—and quickly wrote her name and number and "Call me ASAP."

Carol rifled through the stacks of papers on the counter. It was so hard not to tell her to look under the counter—the letter would be right there.

Sadie tore off her message and held it out to Carol. "Here's my message for Jackie, thank you." She wanted to be gone before Carol found the letter just in case the aide was the paranoid type who would suspect Sadie might have read the letter. Of course, it wouldn't be paranoia if Carol's suspicions were true, but that was immaterial. Sadie would certainly have more questions to ask Carol after she learned a bit more about the reasons behind the letter, and she didn't want to jeopardize that future interview by drawing Carol's suspicions now.

Carol grabbed the message and put it rather carelessly on the counter before resuming her search. She said a very non-Christmassy word under her breath and didn't even apologize for it. Sadie saw her eyes move to the floor a moment before Carol ducked; she'd found the letter.

"See you later," Sadie said as she turned and hurried toward the door that separated the resident areas from the foyer, quickly reorganizing her plans in the wake of this new information. She didn't need to talk to Jackie about which staff had been working during the time the ornaments had gone missing anymore, but she still wanted to look at the visitor sign-in list. She also needed to learn more about this licensing situation with Carol and change into clothes that would be more appropriate for the work she was doing.

Sadie was nearly to her car when she remembered that Joy was still talking to Mary. She considered going back inside but didn't want to encounter Carol again. Instead, Sadie continued to her car, turned it on, and then texted Joy to meet her in the parking lot when Joy was done. Then Sadie flipped on the heated seat and started making a list on her phone of what she needed to do.

- Get list of visitors from Joy
- Shower
- Unload and put away groceries at home
- Cookies?
- Look up Carol Benson's license info
- Background check on Carol?
- Contact visitors from Joy's list
- Get list of visitor sign-ins from Jackie, if possible

Sadie looked over her list. Had she missed anything?

Movement in her peripheral vision caught her attention, and she looked up to see Joy hurrying out of Nicholas House, but not seeming to be looking for Sadie. Maybe she hadn't read Sadie's text.

The cold took Sadie's breath away when she stepped out of her warmed-up car and hurried across the parking lot. When Mary had reached the point where she could no longer drive, she'd given Joy her car—a white 1999 Buick LeSabre. It was a solid automobile by anyone's standard, but as bulky as a tank and thus easy to find in a parking lot full of newer, sleeker vehicles.

"Joy!" Sadie called.

Joy lifted her head and stopped when she saw Sadie.

"How did it go?" Sadie asked when she caught up, her breath clouding in the chilly air.

"I'm late for work," Joy said, casting her eyes around the parking lot and crossing her arms over her chest, an action that could be due to the cold, or could be an evasive movement. There was something tight about Joy's entire demeanor that hadn't been there earlier.

"Did you get the names of Mary's visitors since last night?"

"Oh, uh, yeah. Ivy came by later."

"Okay," Sadie said, opening a fresh page of notes on her phone and typing in Ivy's name. Odd that Ivy would come back after having already been there earlier when Sadie had been there to help with the tree. "What time was that?"

"I-I didn't ask."

"You left at 7:38, so it would have been after that—pretty late for a visit."

Would Ivy take the ornaments? What if she'd learned how valuable they were, and that Mary was planning to give them to Joy?

Ivy was Joy's great-aunt, and from what Sadie had been able to tell, they hadn't really known each other until Ivy had moved back to Fort Collins a year after Joy had moved in with Mary. Any possible tension between them—due, perhaps, to Joy assuming Ivy's role in caring for Mary—had never shown itself to Sadie. Ivy didn't pay Joy much attention.

Could Ivy be jealous of Joy now that she was trying to reconnect with Mary? Sadie thought of how Ivy had offered to paint Mary's nails yesterday but Mary had said Joy had already done them. Possible bad feelings were something to learn more about. Sadie hoped Ivy had nothing to do with this. Such a theft would undermine the improvements Mary wanted to make in their relationship, and yet if Ivy *did* have the ornaments, they would be recoverable.

Joy looked longingly toward her car, drawing Sadie's attention. Why was Joy in such a rush all of a sudden? Joy had said she needed to leave for work at 3:00, but it was only 2:45.

"Did anyone visit today?"

Joy looked at Sadie. "Um, no. That's it." She looked left when she said it, a "tell" Sadie had seen before when people were lying. Joy had seemed eager to help fifteen minutes ago when they had planned things out in the hallway. Now she was acting shifty. Joy was the last person Sadie wanted to suspect. Unfortunately, Sadie had learned a long time ago that rejecting any potential suspects was a novice mistake. And Sadie was no novice.

"What about staff that came into her room?" Sadie already knew who had worked the shift, but which ones had Mary actually interacted with? It seemed that the aides were usually assigned to either the east or the west wing of the hallway. Mary was on the east side.

Joy met Sadie's look with her big, clear, blue eyes, but her shoulders dropped in self-reproach. "I didn't even think to ask about staff."

Sadie had specifically asked her to find out what visitors *and* *staff* had been in Mary's room. That Joy had forgotten one part of a two-part interview was not encouraging. "It's fine," Sadie said, putting her hand on Joy's arm and forcing a bigger smile than she felt in hopes of putting her at ease. Even if Sadie didn't trust Joy, she needed Joy to trust her. "Thanks so much for your help. I'll let you know how it turns out. Have a good day at work."

CHAPTER 10

🍬

The wonderful thing about favorite recipes was that Sadie knew them by heart and could throw them together in a jiffy. Candy Cane Crinkles were just such a recipe, and during the drive home, Sadie determined it was one she could make between the investigative and personal hygiene-related tasks on her growing list of things that had to be done.

She hated that she was rushing to get her neighbor gifts handed out. She'd been waiting because she'd hoped Pete would be home in time that they could deliver them together, but now she'd have to take care of it herself. Which was fine, but now she had an investigation to manage as well, and so she was doubly under the gun. Thank goodness she was an excellent multitasker.

The other great thing about Candy Cane Crinkles was that the recipe made several dozen cookies, if she used her one-inch scoop. Sadie might need cooperation from as-yet-unknown persons as the investigation moved forward, and a few extra plates of cookies could come in handy.

As soon as she parked in the double-car garage beneath their town house, Sadie texted Ivy, asking her to call back as soon as possible. Ivy had said she was working today, but surely it wouldn't be too busy for her to return a call.

Sadie unloaded her groceries and then started throwing ingredients into her mixer. Candy Cane Crinkles required the basic ingredients Sadie always had on hand. Except candy canes, she supposed. She'd crushed up six boxes early in the season and still had plenty on hand, though she'd made sure to set aside enough to sprinkle on top of the Cunningham Candy Cane Cake.

Between the steps of making cookies, Sadie put away the rest of the groceries and checked her phone to make sure she hadn't missed Jackie or Ivy. The cakes from that morning were still on the counter, so she wrapped them in plastic wrap and put them in the freezer until she was ready to work with them again. By the time that was done, the cookie batter was ready to be rolled and the oven had almost preheated.

She was rolling balls of cookie dough in powdered sugar for the second pan when her phone rang. Finally! She wiped her hands on her Feliz Navidad dishtowel and answered the call on the third ring, noting Ivy's name on the ID as she lifted the phone to her ear.

"Hi, Ivy. Thanks for calling me back," Sadie said, holding the phone with one hand and going back to the cookies with the other hand. The powdered sugar, when baked, made a very thin icing-type layer over the cookies—so yummy—but the process was awkward to do with one hand. Still, Sadie had no time to waste.

"Is everything okay with Mom?"

Sadie wished she'd included that Mary was fine so Ivy wouldn't have worried. She herself had made the same assumption when Joy had called her earlier.

"Mary's fine. I called you about something else."

"Okay, but I don't have a lot of time—I'm at work."

"I'll be fast," Sadie said, appreciating the excuse to jump right in. "Did you visit your mom last night?"

Ivy paused longer than necessary. "Yes."

"What time was that?"

Another pause. "What's this about, Sadie?"

Not the reaction Sadie would expect from someone with nothing to hide. Sadie needed to play this as though they were on the same team, however. For now.

"Did you happen to notice anything different about your Mom's Christmas tree when you were there?"

Five full seconds clicked by on the reindeer clock mounted above Sadie's sink before Ivy spoke. Sadie's sugar rolling slowed as she waited for an answer. The oven dinged that it was finished pre-heating. Sadie's rolling rate increased.

"Different?" Ivy finally repeated in a suspiciously even tone. "Like what?"

"There are some ornaments missing from Mary's tree."

"Some ornaments?" She emphasized the plural.

"Five kugels, five Dresdens, and one candy cane—the chipped one that means so much to your mom."

"Really?" Ivy said in a cautious tone after another long pause.

Sadie waited for her to say more. When she didn't, Sadie continued. "You didn't put them away for safekeeping, did you? Maybe your favorites?" Sadie had handed her a reasonable motive on a platter. Ivy could confess to taking them right now and claim she was trying to protect them. Sadie put the last cookie on the pan.

"I didn't do anything with the ornaments," Ivy said. "How's Mom handling this?"

Sadie held the phone with her shoulder while she washed her hands. "I haven't told her yet. I'm hoping to find the ornaments before she discovers they're gone." Sadie put the two pans of cookies into the oven and set the timer for ten minutes before crossing to the desk in the living room. She pulled a notebook and pen—black, .07mm, gel-roller—from the top drawer, flipped to a blank page, and started taking notes about this conversation.

"She'll be so upset." Ivy sounded truly concerned.

"Yes, she will, and I hope we never have to tell her. I'm trying to put together a timeline of when they went missing. Joy was there at six o'clock last night, and the ornaments were there. What time did you visit?"

"A little after eight," Ivy said. "I was on my way home from a dinner with friends, and I brought Mom the peppermint ice cream she wanted."

That was a reasonable explanation, except that Ivy had said a couple of hours before that impromptu visit that she wouldn't be back until today.

"I see," Sadie said.

"And then Mom didn't even want it. She had me put it in the freezer in the kitchen." She spoke as though Mary not wanting the ice cream was a personal offense.

"Did anyone else come into the room while you were there?"

"Um, an aide came in with laundry, and then a nurse came in to do a breathing treatment when Mom couldn't catch her breath after she used the bathroom."

"Do you know which nurse and which aide?" That reminded her to write down the information about the staff Carol had told her earlier, which she did. Harry had been the only nurse on shift at eight, she remembered. Shep was the night-shift aide, and Molly was the one on shift from five to nine.

"Um, I'm not sure."

Something in the way she said it made Sadie doubt that was true. But why not tell Sadie if she knew?

"There were two aides on shift at eight o'clock—Molly and Shep. Which one brought in the laundry?"

"I really wasn't paying attention."

Hmm. "Well, Molly is in her mid-thirties, Caucasian, with brown hair and probably five foot two. Shep is younger, African American, wears diamond studs in both ears, and is at least six feet tall." It wasn't hard to confuse the two.

"Oh, I guess it was Molly."

Sadie circled Molly's name on the list she'd made. Either Ivy hadn't wanted to tell Sadie, or she had been *really* distracted.

"No other visitors while you were there?"

"No, but Mom said Frank would be stopping by after he got off work." Ivy said "Frank" the way someone else might say "sardines" or "toenail clippings." It was the first time Sadie had heard anything about Frank that was less than positive. Mary referred to him as "That dear boy."

"You mean Frank and Joy were stopping by?" Surely Joy hadn't thought she could hide her own visit from Sadie.

"Mom only said *Frank*." Ivy used that same smashed-bug tone. "Joy had already been there earlier with Frank's kid; they brought Mom some sushi."

"Hadn't Frank come with the sushi, too?"

Joy had said "they'd" brought dinner . . . but only specified Star when she'd recounted the evening. Mary had been expecting Frank when she'd told Sadie about the visit earlier though.

"Mom said Frank hadn't come with them, but that he was coming after work to fix her nightstand or something. If you ask me, he's totally the type to steal some old lady's ornaments if he thought they were valuable."

"*Are* the ornaments valuable?" Sadie asked. Mary hadn't thought Ivy knew that information.

"They're a hundred years old," Ivy said. "They've got to be worth something. Marley's Antiques came out and did some bids for Mom last summer, and the ornaments were laid out with the other old stuff when I stopped by that evening. When I asked Mom about them, she waved off the comment and told me that the hair extensions I'd just had put in made me look like a tramp."

Mary, Sadie thought in reprimand. Even if that were true, you never told your daughter she looked like a tramp. "You think Frank would recognize the ornaments as valuable?" Twenty-something-year-olds didn't typically know much about antiques in Sadie's experience. For them, the only things of value were the newest phone model and latest fashion.

"Maybe Joy told him."

"Joy knew the ornaments were valuable?"

"She'd have helped Mom set everything out for the bids, and it wasn't long after those bids that Mom told me Joy was seeing someone. Maybe Joy talked about Marley's Antiques coming out to bid stuff out and put the idea in Frank's head. I mean, that could very well be the reason he's stuck around."

Ouch.

Ivy spoke again before Sadie could think of how to respond. "Have you met Frank?" she asked.

"No, I haven't."

"Well, that explains why you didn't think of him right from the start," Ivy said, animated now that she was gossiping about other people. "Joy tried to hide him from me, too, but I stopped in to visit Mom when they were there a couple of weeks ago. Joy couldn't get him out of there fast enough. He's a total slimeball."

Sadie couldn't bring herself to write "slimeball" next to Frank's name on the list of people to talk to, but Ivy's impression would be easy enough to remember without the notation. Sadie hated that yucky feeling in her stomach that often accompanied judgmental gossip, and yet judgmental gossip was a valuable resource of information for two reasons. First, it revealed details about the person being gossiped about. Second, it revealed an awful lot about the person sharing the gossip.

Sadie thought back to Joy's discomfort in the parking lot an hour ago. She hadn't had any misgivings about finding out the visitors before she talked to Mary, but had been very uncomfortable after. Why? And why hadn't Frank visited along with Joy and Star when they brought in the sushi? Did Frank often visit Mary without Joy?

"Do you know what time Frank was supposed to be there?"

"Well, I was there until about 8:30 . . . Hold on a second." Sadie could hear voices in the background on Ivy's side of the call, then Ivy was back. "Sorry, I've got to go, but I'm pretty sure Frank got off work at nine o'clock so he was coming late. Look, Sadie, Mom has always played her favorites—no one knows that better than I do—and Joy is, like, her favorite person ever, which is great.

More power to both of them. Of course, Mom wants to like the guy who likes Joy, I get that. But if Mom could *see* this guy, she'd think twice about him."

"Huh," Sadie said, writing "appearance?" on the paper and circling it three times. "Do you know Frank's last name?" Maybe Sadie would run a quick background check.

"No idea." She was talking faster now, and Sadie imagined a coworker standing in a doorway, tapping her watch.

"Do you know where he works?" Sadie asked quickly.

"Some auto parts store," Ivy said just as fast. "The kind of job they give to *felons*. Total dead-end job. I really have to go."

Sadie thanked her, hung up the phone, wrote everything down, and checked the timer—thirty seconds left on the cookies. Perfect. She rolled a few cookies in powdered sugar until the timer dinged and then took the two hot pans out of the oven. It took a few minutes to finish rolling the cookies for the next two pans, but soon enough she put them into the oven and set the timer for another ten minutes. Normally she would move the baked cookies to cooling racks and refill the pans with the next batch of cookies, but she *had* to take a shower.

She started peeling off her yoga clothes as she hurried toward the bathroom, planning to take the fastest shower since the years when Breanna and Shawn had been toddlers and she'd had five minutes to herself on a good day.

Sadie glanced at the clock on the bedside table as she passed it—4:08. The day was barreling toward night, and tomorrow was Christmas Eve. Sadie forced her mind to focus and planned out her next few steps:

- Find out where Frank works
- Find out why Joy was acting so weird
- Look up Carol's license information
- Talk to staff—Molly and Bella
- Talk to Jackie
- Find out when Fiona is leaving
- Stay overnight at Nicholas House?
- Put lockpick set into purse—just in case.

Candy Cane Crinkles

2 cups granulated sugar
1 cup butter, room temperature
1 tablespoon vanilla extract
2 large eggs
½ teaspoon kosher salt
½ teaspoon baking powder
½ teaspoon baking soda
3 ¼ cups all-purpose flour
1 cup vanilla chips
10 full-sized candy canes, unwrapped and crushed (about ⅔ cup)
½ cup powdered sugar

Preheat oven to 350 degrees F. Prepare baking sheets with parchment paper.*

Combine sugar and butter, and mix with electric mixer until light and fluffy. Add vanilla extract and eggs. Mix until combined, scraping down sides as needed. Add salt, baking powder, baking soda, flour, vanilla chips, and crushed candy canes (powder and all).

Pour powdered sugar onto a large plate. Scoop 1 tablespoon or use a 1-inch scoop of dough and roll into a ball. Roll in powdered sugar until coated. Place on baking sheet and repeat with remaining dough.

Bake for 9 to 11 minutes or until bottoms are barely brown and cookies look matte.

Remove from oven and cool cookies about 3 minutes before transferring to cooling rack. Makes approximately 4-dozen 1-inch scoop cookies.

*The candy cane pieces will melt, which is why you need parchment paper or a silicone mat. If neither of those is available, simply grease the pan before baking and cross your fingers.

Note: You can crush candy canes in a food processor, just don't turn them to dust. You want the pieces to be smaller than a pea, but still be chunky. You can also crush them by hand by double-bagging zip-top bags and using a hammer or rolling pin to achieve the right texture.

Note: Pete thinks lemon-flavored baking chips are just as yummy!

CHAPTER 11

A text from Pete was waiting for Sadie when she got out of the shower.

Pete: We've got a packed evening so that we can get out of here tomorrow. Flight leaves 1:02 and looks like I'll beat the storm ☺ Cue that love-light!

Sadie considered telling him about the ornaments, but decided it would be best to have more information first. Her investigations had been a source of conflict between the two of them in the past. He was a former police detective who took the "rules" very seriously, while Sadie was more . . . creative. When she'd traded sleuthing for writing early in their marriage, Pete had been almost too supportive of her doing something other than investigative work.

For now, Sadie responded to his text with hearts and kiss emojis. He said he'd call before bed, and she promised herself that she'd tell him then what her day of baking and yoga had turned into.

There was no text or missed call from Jackie, however. Maybe Sadie didn't need those sign-in lists after all, but a quick review of her notes showed that at the very least she needed to verify things like what time Ivy had been there and when Frank had arrived and when he'd left. She hadn't even started looking into Carol yet, but she imagined she'd have some questions for Jackie about her as well. The letter had said Carol needed an assessment from her supervisor. Sadie was pretty sure that meant Jackie, which meant Jackie had to know about whatever license issue Carol was involved in, right?

The timer on the oven dinged, and Sadie threw on her robe and hurried to tend to the cookies. She took the now-cooled cookies off the first two pans, rolled more cookies for another batch, and put the pans in the oven before running back to her room to get dressed. When the final batch was out of the oven eleven minutes later, she finally sat down at her computer.

Joy's Facebook profile was private, which meant Sadie couldn't see anyone on her friends list—including Frank. Her profile photo was her hugging a kitten with an exaggerated grin Sadie had never seen in real life; Joy was usually nervous and quiet, so Sadie was glad to know she had those happy-as-can-be moments that everyone deserved. The cover photo along the top of her profile was of Old Town Fort Collins covered in snow, something Sadie would have appreciated were she not mostly interested in details about Frank, which were not available in the limited information of the private page.

Sadie sent Joy a friend request, waited twenty seconds, and then opened two fresh tabs on her computer to continue working while she waited. In the first search bar, she typed "Department of Regulatory Licenses Colorado." In the second, she typed "Auto parts stores Fort Collins Colorado."

She started with Frank since he was fresh on her mind and called each store in the order they'd appeared on her screen and asked for Frank. When they told her she had the wrong number she thanked them, wished them a Merry Christmas, and hung up before calling the next store. It wasn't until the fifth store—with a four-star rating, as it happened—that the man who answered the phone said, "Yeah, just a minute."

Thank goodness Joy's boyfriend wasn't named something like Brandon or Jake; there was probably one of those at every shop in town. Sadie hung up and wrote down the address for the auto parts store in her notebook. She'd rather talk to Frank in person than over the phone.

Then she turned her attention to Carol Benson and her probationary nurse's license.

Sadie found her way to a page on the Regulatory Licenses website where she could look up disciplinary history on any nurse. A nice Christmas bonus was that the site didn't make her create a profile to access the information; everything was public record. Sadie put in Carol's first and last name and Fort Collins, which was all the information she had. A split second after clicking the "search" button, the record of Carol Benson popped up like a jack-in-the-box, except that Sadie didn't scream like she did with actual jack-in-the-boxes. Sadie scanned the information and then hit print on her computer before going to find her reading glasses. She preferred to read on paper when given the choice; she spent too much time in front of the screen as it was.

By the time Sadie was back to the computer, there were two pages of information about Carol cooling in the printer tray much the same way the cookies were cooling in the kitchen. Sadie smiled at how efficiently she was using her time as she gathered up the pages and then settled into her reading chair—not to be confused with her writing chair.

Four years ago, Carol had been accused of improper medication disposal and fraud at the rehab facility where she worked in Colorado Springs. Her license had been suspended for a year and then reinstated with restrictions for thirty-six months. Sadie did the math to confirm that the timeline matched up with the information in the letter she'd read earlier. Thirty-six months would end mid-January of the coming year, the same time Carol's final assessment was due to the department. Sadie read through everything a second time to make sure she understood as best she could. Technically, Carol *was* a nurse, but with restrictions regarding what she could do.

Improperly disposing of medication was a different sort of crime than stealing vintage ornaments, but the fact that Carol had showed poor decision-making abilities in the past was worth consideration. At the very least, Carol had a secret, and secrets were often the starting place for crime. Unraveling one secret would often lead to another, then to someone else's secret. There was no way of knowing how a case was going to end, which was why the investigator had to be on their toes and ready for action at any moment.

Why was Carol working as an aide and not a restricted nurse? And why was she working at Nicholas House, which had an excellent reputation in the community? It was surprising that they would employ anyone but the very best.

That was something she would very much like to discuss with Jackie.

Sadie spent a few minutes putting the cooled cookies on the

poinsettia-decorated plates she'd bought and then wrapping each plate in cellophane. A plaid ribbon pulled everything together, though she'd have loved to include a sprig of holly in each of the bows if she'd thought of it before now. She put the notebook and printed papers into her purse and grabbed her coat. Sadie wore Christmas sweaters for the twelve days before Christmas— for the American observance—and then the twelve days after Christmas—for the British celebration—and had paired her "Ho Ho Homecookin' for the Holidays" sweater with black jeans and her black snow boots.

When everything was ready, she took three plates of cookies to her three closest neighbors, though only Bob and Janet Bailey were home. Bob was a mostly retired litigation attorney who now did consulting and contract law part-time, and Janet was still teaching drama at the high school even though she was nearly seventy. They were sad that Pete wasn't with her, which was an easy regret for Sadie to share, and they promised to get together and plan a trip in the new year—the Baileys were wonderful vacation friends.

Sadie left plates on the doorsteps of the other two neighboring condos and then texted the owners to let them know to look for them since, like her and Pete, many of them went in and out through their garages and didn't often use their front door. It was all Sadie could do not to apologize for a single-item plate—usually she did a sampler plate with three or four different holiday favorites. Fortunately, good friends would never hold a plate of cookies against her.

As Sadie made her way out of the neighborhood, she saw lights on at Mary's house. Someone *was* there! If not for having important things to do at the moment, she'd have gone over with a plate of cookies and forced an introduction. But there was no time. She needed to meet Frank, who Ivy thought was a slimeball and whose visit Joy had hidden. She was counting on the cookies to help move things forward. Christmas Eve Mass was twenty hours away.

CHAPTER 12

O ne of Sadie's favorite things about Fort Collins was that it was a big enough city to have all the conveniences, yet small enough that she was never too far from any of them. Sadie pulled into the parking lot of the auto parts store exactly six minutes after she'd pulled out of her garage. The squat, blue building was well lit as evening fell. When Sadie pushed open the door a minute later, she was greeted with the acrid smells of oil, metal, and . . . pine, thanks to an oversized, tree-shaped air freshener duct taped next to the door with the words "Pretend I'm Mistletoe" written in marker across the front.

Sadie took a few moments to acclimate to the unfamiliar environment, then moved toward the front desk. Christmas music played through the store, which was bustling with more women than Sadie would have expected, until she realized they were likely looking for last-minute gifts for the men in their lives. The thought was still fresh in her mind when she presented herself at the counter, which that was festooned with rope tinsel held in place with yet more duct tape. An overweight man on the other side of the counter smiled at her, his cheeks bright and jolly. She hoped he moonlighted as Santa when he wasn't running the cash register here.

Sadie put the plate of cookies on the counter, pulling out the big guns up front rather than relying on her personal charm to earn cooperation. There was no time to waste. "Hi, I'm wondering if I can trade you this plate of cookies for ten minutes of Frank's time."

"Absolutely!" he said without a moment's hesitation. He pulled the plate closer to himself, then turned his head and bellowed toward the back of the shop, "Franklin D. Roosevelt! Personal shopper request for you." He pulled a pocketknife from somewhere below the counter and sliced through the cellophane with a single swipe. The knife disappeared as quickly as it had appeared, and just like that, the cookies were fully accessible.

Sadie was feeling pretty pleased with her success until a man she could only assume was Frank—he wasn't really named Franklin D., was he?—stepped out of one of the aisles that stretched behind the counter, fixed his eyes on her, and began moving her way.

She glanced at the embroidered name on his shirt when he was close enough to make sure it said "Frank" before forcing her smile back in place and raising her eyes to meet his again. Frank was tall—at least as tall as Shawn, who was six foot four last Sadie had checked, but she swore he'd kept growing until he turned twenty-five. Where Shawn was dark, broad, and handsome—if Sadie did say so herself—Frank was pale, thin, and . . . punk. Tattoos covered both arms and the right side of his neck. Sadie couldn't identify specific images without staring, and it wasn't polite to stare even when people seemed to make choices that invited scrutiny. He also had shiny black gauges in his ears at least an inch across.

For the love of the North Pole, Sadie could not picture this guy with Joy. Could there be two Franks who worked here? Or maybe Joy's Frank worked at an auto parts store Sadie hadn't called yet because she'd assumed that the Frank working at store number five on her list would be the only Frank employed at an auto parts store in town.

"You're looking for a gift?"

He had a nice voice—low and steady—but his overgrown brown hair was greasy at the part and tucked behind both ears. Was he growing it out so he could wear it in a man bun? A man bun plus gauges plus tattoos added up to a definite not-her-cup-of-cocoa impression of Frank.

She'd planned to be direct about his visit with Mary yesterday, but quickly decided to play up the personal shopper angle instead. She had to make sure this was the right Frank—and she was hoping he wasn't. "Um, yes, something for my husband."

Frank nodded.

"These are really good, ma'am."

They both turned to look at the guy behind the counter—his name tag said "Clint." Half the cookies beneath the splayed cellophane were gone. His smile suddenly fell. "Shoot, was I supposed to save some for Pine-head?"

Pine-head?

She looked at Frank, her eyebrows together.

Frank quirked a half smile. "He means me."

"Oh." Sadie turned back to the cookie monster. "I've got another plate in the car I can give . . . Frank."

The fat man grinned and picked up the last cookie while a woman approached the counter with a case of motor oil. Wasn't that kind of like a man buying his wife a bunch of vacuum bags for Christmas?

"So, what did you have in mind?"

Sadie turned back to Frank. "Excuse me?"

"For your husband? What are you looking for?"

"Oh, um, I'm not sure. What would you suggest?"

"Well, is he the kind of guy who likes to work on his car himself or is he more into accessories?"

To Sadie, accessories were earrings and necklaces, maybe a brooch for formal occasions, and it took her a moment to twist her interpretation to include automotive parts that could accessorize a vehicle the same way a scarf could dress up a sweater.

"Um, probably accessories. He drives a Toyota Corolla."

"Year?"

Sadie had to think back to when she'd last registered the car. "Um, 2011."

"Any aftermarket props?"

"Props?"

"Lift kit, trims, decals?"

"Oh, yes, we've got thirteen little foxes along the back window to represent our grandkids. Get it, foxes, cause they're so cute? Like, foxy."

Frank smiled awkwardly. "Ah, I get it. That's clever."

Sadie glanced around the shop, looking for something to save her, and her gaze landed on a sign on the far wall. "What about floor mats?" The driver-side floor mat was still stained from a long-ago ketchup incident. People underestimated the stain power of condiments all the time.

"We have Classic or WeatherBeater styles. Is his car a manual or automatic transmission?"

"Automatic."

She followed Frank to the far side of the store. It wasn't hard to picture him in a sleeveless biker jacket with a switchblade in his hand while he held up a convenience store. In fact, that was an easier mental image to conjure than him sitting in Mary's room at Nicholas House. If someone were to base their impression of him based only on looks, then "slimeball" could fit. But Sadie had always felt such terms to be much more fitting for a character assessment. After all, a corrupt politician could be a slimeball even if he wore a nice suit and washed his hair every day.

They approached a row of floor mats hung along the wall, and Frank started thumbing through them. He lifted two sets off the rack: one was rubbery plastic and the other was gray carpet.

"What color is the interior of his car?"

"Oh, um . . . tan, I think." Right? Or was the interior of her car tan and Pete's was gray? Neither of them was all that into their cars.

Frank put the carpet mats back. "These are the only mats that fit the automatic Corolla and would match his interior, then. What do you think?"

"They're perfect," Sadie said even though they looked awfully utilitarian. The upside, however, was that they would never be stained by anything ever again. They could be hosed off at the same time Pete washed his car, which was every other Saturday; Sadie had bought him a yearly pass to the Peachy Kleen for Father's Day last year.

"Great. Clint can ring you up and—"

"What about some other accessories?" Sadie asked because she'd managed to learn exactly nothing about Frank so far. "Like, something to hang from his rearview mirror."

"Um, sure," he said, leading the way toward another part of the store.

"You really know your way around this place," Sadie said casually after they'd crossed a few aisles together. "Have you worked here long?"

"About a year," he said, stopping in front of a variety of decorative items—key chains, lanyards, and rearview mirror hangers. Some were definitely rated PG-13. Frank waved his hand in front of the display, and Sadie made out one of the tattoos on the back of his hand—Spider-Man. Was the rest of him tattooed with comics? Did Spider-Man have some sort of special significance to him?

"Here's what we have."

Sadie pretended to be interested in a rather cliché pair of fuzzy dice, though smaller than the ones that had been popular in the 1950s.

"Are you from Fort Collins originally?" she asked.

"Um, no, my daughter and I moved up here last November."

Joy's Frank had a daughter. This could really be Joy's boyfriend! "So, you've been working here since you moved; that's a good job history. What brought you here? Family, maybe?"

"Um." He shifted his weight. "Just needed a change of scenery, I guess."

"It *is* lovely here," Sadie said, keeping the smile on her face. She moved her attention to a different hanger, this one with a stuffed Tom and Jerry from the cartoon wearing old-fashioned riding helmets and goggles. Did Pete like *Tom and Jerry*? Sadie was indifferent to that particular cartoon. "Have you been to the Rocky Mountain National Park? It's so pretty there."

"No, not yet."

"Maybe this summer, then," Sadie said, giving him a smile as she moved her attention to a SpongeBob SquarePants hanging. Would Pete choose Tom and Jerry over SpongeBob? The grandkids would think SpongeBob was much cooler. "Where are you from, originally?"

"Um, Pueblo."

She gave him another glance. Was she making him uncomfortable? If so, why? Did he have something to hide? She went back to the mirror hangers and tried again to picture this man and Joy standing side by side, his arm over her shoulder and her smiling up at him adoringly. Like pieces from two different puzzles, the image just wouldn't come together.

"What's your daughter's name?" Joy had said it was Star, and it was the final confirmation Sadie needed to accept that, against all odds, this *was* Joy's boyfriend. Two Franks who worked in auto part stores in Fort Collins, Colorado, with daughters was already nearly an impossibility.

"Um, we call her Star."

"We?" She looked at him expectantly. Would he account Joy in the "we"?

He took a step backward. "Look, lady, I'm flattered, but I've got a girlfriend."

The heat of embarrassment started at the back of her head and rushed forward and then down the length of her body. "O-oh." Sadie tried to laugh, but it sounded like she was choking. A man in coveralls entered their aisle, and Sadie flushed even hotter. The only thing worse than Frank assuming she was flirting with him was for someone else to think so, too. She was fifty-nine-ish-years old, and Frank was in his twenties.

She lowered her voice, casting a wary look at the new man in the aisle. "I wasn't trying to, um, ask you out or anything . . . See, the thing is . . ." Oh, gosh, how did she explain having pretended to be a customer? Because she hadn't thought it possible that he was really Joy's boyfriend, so she'd taken on the covert identity of an innocent shopper?

The man in coveralls stopped a few feet away. She leaned closer to Frank and dropped her voice to a whisper. "Um, is there somewhere we could talk?"

Frank took a step away from her, and her cheeks burned hot enough to roast chestnuts without a fire.

"Pine-Sol!"

Frank turned toward the front of the store, and Sadie, confused at why he answered to the name of a cleaning product, turned her head with him.

Clint at the cash register made eye contact with Sadie. "Sorry, ma'am, we've got a delivery truck—last one of the year—just pulled up a little early. Frankie's got to get them checked in."

"Do you, uh, want me to take these to the desk for you?" Frank asked, lifting the floor mats he still held and looking relieved for a reason to escape. He couldn't be more relieved than she was, however. She'd really lost her touch—no one she'd interviewed on past cases had ever thought she was hitting on them. "You can take all the time you need with the rest of your shopping. For your husband."

She couldn't look him in the eye. "Y-yes, it would be wonderful if you would leave them at the counter. Thank you."

He was halfway down the aisle before she finished talking, eager to get away from the cougar who he thought had put her sights on him.

Humiliated, Sadie spent a couple more minutes browsing, and thinking, before making her way to the front desk with the Tom and Jerry mirror hanger. She grabbed a digital tire gauge from a box near the cash register to round out her purchases and justify the amount of time she'd spent here. Pete was going to be so confused by his gifts. Could she return the items at another store?

"Those were seriously the best candy cane cookies I've ever had," Clint said as he rang up her purchases. "Sometimes people will make a candy cane-themed dessert and the candy canes get stuck in my molars, ya know? These, well, these were perfect."

"I'm so glad you liked them," Sadie said, trying to use his compliments to boost her currently low levels of self-esteem.

"Alright, that will be $212.36—cash, check, or card?"

She handed over the credit card she'd promised not to use anymore after having overshot her Christmas shopping budget weeks ago.

"Did Frankenpine help you out good?" Clint asked as he ran her card through the scanner.

"Frankenpine?" she asked.

He laughed and handed back her card. "I call him about a dozen different things—Frankie, Frankincense, Frankenpine, Pine-Sol, Pineapple Head." He shrugged good-naturedly. "He's just got one of those names that's easy to mess with, ya know?"

"His last name is . . . Pineapple?"

Clint laughed again—a rich belly laugh that made Sadie smile. He really would make an excellent Santa. "Just Pine. I tell him if he could clean off the paint, put on fifty pounds of muscle, and master a smoldering look, he could be an actor like that Chris Pine guy." He laughed at his joke, and Sadie smiled politely. She couldn't remember who Chris Pine was. Captain America?

First name: Frank. Last name: Pine. Approximate age: 27. Former address: Pueblo, Colorado.

Sadie hadn't confirmed his visit to Mary last night—without Joy—or what he'd done there, who he'd seen, or when he'd left. But without meaning to, Sadie had managed to gather enough information for a background check. When she was online, she could also review the store's return policy and find the next-closest location to make her returns to. Since she had to go back home for the computer work, maybe she could add "Make meringues" back onto her to-do list. It was another of the Cunningham family favorites and one that would be nice to get out of the way. Oh, and she still needed to mix up the Cunningham Cheeseball—that was one she definitely wanted to make ahead of time so the flavors had time to blend.

She thanked Clint, threw her purchases on the back seat, and drove the six minutes back home for the next round of fact-checking via Google.

Over the river—literally, the Cache la Poudre River went right through town—and through the woods, to grandmother's house she went. Except it was her house. Well, her town house. She shook the mismatched reference from her mind and just focused on the drive.

CHAPTER 13

🍭

Sadie was almost home when a glance at the clock alerted her to the fact that she'd known Mary's ornaments had been gone for almost four hours—it was 5:49. Every minute that passed was one minute closer to the possibility of Mary discovering the theft. It also renewed Sadie's commitment to find who had absconded with the eleven stolen ornaments as well as make sure none of the other ornaments went missing.

With determination fresh in her veins, Sadie called Nicholas House again—hands-free, of course—in hopes she could catch Jackie before she left for the day. Assuming she left at six o'clock, which Sadie wasn't sure of. She saw Jackie at the facility quite often, but didn't track her office hours.

"Nicholas House, Carol speaking."

It was temping to grill her, right now, but phone interviews were not optimal, and Sadie still felt scattered after her exchange with Frank and didn't trust herself to ask the right questions. There was usually only one chance to interview hostile suspects, which Carol would certainly be.

"Can I speak with Jackie, please?" Sadie said.

"She's gone for the day. Can I take a message?"

"No, thank you," Sadie said politely, then ended the call. Had Carol even given Jackie the message Sadie had left? Sadie considered her options for a full fourteen seconds, then used voice commands to text Carla Meadows. Carla was in Sadie's book group, but she also worked at the chamber of commerce and was one of the sponsors of the health fair Sadie had worked with Jackie. It was because of Carla that Sadie had offered to be on the committee after she'd lamented the lack of volunteers a few years ago.

Carla texted back that she didn't have Jackie's personal cell phone number, but she said Linda Abramson might because Linda had been over the senior health portion of the fair.

A text to Linda turned up the number for Hannah Litchfield, whose cousin's neighbor had dated Jackie's son a few years ago. By the time Sadie was home, Hannah had found Jackie's cell phone number and Sadie was gushing her thanks via texts. This was what Christmas was really about—friends helping friends.

Sadie called Jackie as soon as she was parked in the garage, then let out a frustrated breath when the call went to voice mail. She left an urgent message.

Once back in the kitchen, Sadie preheated the oven, prepped two cookie sheets with parchment paper, and organized the ingredients for the meringues and the cheeseball. She set her laptop on an overturned 9x13-inch pan so she could beat the egg whites with one hand and use the other hand to peck out the details into the computer in order to run a background check on Mr. Frank Pine of Pueblo, Colorado.

Back when Sadie had worked as a private investigator, she'd run background checks all the time and had used a variety of websites to gather the necessary information to get the full view of a person's history. She'd let her membership to many different websites lapse over the years, except for one. It came in handy when she needed to know if the plumber coming to fix a pipe was the sort of man she could trust to leave alone in her bathroom, or if the guy who moved in on the corner really smelled funny because he worked at a chemical warehouse or because he was making meth. Turned out to be the former, but it had been nice not to have to wonder.

That the results of Frank's search began to appear almost instantly did not bode well for Frank. Criminal charges were the first database the program scrubbed, and the egg whites were just getting foamy as Sadie leaned forward and read the details.

When she saw the prison sentence, she would have stopped beating the eggs if she could, but she would not have time to do this again if this batch didn't work. She enlarged the text on her screen so she could read without straining her eyes too much.

Finally, the egg whites got that dry look of stiff-peak stage, and she stopped the beaters. She scrolled through the public record, growing more and more concerned with every line. Concern turned to worry which turned to a rock in her stomach by the time she'd finished reading through everything.

Multiple arrests, starting within a few weeks of his eighteenth birthday, a state-funded rehabilitation program that he flunked out of when he was twenty, and then pleading guilty to an assault a year later didn't leave much doubt as to Frank Pine's character. He'd been out of prison for almost three years now, off probation for only sixteen months, and here in Fort Collins for the last thirteen.

Yet he had custody of his daughter, and he'd kept a steady job since coming here. Did Clint from the auto parts store know of Frank's history? He must, right?

But did Joy know?

Sadie poured in the crushed candy canes for the meringues and used her rubber scraper to fold them into the egg white-and-sugar mixture nice and easy so as not to deflate the lift. While she filled up a frosting bag so that she could make perfect little meringue stars, she continued to contemplate the situation.

If Mary knew about Frank's past, she'd have said something to Sadie. But was Mary's ignorance because these two young people were hiding the information or because poor Joy had no idea who Frank really was? Ivy had made up her mind about him after one meeting, and the facts pointed to Ivy being right. The comment about Frank having "the kind of job a felon would have" had seemed to be tongue-in-cheek, but she'd been right. Yet as put off by him as she was, Ivy hadn't told Mary about his appearance. Again, if she had, Mary would have told Sadie. If Joy was hiding these things about Frank, wouldn't she be afraid Ivy would tell? And why hadn't Ivy told? Maybe Ivy's eagerness to share her thoughts on Frank was a diversion.

Sadie put down the decorator's bag, wiped off her hands, and put a star next to Ivy's name, then tapped her pen on Joy's name.

How long had they been dating? How old was Star? Why did Frank—a felon—have custody of his daughter? Would Joy protect Frank instead of Mary? Maybe Joy's discomfort when they'd talked in the parking lot earlier that day was because she had been hiding Frank's visit to the facility. But maybe that discomfort was fear.

Sadie started making meringue stars on the parchment-covered pans she'd set out. As soon as she finished, she put the bowl, beaters, and spoons in the sink to soak and put the pans in the pre-heated oven. Then she texted Joy.

Please call me ASAP!

Sadie googled "Frank Pine Colorado news article," bringing up several articles about his arrests. Regarding the arrest that sent him to prison, one article said that Frank had been yelling racial slurs at a man he then attacked. Another said it was the man he'd been with who had yelled racial slurs, but then Frank got involved in the brawl. Neither option spoke well of him.

He wasn't on Facebook, unless he went by another name, and Joy hadn't yet approved Sadie's friend request so she couldn't see if there was any information linked that way. Sadie printed out the pages she needed and was paper clipping the pages together when her phone rang, startling her so much that she hit her hip on the open silverware drawer and knocked a package of cream cheese off the counter. Her irritation with her clumsiness was forgotten when she saw that, according to her phone, the call was from Jackie.

Finally!

Meringues

4 egg whites (½ cup)
1 cup white sugar
1 teaspoon vanilla extract
1 teaspoon lemon juice
2 tablespoons cornstarch

Preheat oven to 275 degrees F. Line two baking sheets with parchment paper.

In large glass or metal bowl, beat egg whites until stiff peaks are achieved, but not dry. About 3 minutes.

Gradually add sugar, 1 tablespoon at a time, beating well after each addition until thick and glossy. Gently fold in vanilla, lemon juice, and cornstarch. Mix well.

Drop mixture by teaspoons or use a pastry bag to pipe teaspoon-sized dollops onto parchment paper, about an inch apart.

Bake 25 minutes. Turn off oven, prop door open, and leave in oven for 35 minutes or until pan is cool to the touch.

Store in an airtight container

Variations
- 1 tablespoon lemon zest
- 1 tablespoon lime zest
- ½ teaspoon peppermint extract
- ½ cup crushed candy canes

Add any of the variation ingredients along with the vanilla and cornstarch. Omit the lemon juice if not doing a citrus flavor.

CHAPTER 14

🍬

This is Sadie," she said breathlessly, ignoring the pain in her hip as she put the cream cheese—still fully packaged—back on the counter. She could put most of the cheeseball together while she talked and mix it after she finished the call. It would be a relief to get one more recipe out of the way.

"Hi, Sadie, it's Jackie. I'm on my way to pick up my son from the airport, but I just got your message. What's wrong?"

"Thank you for calling me back," Sadie said as she reordered all the thoughts in her head, reminded herself of her goals, and pulled out her notebook. She wrote "Call from Jackie 6:29 PM" so that when she sat down to update her detailed timeline, she would know where this call fit.

"Of course, it sounded urgent, but I called the facility first and they said Mary was fine. Fiona's spent the day with her, which always puts her in good spirits."

"It is urgent, but not regarding Mary's health."

Jackie paused, and Sadie shifted her weight, aware that Jackie might not be exactly pleased by the news Sadie had to share about Mary's missing ornaments.

Jackie sighed when Sadie finished, and Sadie unwrapped the cream cheese as quietly as possible. "Are you absolutely certain?"

The timer dinged for the meringues, so Sadie turned off the oven and propped the door open so they would cool. They looked perfect.

"I'm certain. Her granddaughter helped me identify which ones were missing. Five of the glass type are gone as well as five of the shaped ones, and one candy cane." She put the cream cheese in the mixing bowl, and tore open the bag of shredded cheese—also quietly. She didn't want to distract Jackie, or make Jackie think she was distracted. Which she wasn't.

"A candy cane?"

"Mary's favorite—there's a whole story attached to it. Anyway, they disappeared sometime between 6:00 last night and 1:30 this afternoon. So far, Mary doesn't know this has happened, and I am hoping to find them before she has to know, but I could really use your help."

"Help with . . ."

"Finding the ornaments," Sadie said when Jackie didn't finish the sentence. Mayo, garlic—goodness, she'd almost forgotten the cheese spread!

"Well, you can file an incident report—is that what you mean?"

"Not necessarily," Sadie said. "I would like to try to find them myself. I imagine that both of us would prefer this not become common knowledge." Did that sound like a threat? "What I mean is that not upsetting Mary is my main goal, and I'm working very hard and very carefully to keep her from learning the truth. I would imagine an incident report would need her to verify things, which would necessitate telling her what's happened, which is exactly what I'm trying to avoid for now. Does that make sense?"

"It does," Jackie said slowly. "But as an administrative employee, I'm required to follow procedure, and our procedure is to file an incident report when something is missing."

"You probably don't know this about me, Jackie, but before coming to Fort Collins, I was a private investigator. I won't tell anyone where I got the information from. I just want to get the ornaments back, but in order to do that, I have to know who had opportunity to take them in the first place. I'm willing to comply with the procedures your company has if it doesn't interfere with what I'm trying to do, does that make sense?"

Jackie was silent, and Sadie feared she'd come on too strong. She'd hoped that their friendship and mutual affection for Mary would put them on the same side. She'd also finished putting everything for the cheeseball into the bowl. She began to quietly straighten the kitchen. A minute saved was a minute earned.

"So, is that all you need from me—visitor and staff lists?" Jackie asked.

Hope bloomed in Sadie's chest like an amaryllis flower in winter. "As far as I know, that's all I need from you. I'd sure appreciate your support and your discretion. The fewer people who know I'm trying to track down the culprit, the better."

"And I would appreciate no one knowing that I've given you these lists. It doesn't necessarily violate the privacy act on behalf of the residents, but it's certainly not something the corporate managers would want me to do. I see what you're saying about this situation; it's the holidays, and your efforts will likely be more helpful than filing an incident report through the corporate. I'm just sick about this, though."

"So am I."

"Are you planning to talk to the staff?"

"Yes, but cautiously. I'm hoping to get information without revealing too much. Those lists will be very helpful in confirming information I get from them."

"Okay, tomorrow is a crazy day. We have the facility Christmas party, and then several residents are going home with their families for the holiday, but I could meet you at the facility first thing to-morrow at, say, eight o'clock. Does that work?"

Eight o'clock? That was thirteen hours away! But Jackie was going out on a limb for her already, and Sadie didn't want to jeopardize that by being too demanding. And Jackie wasn't even at the facility right now. Sadie couldn't get the lists this minute even if she insisted. Yet, Sadie still needed to take advantage of every minute available to her.

"That will work. I'm actually going to stay overnight in Mary's room to keep an eye on the tree. I want to make sure none of the other ornaments disappear."

"That's a good idea. Make sure you let the nurse on staff know you'll be staying over. Is there anything else I can help with?"

"Actually, yes, there is one more thing. I have some questions about one employee in particular. Carol Benson."

Jackie was silent, and it perked up every one of Sadie's investigative instincts. So much that Sadie stopped cleaning the kitchen and leaned against the counter, giving the phone call her full attention. "What about Carol?"

"She gave me an odd . . . vibe when I talked to her this morning.

Because of that reaction I, um, checked her out on the Department of Regulatory Licenses. I know she's had some trouble." It sounded like weak motivation, but she wasn't about to tell Jackie she'd snuck Carol's letter out of her pocket.

Jackie's tone lowered. "I really can't discuss an employee, Sadie."

"You don't have to discuss her—everything I learned was public record—but you'll understand that her name has floated to the top of my 'persons of interest' list, and I'd like to better understand her situation so I know if that's appropriate or not. I have to admit I'm surprised she works there at all. From the information I found, she has her nurse's license, yet she's working as an aide."

Jackie was still silent, and Sadie waited, even though patience was not one of her talents. After Sadie had taken a few yoga breaths, Jackie finally spoke. "Carol and I went to nursing school together, gosh, almost thirty years ago at Colorado State. After graduation, she moved, and we fell out of touch. I wasn't aware of the *trouble* when she went through it, but she moved back to Fort Collins and called me for help in finding a job in the medical field again. She wondered if I knew of anyone who might hire a nurse on probation, and I asked what she would be willing to . . . settle for.

"We only run one nurse at a time here, and Carol has too many limitations to be the only nurse on the floor. She was open to finding something that was a good fit for her and for us, and so I went to corporate. They agreed to hire her as a sort of a hybrid nurse and nurse's aide. She supervises the aides, trains new employees, helps with the nursing care she's able to do, and yet does all the nurse's aide responsibilities as well. She's an excellent nurse, and I've never regretted the arrangement."

"What are her limitations?"

Jackie paused.

"I can read this online, Jackie," Sadie reminded her, though she wasn't sure that was exactly true.

"She can't have access to controlled substances—narcotics, sleeping pills, things like that—or work the floor by herself. And she has to submit to monthly, as well as random, drug screenings."

"Are there other employees on your staff with licensing problems?" Sadie imagined half a dozen staff members poised at a starting line to race toward Mary's tree and see who could steal the ornaments first. It was a terribly distressing mental image.

"No, Carol's the only nurse with a licensing issue I've even considered hiring in the years since I've been in this position. Patient care is my top priority, and I would not have hired her, or kept her, if not for her being an excellent caretaker."

"I have no doubt in your judgment, Jackie, and appreciate you helping me understand the situation. What does it mean that she improperly disposed of medications?"

Jackie hesitated again. "When a prescription is no longer needed, or a patient has been discharged, there's a procedure for disposing of those medications. It requires two nurses to sign off on it. Carol falsified a second signature on four different occasions, claiming that the second nurse hadn't wanted to help her and told her to sign her name each time."

"Is that true?"

"According to Carol, yes."

"You don't believe her?"

"Well, if the second nurse refused, Carol should have notified her administrator as soon as possible. Instead, she continued to falsify the documents on three other occasions. The second nurse denied refusing to sign and claimed she knew nothing about Carol disposing of anything. Since Carol didn't follow procedure, there's no way to know what really happened to those medications, which means Carol could have been diverting the medications."

"What does *that* mean?"

"Taking them or selling them."

"That's why she has to take random drug screens during her probation," Sadie reasoned. "Because she may have had a drug problem, which could be the real reason she ignored procedure with those medications?"

"Right."

"Why don't you believe Carol's version of the story?"

Jackie let out a breath. "I've already said more than I should, Sadie. She's a good nurse, and I'm glad to have been able to play a part in helping her get back into full fellowship of her license. Could we talk more in the morning? I'm almost to the airport."

"Yes, of course," Sadie said. "Thank you for this, Jackie. And for the lists. I'll see you in the morning."

Cunningham Cheeseball

2 (8-ounce) packages of cream cheese, room temperature
1 jar Kraft "Old English" cheese spread
1 to 2 cups shredded sharp cheddar cheese
1 tablespoon mayonnaise
1 ½ teaspoons lemon juice
½ teaspoon (or 1 clove) minced garlic
1 cup walnuts or pecans, chopped

Mix cream cheese and cheese spread together with an electric mixer until smooth. Add remaining ingredients, except the nuts. Mix well.

Spread a sheet of plastic wrap on the counter and scoop the cheese mixture onto it. Using the plastic wrap to protect your hands, mold the cheese into a ball shape, then wrap it with the plastic wrap. Refrigerate 30 minutes.

Put chopped nuts on a tray or another sheet of plastic wrap. Unwrap chilled cheeseball and roll over nuts until the cheese portion is covered.

Rewrap with plastic wrap and refrigerate until serving. Serve with crackers or celery sticks.

Note: Lasts up to two weeks in an airtight container in the fridge.

Note: Flavors get stronger as it ages, so it's best to make this a few days ahead of when you'll be serving it.

CHAPTER 15

S adie mixed and formed the cheeseball before putting it in the fridge. She could hold off rolling it in the chopped nuts until right before the party if she had to. Then she gathered up the printed reports, her notebook, and laptop, and loaded all of it into a shoulder bag—the kind with the cushy section to protect a laptop from damage. She also packed an overnight bag and texted Joy again. Fiona had never answered her earlier text and, knowing the older generation didn't always monitor their phones very closely, she called.

"Hello," Fiona said after the second ring—thank goodness.

"Hi, Fiona, it's Sadie. Just wondering how Mary's doing."

"You mean other than being an absolute pain in the neck?" Sadie heard Mary laugh in the background, and then Fiona laughed, too. "She's doing great, says she feels a lot better tonight than she felt this morning. We're just back from dinner—pot roast and potatoes, yum-my. Mary took like four whole bites like a big girl."

"I ate almost all of it, Sadie," Mary chimed in from the background.

"She lies," Fiona said simply, and Sadie imagined the older woman shrugging her thin shoulders. "Now we're going to have this peppermint ice cream Ivy brought by last night, and Mary wants to listen to *It's a Wonderful Life*."

"So, you'll be there for another couple of hours?" Sadie checked her watch—getting back to the facility by nine o'clock shouldn't be a problem at all.

"At least," Fiona said. "I've still got two scarves left to do, if you can believe it. Plus, Mary said that after *It's a Wonderful Life*, she'll watch *Elf* with me."

Sadie laughed. "Mary doesn't like *Elf*."

"And I don't like *It's a Wonderful Life*, so it's all fair. That movie came out when I was a kid, and when networks started showing movies on TV, they showed it every Christmas. Every single Christmas. Don't even get me started about VHS tapes, movie channels, and Netflix! I bet I've seen that blasted thing a hundred times, and yet Mary's making me watch it *again*. Here—she wants to talk to you."

When Mary was on the line, Sadie asked if she could stay overnight.

"Oh, Sadie, you don't need to babysit me."

"I'm not babysitting; I'm spending time with a friend. Pete's still out of town, and my kids and grandkids are about to descend upon us. I'm not sure how much time I'm going to get with you once all that happens."

"I should warn you, I snore something awful."

"Thank goodness," Sadie said with exaggerated excitement. "So, does Pete, and I can't hardly sleep without it."

"Well, suit yourself, then," Mary said, but she sounded pleased.

They finished the call, and Sadie headed for the car. The meringues would continue to dry out in the cooling oven overnight; she'd put them in a container tomorrow. One more Cunningham recipe finished.

Relieved that Fiona could act as unknowing sentry over the tree, Sadie turned her mind to the next person on her list: Joy.

The fact that Joy hadn't answered Sadie's texts could be because she was working—she managed the mall's Christmas village this time of year—but it could be because she was avoiding Sadie. Something had happened between the time Joy had agreed to get a list of Mary's visitors and relaying that list to Sadie. Beyond that, Joy was also dating a man with a dangerous past. If she didn't know about his criminal record, she needed to. Therefore, Sadie had a terrible, awful task: she had to go the mall two days before Christmas.

Sadie wasn't one of those fanatics who got all their shopping done before December, but she *was* one of the wiser holiday shoppers who *did* get all of their big-box and mall shopping done by Thanksgiving. In fact, as Sadie pulled into one of the only available parking spaces roughly two miles from the actual mall entrance, she could not remember the last time she'd been to a mall in the week before or after Christmas. Maybe when Breanna had been in high school and simply had to get the black Vans Sadie had given her a gift certificate for.

It took twenty seconds of reminding herself why this was absolutely necessary before Sadie felt prepared to leave her car. She repeated those reasons during the long walk through the rather perilous mall parking lot. Harried shoppers tried to beat each other out of closer spaces and pulled out without checking behind them. One man flipped off Sadie for no reason.

Once she reached the entrance, Sadie straightened her red coat over her hips and then thanked a man who held the door open for her despite his arms being weighted with bags. Christmas really did bring out the best in people. Well, most people. She didn't count the people who had tried to kill her in the parking lot or the man who had flipped her off.

Just inside the door was a sign pointing toward Santa's Village, and Sadie followed the directions, weaving between what felt like a thousand shoppers with expressions ranging from excitement to frustration to pure rage. She saw a big man standing outside a jewelry store, muttering to himself and flexing his fingers as though getting up his nerve to go inside; the store was packed. As she passed him, he turned suddenly and headed straight for the exit. No doubt his wife was getting Walmart perfume this year, or maybe a case of vacuum bags. Another casualty of the season. Poor guy.

There were signs posted every few feet until Sadie saw a two-story gingerbread house poking above the masses of people. Larger-than-life gumdrops surrounded the edges of the windows, and big peppermint candies decorated the very realistic house, though Sadie was sure it was Styrofoam painted to look like gingerbread—she'd seen that process on *How It's Made* once. The detail was impressive, the walls showing the same texture of actual gingerbread.

Surrounding the house were a dozen Christmas trees of varying heights, making it look as though the house was set in the middle of a forest. Bright ornaments of green, gold, and red popped from the trees, and a white picket fence separated a line of children from jolly old St. Nicholas himself, who sat on a big velvet chair in the front yard of the gingerbread house.

Sadie scanned the crowds as she got closer, looking for the CSU sweatshirt Joy had been wearing before work.

A little girl with frizzy black hair currently sat on Santa's lap, looking up at him with abject terror as he tried to ho-ho-ho his way into her heart. An elf standing beside an old-fashioned camera with a retractable-accordion-type lens told Santa to look her way and say "Merry Christmas," which he did in preparation for the camera flash.

As soon as the photo was taken, another elf picked up the child and put her on her hip, giving her a candy cane as she took her to the other side, where the child's mother put out her arms. It was that second elf that Sadie fixed her eyes on as she came to a stop at the fence. Joy?

The elf had pointed, rubber tips on her ears and a felt cap with a pointed top that hung down her back and ended in a big, white pom-pom. She wore red-and-white-striped tights beneath a green Peter Pan dress and pointed shoes that curled around three times before ending with the essential bell at the end. Joy's dark hair was in two braids, and she wore fake lashes and bright-red lipstick. She also seemed . . . happy. Happier than Sadie was used to seeing this girl, whom she'd described to Breanna as "quiet but cute."

Sadie walked around to the parents' side of the fence and watched as Joy went to the next child in line, expertly separated him from his mother, and escorted him to Santa, holding his hand. Then Joy stood back and watched as the little boy beckoned Santa to lower his head so he could whisper his Christmas wishes in Santa's ear, to which Santa said, "Ho ho ho! That sounds like a mighty fine Christmas present to wish for. I'll be sure to tell the elves to make lots of room in my sleigh."

The picture was taken, and Joy gave the boy a candy cane and escorted him to the side, where the mother, and Sadie, were waiting. Joy's eyes met Sadie's and went wide. After a moment of staring, Joy turned to the elf manning the camera and made a time-out sign. The camera elf turned and said in a voice much louder than her petite frame suggested was possible, "Five-minute break. Please keep your place in the line."

Groans and whining rose from the parents and children in line, respectively, and Santa stood up rather quickly, saying that he needed to visit the little elves' room. The photographer elf nodded in a somewhat militant fashion and then led the way through a back door in the fence and toward the public restrooms, putting her arms out when people tried to approach Santa, who waved and ho-ho-hoed as they went, though he was walking fast.

Joy crossed the remaining distance to Sadie, standing outside the fence. "Has something happened to Grandma?"

"Mary's fine." Joy's eyes closed in relief, then opened to look at Sadie with trepidation. She knew if Sadie wasn't there about Mary, she was there for something else. Sadie decided to take a softer approach than she'd previously planned. "You look great, Joy."

Joy smiled self-consciously and tugged at her skirt. "It's all the bright colors."

"And that the dress is fitted and . . . you are really good at this." She waved toward the kids in line.

A real blush augmented the pink circles on Joy's cheeks. "Thanks," she said shyly. "I really like working with the kids."

"That," Sadie said, "is a gift, and I am thrilled to see that you have found a way to use one of your gifts."

Joy blushed again and looked at the ground.

Sadie counted to three Frostys and then said gently, "I know Frank visited Mary last night."

Joy's head snapped up, and her eyes went wide.

"Why didn't you just tell me?" Sadie asked.

"I just . . . I needed to talk to him about it first."

"You didn't know he'd visited? Mary told you?"

Joy paused, but then nodded. "I called him on my way to work, and he explained that he'd gone over to fix her nightstand."

"Why didn't you know beforehand?" These days, young people texted and liked each other's photos twenty-four-seven. More's the pity that they would never know the excitement of the home phone ringing and *wondering* if it was their sweetheart.

Joy shifted her weight to her other curly-shoed foot. "We'd had an argument on Saturday, and so we weren't really talking. But we're fine now, and I understand why he was there, and I can assure you that he did not steal those ornaments."

"What did you argue about?"

"No offense, Sadie, but that's none of your business. It doesn't have anything to do with Grandma or her missing ornaments."

Sadie held Joy's eyes. She had seen enough TV movies to know that a lot of girls with low self-esteem often ended up in unhealthy relationships with disreputable men. Joy's defensiveness of Frank was a huge red flag. She leaned in slightly and put her hand on Joy's arm.

"Are you afraid of him, Joy? Because if you are, I can—"

Joy's jaw hardened, and she stepped back from the fence that separated them, pulling her arm away in the process. Sadie's hand fell to her side, and when Joy spoke, it was with more confidence than Sadie had ever heard from her. "I don't need help, Sadie. I'm not afraid of Frank, and he didn't steal those ornaments. I'm sorry I didn't tell you he'd been there, but you don't need to waste time worrying about him." She looked around, saw Santa coming back to his seat and took another step away from Sadie. "I can't talk anymore. I'm working."

She turned on her heel and walked to the other side of the gingerbread house, where she fiddled with the basket of candy canes and straightened the velvet covering on Santa's chair.

"Joy!" Sadie said in a hushed yell. She wasn't finished with this conversation, and Joy's avoidance did nothing to put her at ease.

Joy ignored her.

Well, Sadie wasn't going to stand for that. She knew things about Frank, and Joy simply telling Sadie he was innocent was going to fly about as well as Santa's sleigh without Rudolph in the lead. Sadie walked through the designated exit and around the back of the village until she was on the same side as Joy. Due to the decorations and fence, however, she was still nearly six feet away from her.

"I know things about Frank that you don't know," Sadie said.

Joy's gaze flickered up to her, and her eyes narrowed. She turned and walked to another section of the gingerbread house behind Santa's chair and out of conversation range, where she fussed with some of the decorations there. Sadie would have to yell, which she would have done if not for fifty kids with frazzled parents waiting to check "visit Santa" off their Christmas to-do list. Was Sadie really prepared to confront Joy with hard truths in front of a crowd? Was she willing to endanger Joy's job?

Suddenly someone took hold of Sadie's shoulder and spun her around. The tall woman had dark hair that fell in waves over her shoulders, and she wore a fuzzy Santa cap that was the same bright red as her high-heeled shoes. Other than the hat and shoes, she was dressed in all black. A gold name tag said "Holly Hamstead, Event Coordinator."

She looked Sadie up and down, her eyebrows pulled together while Sadie stared at her, too stunned to react.

"It's about time," Ms. Hamstead said, then pulled Sadie with her as she marched in the same direction Santa and the other elf had gone earlier.

CHAPTER 16

For the sake of the children watching, Sadie waited until Ms. Hamstead had pulled her a solid twenty feet from the village before she dug in the heels of her snow boots as best she could and pulled her arm from the woman's grip. It had been years since Sadie had needed to break a hold, but by jerking fast in the direction of the pinky finger—the weakest part of any person's grip—her wrist slid out as though the woman hadn't even been trying.

Ms. Hamstead looked at her now-empty hand and then at Sadie. For half a second, her expression was a combination of surprise, confusion, and frustration. Then her jaw went tight, her chin went down, and she took a step closer to Sadie. She leaned in until her nose was only a few inches from Sadie's. Her breath smelled like pretzels.

"Look, lady, it's bad enough we're paying you a hundred bucks an hour to play the big guy's bimbo, but you're an hour late and dressed like . . ." She backed up and scanned Sadie up and down again. "A discount shopper who—"

"Whoa!" Sadie said, putting a hand, literally, in front of Ms. Hamstead's face, which caused the woman to stand at her full height. It was unfortunate for Sadie that Ms. Hamstead was a solid six inches taller than she was, even with Sadie's snow boots on. At least standing on the higher moral ground gave Sadie some stature. "First of all, you didn't hire me for anything; I came to talk to Joy Hallmark. Second, you have no right to disparage the relationship between two international heroes who are obviously married—her name is Mrs. Claus, for heaven's sake. And third, you have no right to drag me around the mall and use the term 'discount shopper' in such a derogatory way. There is nothing wrong with getting a good deal."

The woman blinked as the anger drained out of her expression. "You're not Mrs. Claus from First Impressions Employment Agency?"

"No, I am not."

The woman's face turned a hot pink, and she sputtered apologies like a teapot. "Oh, my gosh, I'm so sorry. This whole Santa thing is going to kill me." She started blinking fast, as though she might cry, then she put a hand over her mouth, and Sadie's already big heart grew ten sizes in the same moment that a few different ideas melded together in her mind.

Her indignation spent, Sadie put a hand on the woman's arm, much like she'd done with Joy a few minutes earlier, and smiled. "Now, now, why don't you tell me what's happening? Maybe we can get it all sorted out."

Ten minutes later, Sadie bustled—literally, the bustle on the Mrs. Claus costume was rather extreme—back to Santa's Village, wondering if she should have looked at herself in the mirror after all. The storage room that had doubled as a dressing room for the "cast" was equipped with a full-sized mirror, but Sadie had avoided it. Sadie wanted to do a good job at anything she did, and yet if she pulled off being Mrs. Claus too well, it could bring on an existential crisis, which was something she couldn't afford right now. She was playing a role in order to get close to Joy in an environment where Joy could not get away from her, that was all.

"Thank you so much, Mrs. Cunningham," Holly gushed as she brought up the rear, her red-heeled shoes tippity-tapping much like Sadie imagined the hooves of eight tiny reindeer might sound. "You've saved my job, and the day, and . . . and Christmas, really."

Sadie smiled good-naturedly and adjusted the wire-framed glasses a little farther down her nose. The idea of saving Christmas was a very nice thought. "Consider this your Christmas present, Holly."

Holly laughed a little too hard at that, then stepped ahead of Sadie and led the rest of the way through the crowd. "And you look amazing! Are you sure you've never done this before?"

Sadie had learned that this was Holly's fifth year managing Santa's Village, and possibly her last. There had been one problem after another since they'd opened the Sunday after Thanksgiving. She'd told Sadie all about it while they put her into the costume, an extra kept on hand for parts if there were wardrobe malfunctions in the costumes the actual Mrs. Claus wore. The dress portion was a little big—which Sadie appreciated—but once the apron was on, the sizing wasn't too noticeable.

The first problem Holly had encountered was the gingerbread house—a new addition this year. Three days in, it had cracked along the west wall and had to be replaced on a Sunday night be-tween Santa sessions. The next week, a bunch of teenagers had gotten into a Christmas light bulb fight, and last, but certainly not least, due to the ongoing nature of the difficulty, there had been *four* different women coming as Mrs. Claus, not one of them in a "set" with either of the two Santas.

The Mrs. Clauses split shifts without telling her, wore shades of red other than Christmas red—which was required in order to match the decorations—and one of them was in her thirties and wore a low-cut dress that made some of the parents very uncomfortable. Today's Mrs. Claus hadn't shown up at all, and the agency had said they couldn't guarantee a replacement until tomorrow, which was the last day for the village.

To be without a Mrs. Claus two days before Christmas was unacceptable to Holly, and yet it had seemed like she had no choice. Until Sadie had shown up and, well, saved Christmas. Since Sadie didn't have to be to Nicholas House until two movies had been viewed in full, playing the role worked rather well into Sadie's schedule and provided her an opportunity to be close enough to Joy to finish their conversation.

"I can't tell you how grateful I am," Holly said yet again as she held the back gate open for Sadie. "Are you sure I can't pay you?" she asked quietly so none of the parents would overhear. Knowing that Santa and Mrs. Claus were hired help would certainly break that essential Christmas magic.

Sadie kept her answer a whisper, too. "If I were doing this for money, you could never afford what it would cost for me to take this on."

But there were things far more valuable than money. Like information. Holly had explained that Joy was the administrative representative for the village and managed the other elves, who were from a local temp agency. She'd been working fifty hours a week at the village since November but doing an excellent job, according to Holly. What that meant to Sadie was that Joy wasn't going to storm off when she realized Sadie had her cornered.

"Wait here," Holly said to Sadie, then fetched a Queen Anne chair from inside the gingerbread house and settled it next to Santa.

Sadie adjusted the white knitted shawl on her shoulders and repositioned the glasses again; they didn't have those nice nose cushions, which Sadie would never take for granted again.

Joy noticed the chair first as she was leading a little girl to Santa. When she looked past the chair to Sadie, her eyes went wide and her mouth fell open. Sadie smiled at her knowingly.

Oh, yes, indeed, there were many things in this world that were more valuable than money or even one's self-respect. The truth rarely came easily, but Sadie had never been afraid of hard work.

CHAPTER 17

Sadie moved forward to the Mrs. Claus chair, passing Joy in the process. "I don't give up easily," she said under her breath. "What do you know about Frank's past?"

Joy didn't have time to answer, but Sadie knew the girl would have no choice but to continue thinking about the question. She'd have time to play out a dozen different scenarios of what she could do to put Sadie off, until she realized that if Sadie was willing to dress like Mrs. Claus, she meant business.

"Ho, ho, ho," Santa bellowed when Sadie settled herself in the chair beside him. His belly looked as real as his snow-white beard. He put his arm around Sadie's shoulders to give her a side hug more fitting for the wife of a football coach than a jolly old elf. His belly-shaking laughter nearly bounced her glasses off her nose, but she donned a patient smile and said in a musical voice she felt fitting for the role how sorry she was that she was late.

Santa removed his arm from her shoulders, leaned his cheek toward her, and tapped it with his gloved finger. "How's about you give Santa a little sugar, huh?"

Sadie shot a questioning look at Holly. Was fraternization a requirement of this job? Holly gave her a shrug that seemed to say she had no answer but would really appreciate Sadie's cooperation. Sadie hesitated, then kissed Santa quickly on the cheek, which set off another round of ho-ho-hoing. Sadie's cheeks flushed under the clapping and giggles of the crowd, and she made eye contact with Joy, who was holding a nervous little girl by the hand. Joy looked unsure about what was happening, but she also looked less irritated than she had before when she was dodging Sadie's questions.

Holly cleared her throat, and Joy startled back to the moment at hand.

Joy stepped forward to present the little girl to Santa. "Isn't this wonderful, Karishna, Mrs. Claus is here too." She helped settle the girl on Santa's lap.

"What's she supposed to do?" the little girl asked suspiciously.

Excellent question.

"Well, she's going to check your name in Santa's book," Holly said, lifting a huge binder covered in bright-green velvet and trimmed with lace from under one of the Christmas trees. She put the book on Sadie's lap, and Sadie opened it to find a script inside. Thanks be to all the stars in heaven above.

"Santa," Sadie said in that same singsong voice, "you remember . . ." The script read "INSERT CHILD'S NAME HERE," and luckily Sadie remembered the little girl's name from Joy's introduction. ". . . Karishna. Her name is right here on the nice list, Santa." She turned to the child. "What would you like Santa to bring you for being such a good girl this year?"

The child's eyes suddenly filled with tears, and her chin began to tremble. "I killed all the fish!" Karishna wailed.

"Ho, ho, ho." Santa laughed awkwardly but the child cried

harder, covering her face with her hands and leaning so that her hair fell forward.

Sadie had taught second grade—never mind having raised two children—and knew a thing or two about how to handle children in distress. She set the book aside and stood up. Taking the child into her arms, she held the girl against her shoulder and paced in front of the gingerbread house while Karishna confessed the whole story. Her mother hovered on the parents' side of the fence, and Sadie gave the mother a reassuring smile. Once Karishna was reduced to huffy gasp-sobs, Sadie put her down and let her choose a candy cane from the basket.

"Next time, you make sure to leave the fish in the tank, okay?" Sadie said as she walked Karishna back to her anxious mother. "Only toy fish can go outside to jump on the trampoline. You're still on the nice list, though, because you only made a mistake. Now that you know better, you won't do it again, now will you?"

"I won't never, Nana Santa," Karishna said, shaking her head, her eyes brimming with conviction.

Sadie suspected there was more to the story of why Karishna took eight hundred dollars'-worth of tropical fish out of her step-father's fish tank for a play date, but it wouldn't likely come out until Karishna was in therapy ten years from now.

Sadie opened the gate so Karishna could be reunited with her mother, then she returned to her place on the chair and picked up her book, glancing toward Joy, who was busy managing the line of children but glanced at Sadie long enough to give a grateful smile. Santa had heard the wishes of four other children while Sadie had soothed Karishna's troubled soul. There were easily three dozen more kids in line, and Sadie was beginning to think she might not get the time to extract a full confession from Joy the way she'd hoped. If only Joy could be a bit more like Karishna.

"Oh, Santa, you remember . . ." she said in her high-pitched "Nana Santa" voice after Joy had deposited the next child onto Santa's lap and said his name. "T-Trey-zor-o. Well, he's been a very good boy this year. His name is right here on the nice list. What would you like Santa to bring you this year for being such a good boy?"

Treyzoro looked from Sadie to Santa and then his chin began to tremble just as Karishna's had. Goodness. "I stoled the Pokémon," he whispered.

"Ho, ho, ho!" Santa said as he handed the child off to Sadie without hesitation.

Half an hour later, Sadie had given out seventeen candy canes, wiped eight noses with the ends of her shawl, helped get chocolate out of Santa's beard, and forgiven nine deviant children of their crimes. Changing the script had helped some, but there seemed to be something about her—or, rather, about Mrs. Claus—that turned the Christmas village into a confessional. Sadie had had exactly three meaningful looks with Joy, but that was all she'd had time for. Would she have to take satisfaction from helping to spread Christmas cheer rather than furthering this investigation? It didn't feel like a balanced trade. Maybe she was a better Mrs. Claus than she was an investigator. The thought made her frown as she looked into the basket of candy canes next to her chair and did a quick count.

"Oh, Elf Joy?" she said as Joy was making her way back to the line of children.

Joy turned, looking as wary as she had every time Sadie had made eye contact with her.

"We're running short on candy canes," Sadie said when Joy approached the chair. "Is there somewhere I can find a few more?"

"I'll get them," Joy said, then disappeared into the gingerbread house a moment before coming back with another handful. She put them in the basket and then whispered, "You've been amazing to help this way, Sadie. Thank you."

"I did it so you couldn't run away from me."

Joy looked down for a moment, then said softly, "I'll talk to you after we close up."

Sadie nearly shouted hallelujah to know her efforts had not been in vain.

"Thank you, Elf Joy," Sadie said out loud, then turned to the next creatively named child—Ameenia—with a sincerer smile than she'd managed for several minutes.

Sadie and Santa worked through the line of children until 8:00. The village was supposed to have closed at 7:30, but they weren't about to turn away the last few children in line.

The mall remained bright and bustling thanks to the shops staying open until midnight, but Sadie was glad to hear Holly say, "That's a wrap," and to see the lights in the Christmas village go out.

Santa stood from his throne and stretched out his shoulders. "Man, what was with this last batch of kids? It's like future-delinquent day or something; I'm glad it's over. I'm going to miss my lovely missus, however." He winked at Sadie, who winked back, eliciting a non-Santa laugh that made his belly shake some more.

Holly turned to Sadie with a hopeful smile. "Could I convince you to come back tomorrow? You're absolutely terrific. A Rudolph among other reindeer."

"Well, thank you for that," Sadie said, patting her lacy mob-cap to make sure it hadn't deflated. "I'm afraid my schedule is full though." Jackie would have those lists for her in the morning, and Mass would be only hours away. Thinking about tomorrow made Sadie examine what she'd accomplished today. It was a discouraging accounting since she didn't feel any closer to finding the ornaments now than she'd been that afternoon. She knew, however, that an investigation often resolved quickly when the last stone was overturned. The only way to solve anything was to work every lead, but it was so hard to be patient.

Santa and Holly both frowned at her response.

"You will be missed," Holly said, then turned back to Santa. "Penny's on the schedule. I asked her not to smoke in her costume anymore, so hopefully that will be better."

"But did she keep the cats from sleeping on it? It's the cat dander that gets my allergies in a fiddle." Santa raised his eyebrows and stretched out his back again. "They just don't make Mrs. Claus the way they used to." He sighed, then put out his elbow to Holly. "Can I interest you in an Orange Julius, m'lady?"

Holly laughed and slid her arm through his. "How could I say no to that?"

The photographer elf packed up the camera and departed, leaving Sadie and Joy alone in the darkened Christmas village.

Joy shifted her weight from one foot to the other, then met Sadie's eyes. She tugged at the hem of her elfin dress as though to make it longer than its mid-thigh length. "That was really generous of you to help out, Sadie. Holly's had a hard time this year." She paused to take a breath and perhaps draw in some confidence.

"Starbucks makes a great peppermint cocoa. Would you like to join me for a cup?"

Sadie hadn't expected the need for a cocoa-long conversation, but knew better than to turn it down. "Should we change first?" She fanned her apron to emphasize that she was terribly overdressed.

"Nah," Joy said, shaking her head. "People love it when we wander the mall in costume."

CHAPTER 18

Sadie was more than a little uncomfortable staying in costume, but felt better with every harried shopper who smiled when they passed.

"Merry Christmas, Mrs. Claus," one lumberjack of a man called out to her.

"Merry Christmas," she called back, then waved her white-gloved hand the way she imagined Mrs. Claus would do if she were on a Christmas parade float. Sadie felt like an honest-to-goodness celebrity by the time they reached Starbucks, which was filled with shoppers in need of sugar and caffeine to sustain their last-minute searches for the perfect gift. Pete would make a wonderful Santa, though he'd need to rent a beard—his still had some black streaked through the gray and wasn't nearly long enough. They could be quite the Santa power couple, though, if he would agree to do it.

The Starbucks employee gave them free cocoa, which Joy admitted was another perk to staying in costume. Sadie almost protested—she wasn't a *real* hired Mrs. Claus—then realized she'd left her purse and phone in the dressing room and had little choice but to be a gracious recipient of the cashier's generous Christmas spirit.

"When you said you managed the Christmas village, I didn't realize you were part of the cast," Sadie said to Joy once they were tucked into a table in a far corner. The chair's open back allowed Sadie to sit with the bustle, though she tried not to think how it must look to people walking past. John Lennon sang "So this is Christmas" overhead, and Sadie tried to block it out. She did not appreciate the shaming in that particular song and did not count it as a Christmas carol at all.

Joy sipped her cocoa, and though she was trying to appear relaxed, the jingle of the bell on her elf shoe as she tapped her foot revealed her anxiety. "I took the seasonal job as an elf the first Christmas I was in Fort Collins to get a little Christmas money, and then Holly started hiring me for different events after that—Easter Bunny visits and Witching Night at Halloween. I'd mentioned to her last summer that I needed something full-time, and a couple of weeks later, she told me about the administrative assistant position here at the mall and wrote me a letter of recommendation." Joy shrugged. "Mostly the job is running errands and doing the work no one else wants to do, but Holly and I worked it out so I could manage the elves and keep my position with the Christmas village this year too, and it's been fun."

"You're very good with children."

Joy took another sip of her cocoa and shrugged, but looked pleased by the compliment. "I really like kids. I'm thinking of going back to school and becoming a teacher, or maybe opening a day care or something."

"I think you'd be wonderful at either of those jobs," Sadie said. "You have a nurturing heart."

"Thanks," Joy said in a way that didn't sound as though she

believed the compliment but wanted to be gracious. She took a long breath, then met Sadie's eyes with an expression of anxious resignation on her face. "I met Frank when I was working at the village last year," she said, suprising Sadie by volunteering the information. "He brought Star in to see Santa."

She paused, and Sadie was afraid that Joy had lost her nerve. She offered a prompt. "And was it love at first sight?" Only after she said it did she hear the sarcasm.

Thankfully, Joy gave a soft laugh and shook her head. "No, he freaked me out," she admitted. "But they came back night after night. We don't get a lot of repeat customers, and he kind of stands out. After a while, I stopped noticing how out of place he looked and instead noticed how sweet he was with Star. We started chatting a little after that first week and, well, here we are a year later."

"That's . . . a great story," Sadie said. And an unexpected story, too. "I'm glad to hear that he's a good father. What do you know about his history?"

Joy's expression closed slightly, and Sadie hurried to get her words out. "I went to his work this evening, Joy. He's nothing like the kind of man I would expect you to be in a relationship with, and I—"

Joy leaned forward, her false eyelashes making her wide eyes look huge. "You met Frank?"

"He doesn't know who I am. He thinks I was just shopping for a gift for my husband." Sadie wasn't sure how best to explain their interaction. "But I left with a lot of questions, so I ran a background check on him and—"

"You ran a *background* check on him?"

Oh, right, most people did not regularly run background checks on other people. She sat up straighter in her chair and hoped it made her look confident. "I used to be a private investigator, Joy, and I'm honestly surprised more people don't do them on a regular basis. Yes, I ran a report on Frank, and I have some *serious* concerns. You can't base your beliefs in a person's character only on who they appear to be now. I'm worried, Joy. My main concern here is your well-being."

Joy looked into her cocoa, then laughed under her breath and shook her head as though responding to something Sadie couldn't hear. Finally, she took a deep breath and met Sadie's eyes. "I was sixteen years old when I got pregnant."

Sadie had not seen that coming. Fortunately, Joy wasn't waiting for a response.

"Most people think 'homes for unwed mothers' don't exist anymore, but they do. My parents sent me to one in Connecticut a week after I told them I was pregnant. I was four months along by then and having a hard time hiding it. My family moved from San Luis Obispo to Bakersfield while I was gone, and I kept up with my schoolwork online. I went home to a new house in a new city and started my junior year at a new high school as though nothing had happened." She held Sadie's eyes. "No one knows. Not my younger brothers and sister, not my aunts and uncles. Not even Grandma Mary. My parents and I are straight out of the 1940s the way we pretend it never happened."

Sadie opened her mouth but realized she had nothing to say so she closed it again. Just as she'd struggled to picture Frank and Joy as a couple, she could not picture Joy—awkward, shy Joy—as a pregnant teenager. A great well of sympathy rose in her chest.

Joy cleared her throat, rotated her cup a quarter turn on the table and held it with both hands as though it were an anchor keeping her in place. "I kept my head down and my grades up through the rest of high school. I didn't join any clubs or sport teams. I didn't care what I wore or what I looked like or what anyone thought of me. In fact, I preferred they didn't notice me at all, and most of them didn't.

"In Bakersfield, I became someone totally different. Protected myself. I had no friends. I was asked to one dance my senior year, and I told him I would be out of town that weekend. After I graduated from high school, I did data entry for a friend of my dad's and then stayed in my room playing video games because I had no other reason to leave the house. My parents took me to a couple of therapists—in a different town, of course, so no one would talk—but I wouldn't open up and eventually my parents decided not to waste their money. I know people think I'm weird and socially awkward." She shrugged, and Sadie sensed that she really didn't care. "In reality I was just a girl who didn't want to care about anyone ever again, who battled depression, and who struggled to trust my parents after they pushed me into a decision I didn't understand well enough to make. I've spent most of the last seven years of my life absolutely hating myself." Joy looked up with dry, clear, and maybe even wise eyes. Her normal aura of anxiety had dissipated, and she sounded oddly confident despite the vulnerable nature of what she was sharing.

"I'm sorry, Joy," Sadie said, hoping the words were the right ones. They felt far less than they should be.

"Thank you." She offered a small, sad smile. "Frank's childhood was a disaster—never knew his dad, his mom would leave him with friends for weeks at a time, no one did his laundry or read a book to him or cared if he went to school. He was arrested for shoplifting when he was nine years old and started smoking pot in the seventh grade.

"He learned how to do stick-and-poke tattoos when he was fourteen and did all kinds of weird words and pictures and things all over his body that looked as though he'd drawn on himself with ballpoint pen. As he got older, he covered those with more professional tattoos, which also helped him create an identity that made him feel like he had some power in his life. The piercings and gauges were part of that, too, because—like me living in my parents' basement and not making friends—he didn't want to trust people. If you don't let people close, you don't worry if they'll hurt you.

"He was in prison when he learned about Star, and it changed him because, for the first time ever, he had purpose. Someone needed him, and he was determined to be the kind of dad his daughter would want in her life. He finished his GED, found he had a knack for mechanical work, and starting thinking about where he wanted to be in five years.

"When he got out on probation, he found Star's mom in Denver. They tried to make things work, but it didn't turn out. He stayed close and got a job at an auto parts store. About a year and a half ago, Star's mom was killed in a horrible car accident with her new boyfriend, who was driving while high. Frank had Star that weekend, and after he was given legal custody, he requested a transfer at work. That's how he ended up in Fort Collins.

"His manager, Clint Everlight, lets Frank work the same hours Star is in school as much as possible, and his wife watches Star the other times. The reason Frank brought his daughter to see Santa every night for two weeks last Christmas was because it's free if you don't buy the photo and within walking distance of their apartment, but mostly because it made her happy." She blinked back tears and took another breath.

"He'll tell you that he first noticed me because I was so nice to Star." Her cheeks flushed slightly. "We started chatting, like I told you earlier, and then he started coming right before we closed and walking me out to my car. One night, my car wouldn't start. He doesn't have a car, but he found someone leaving the mall who would give me a jump, and then he told me to come by his work the next day and he'd get me a new battery. He'd only seen me like this." She waved a hand toward her costume—the eyelashes, the minidress that made the most of her curves, the bright red lips, and braided hair. It wasn't what Sadie would call sexy, but it was different from what Joy normally wore. "I showed up at his work in an oversized T-shirt and sweats with a hole in the knee, knowing he would not look at the real me the way he'd looked at Elf Joy. Except"—her voice got lower—"he did."

Sadie blinked back tears she had not felt creeping up on her.

"Our first date was to McDonalds because he had a buy-one-get-one-free Big Mac coupon and the PlayPlace is free . . . and within walking distance from his apartment. I drove myself and met them there. While Star played on the slide, he told me everything I've just told you about himself—his childhood, his tattoos, his prison record, Star's mom. He said that he liked me and liked how I treated Star and he'd like to eat a hamburger together now and then, if his past didn't scare me. It didn't scare me." She shook her head and smiled, but was still nervous, turning her hot cocoa cup in her hands as she spoke.

"It took eight months of Big Macs before I dared tell him my story. He was the first person I had ever told, and it felt . . . amazing. He didn't judge me or back away. It felt so good to be honest." She smiled, but only for a moment. "I thought about telling Grandma. Of everyone in my life, I knew she loved me no matter what. She had a doctor's appointment that next day that she was worried about, though, so I decided to wait and, well, then we learned how sick she was, and she wanted to get everything in order and there was no way I could tell her then.

"I introduced her to Frank a few weeks after that, but I didn't tell her about his looks or his history or anything like that because he has to deal with people judging him for those things all the time, and he didn't have to with her. When Ivy met him, I thought for sure she would tell Grandma, but she didn't. Or at least she hasn't yet, and maybe Grandma won't care—I don't know—but I haven't wanted to mess things up. It's hard enough coming to terms with the fact that she's . . . dying. She's been an absolute miracle in my life, Sadie. So has Frank."

CHAPTER 19

The Carpenters were singing "Merry Christmas, Darling" over the speakers, and Sadie stared at Joy. She really was in love with Frank, pure and sincere. Their story would make a great romance novel, if Sadie ever tried her hand at the genre. Mysteries were more her story of choice, however.

"He's been taking this personal-finance class at a local church for a few weeks, and so after we saw Mary on Friday night, he took me home and then borrowed my car. The church is in Harmony Crossings, but they have a playroom for the kids and things so Star went with him. He was supposed to pick me up for work Saturday morning but forgot to set the alarm on his phone and he'd turned off his ringer. I called and called and finally had to take an Uber. I was fifteen minutes late, and Holly bit my head off for it, though she apologized later.

"I called him on my lunch break, but between the hours we've both been working and the pressure of Grandma's cancer and Christmas and living in two places but trying to share a car . . . I was just so mad. I ranted and hung up on him and wouldn't answer his calls for the rest of the day. He picked me up from work that night—I'd worked a double shift—and I took him home. The only thing we talked about was that I'd watch Star yesterday since he had to close at the store and then I'd take her to the Everbrights', where she was sleeping over. It was our first fight, and it's been horrible."

She paused to blink back her own tears and take another sip of her cocoa. Sadie took a sip of her cocoa too because she was afraid she might say something and ruin the moment.

Joy took a breath and continued. "Star and I took sushi to Grandma, then I took her to the Everbrights' and went home. I guess Frank took an Uber to Nicholas House after he got off work. Grandma had told him a few days ago that the nightstand was too wobbly for her to put her tea on, and Frank wanted to fix it for her. Because he and I weren't talking, I didn't know anything about it. I was surprised when Grandma said he'd been there during the time the ornaments had gone missing, but not because I thought he had anything to do with the theft—he would never do anything to hurt Grandma or me or risk custody of Star—but because I had missed him so much those last two days and I hated that we were having this stupid fight. What kind of guy goes to all that trouble to tighten some bolts on a nightstand for his girlfriend's great-grandmother, Sadie?"

She didn't wait for an answer.

"I called him as soon as I finished talking to you this morning and asked him about his visit. Then he apologized, and I did too. I'm going to his place after work tonight so we can talk it all out like we should have on Saturday." She paused for a breath. "The other reason I didn't tell you he was there was because he can't just put his head down and become invisible the way I can. He's marked by his past and judged by it every time he meets someone, which I knew meant that as soon as you knew he'd been there and saw him in person you would assume he'd stolen the ornaments, which would only distract you from the person who really *did* steal them. So, yes, I didn't tell you, and, yes, I realize that makes both of us look suspicious, but, no, he did not take those ornaments. I would bet my life on that."

Sadie stared at Joy across their cups of cooling cocoa. Joy's eyes held a glimmer of fear that Sadie was going to judge her, or him, or both of them.

"How old is Star?"

Joy paused and then tears rose in her eyes. "Six," she whispered. "A month and two days older than my daughter."

"And where is your daughter?"

Joy blinked her heavily lashed eyes and sent two fat tears racing down her rouged cheeks. "I have no idea. It was a closed adoption, so it will be another twelve years before I can try to find her. Star fills a hole I never thought could be filled, but she's not the reason I'm with Frank, she's just a bonus."

Sadie reached her white-gloved hand across the table and placed it on the arm of a girl she thought she'd figured out a long time ago. She said nothing, and they sat in silence for several seconds.

"You're going to tell me to tell Grandma Mary about my baby, aren't you?"

"That's none of my business," Sadie said, biting her tongue to keep from saying that exact thing.

"It will make her so sad," Joy whispered. "And she'll feel bad that I didn't tell her sooner. She deserves to be happy for the time she has left, and I don't want her to worry about me."

"I think she would put her arms around you and tell you how sorry she is for your pain, and how proud she is of you for pushing forward, and how much she wishes you every happiness. I think she would want you to have those words with you forever and be glad she had the chance to say them."

Sadie watched Joy absorb those words, felt how hard it was to believe them but also how much Joy wanted them to be true. After several seconds, Joy nodded. "I'll think about that." Some new Christmas pop song Sadie didn't know came over the speakers. "You believe me, don't you—about Frank not stealing the ornaments?"

Sadie weighed telling this girl what she wanted to hear against telling her the truth. "I'd like to talk to him about his visit."

Joy tensed on her side of the table.

"I'm talking to anyone who might have seen anything," Sadie explained in a hurry. "This isn't about how Frank looks or anything like that, but until I know who *did* take those ornaments, anyone who was there during the time they went missing is going to have to answer some questions."

Joy let that sink in. "Okay, I guess I can see that. What can Frank do to help?"

Sadie assumed that by "help," Joy meant help prove himself innocent. "He can tell me everything he saw and hold nothing back."

"He'll do it," Joy said without hesitation. "We both get off at noon tomorrow. He can meet you after that but before Mass."

"That would be great," Sadie said, though she hated the idea of having to wait that long. "You have my number, so call me when he's ready, and we can arrange to meet up."

They both took another drink of their cocoas, agreed it wasn't as good cold, and got up from their table. But Sadie's bustle had gotten wedged into the back of the chair, and when she stood, the off-balance chair knocked her forward into the table, which knocked over both cups. The lid on Sadie's cup popped off, and though Joy sprung away from the table with enviable agility, Sadie wasn't fast enough, and the cocoa spilled right down the front of her dress and apron.

"Ah, nutcracker," Sadie said, trying to back away from the table. With the chair still stuck on her ample bustle, however, she knocked over another chair.

A man sitting nearby jumped up to help, while Joy came around the table and put a hand on Sadie's arm to keep her from knocking into anything else. The cashier came next, with a bar cloth to clean things up, but also trying to hide a smile at the whole scene.

Sadie's cheeks flamed with embarrassment as she had to stand still while three other people scurried around, trying to clean up the mess she'd made and get the chair off her bustle. She wanted to explain that this was a fashion choice of the Victorian era and entirely appropriate to the costume, not her actual backside, but suspected that wouldn't help. A few shoppers stopped on the other side of the glass wall to laugh and point. Sadie put on her biggest, fakest smile and waved her cocoa-spattered gloved hand at them as though this were all part of her role.

"Thank you," she said to both the kind patron and the cashier once she was freed from the chair and as cleaned up as she could be. She took off the apron, the brown stain dark against the white fabric. The red of her dress hid the rest of the cocoa much better.

"You're sure you're alright?" the cashier asked.

Sadie nodded and smiled as she moved toward the exit of the Starbucks as fast as she could. "Yes, certainly, thank you so much. Merry Christmas."

Joy walked quickly to keep up. "Are you really okay, Sadie?"

"Just humiliated," Sadie said quietly. She accidentally made eye contact with a shopper, and the way their face lit up at seeing her helped lighten her mood. She waved at the shopper, then said Merry Christmas to the next man who caught her eye. They didn't seem to notice the cocoa stain on her white gloves or that she held her apron balled up in one hand. She wasn't Sadie Cunningham to any of them, just Mrs. Claus. That helped cool her embarrassment even more.

Still, Sadie was relieved when the door to the storage-slash-dressing room came into view. She was quite ready to leave Mrs. Claus behind her.

"Do you need help getting out of your costume?" Joy asked once they were inside.

"If you could just undo the zipper," Sadie said.

"Of course." Joy unzipped the back of the dress. "What else can I do?"

"Nothing, I can do the rest."

"Okay, then I'll see you later. I'm supposed to pick Frank up at nine o'clock."

Joy was halfway through the door before Sadie called her name, remembering something. Joy turned to look at her expectantly.

"Um, when Frank learns that the woman he helped pick out

floor mats for earlier today was me, will you assure him that I am happily married and was only being friendly?"

Joy pulled her eyebrows together. "Sure, but why?"

"Um, I just think I gave the wrong impression." She turned around and started searching her purse for her phone so as not to prolong the conversation. "Good luck with the discussion. I hope you guys can finish sorting everything out."

CHAPTER 20

The relief Sadie felt when she held her phone in her hands made her feel like a teenager who'd been ungrounded from social media. Her generation often joked about kids and their addiction to their cell phones and instant communication, but Sadie was just as bad. She sat on a bench against the wall of the storage-dressing room, but the blasted bustle forced her to balance on the edge of the bench as she scanned all the life that had gone on without her while she'd played Mrs. Claus.

She'd missed a text from Breanna that said they were just getting on a plane at Heathrow and a text from Maggie asking if Sadie had almond extract at the town house for a family recipe she wanted to make. Sadie scoffed. Of course, she had almond extract. As well as butter, rum, lemon, spearmint, peppermint, orange, maple, and, of course, the good vanilla from Mexico—as well as vanilla paste and vanilla powder. She limited her response to a simple "yes," and that she was excited to see them in a couple of days.

Sadie set aside her phone and caught her reflection in the mirror she'd avoided earlier. She stood from the bench and walked forward until she had a full view of Mrs. Sadie Claus.

The bodice was looser now that the zipper had been undone, but the bustle made her waist look smaller and the full skirt balanced out her figure in rather flattering ways. It would look better with the apron breaking up so much solid red, but overall, it wasn't half bad. For an old lady costume.

Sadie frowned at the cocoa stain, then shimmied out of the costume and put it back on the hangers. She pulled a piece of paper from her notebook and wrote a note, apologizing to Holly for making such a mess and offering to pay for the dry cleaning if needed, though she didn't think Holly would take her up on that.

Sadie reached up and undid the hairpins holding the lacy mobcap on her head and then frowned when she lifted it off her head. Holly had only sprayed the hair curled around her face with the white hair spray, which meant the hair under the cap was still spiky and gray; it looked positively dirty next to the bright-white curls. Sadie took off the gloves and tried to finger-comb her hair into some semblance of symmetry, but the white-sprayed portion was stiff and unwieldy. She gave up and replaced the mobcap, deciding she'd rather have a cap on her head than have people wonder what she'd done to herself.

Her phone made a kissing sound—Pete's text tone—and Sadie hurried to retrieve her phone from the bench. She'd missed their usual nine o'clock good-night phone call.

Pete: Can you explain this to me?

Sadie furrowed her brow and was typing out a line of question marks when a picture came through. A picture of her in costume handing a candy cane to the little deviant Treyzoro, who looked at her as though she were deity.

Sadie let out a breath and replied.

Sadie: Can I call you in 10 minutes?

Pete: I don't know, can you? Santa looks like maybe he's got other ideas for you.

Sadie looked at the photo again and noticed Santa in the background for the first time. The look on his face could only be described as leering. Goodness, how embarrassing. And yet she didn't mind that Pete was a tiny bit jealous.

Sadie: 10 minutes. I need to get to my car.

Pete responded with a very neutral thumbs-up sign.

Sadie hurried to put on her coat, scarf, and boots before quick-stepping her way out of the mall and its frightfully anxious energy. The temperature had dropped since she'd entered the mall two hours earlier, and she checked the temperature on her watch—11 degrees. She would get an update on the storm as soon as she was settled in at Nicholas House, but hoped that at the very least it let Pete get home before it broke open.

Fewer cars in the parking lot meant that Sadie didn't have to fear for her life even once, and no one flipped her off. Once in her own car—parked twenty-seven miles away, it seemed—she started the engine, turned on the seat heater, adjusted her phone in the hand's-free holder, and cranked the heat all the way up before she called Pete back.

"It's been thirteen minutes," Pete said instead of hello.

She did not appreciate his tone even though she realized she deserved it. If the roles were reversed, she'd be quite concerned with him unexpectedly showing up on Facebook in a Santa costume being eyed by a nefarious Mrs. Claus. "I was leaving the mall, and it took longer than I thought it would."

"Explain what's going on, and don't leave anything out."

She took a breath, let it out, and then told the tale, starting with the call from Joy as she'd been leaving the grocery store earlier that morning. She left out a few details she'd determined unimportant—such as Frank assuming she'd been flirting with him and the fact that the bustle had gotten stuck in the chair at Starbucks.

Pete was uncomfortably quiet through the duration of her explanation, making her wish she'd made more progress toward actually finding Mary's ornaments so that her means would have more apparent justification.

"So, now I'm driving to Nicholas House, where I will be watching over the tree to make sure no one else comes to borrow any of Mary's ornaments." The light turned green, and Sadie hurried to put the mall behind her. She would feel better the farther away she got from that mad, mad world.

Pete was still silent. So silent that she worried their connection had been lost, which might not be all bad, really. Saying everything out loud made it sound more neurotic than it had seemed before.

Sadie counted five Rudolphs and five Frostys in order to make sure she gave him plenty of time to share his thoughts. "Um, Pete? Are you there?"

"I'm here," he said in a flat tone.

"Are you . . . mad?"

"Let's go with *concerned*."

"I know it sounds crazy when I lay it all out like that," Sadie said quickly. "But this is Mary's last Christmas, and I've promised to do everything I can to make it the best it can be. I have to find those ornaments in order to keep that promise. Plus, I haven't done anything illegal, so there really isn't anything you can get mad about."

"You haven't picked any locks?"

"No." She thought about the lockpick set in her purse but decided not to volunteer that information.

"You haven't broken into anyone's house?"

"Those are basically the same thing, but, no, I haven't." She felt quite virtuous about that. In fact, the only house she'd even considered breaking into was Ivy's, but she didn't have cause yet to justify the intrusion. Sadie had always tried to limit her breaking and entering to situations where she was quite certain she would find physical evidence she would not find otherwise.

"Have you taken any documents that are meant to be confidential?"

"No." Sadie didn't count the lists she would get in the morning because Jackie was giving them to her. She stopped at another light and gritted her teeth. It didn't seem fair that she should have to deal with traffic on top of everything else today.

"Has anyone been hurt?"

"No," Sadie said, her tone getting sharper. "I've been gathering information about possible suspects, Pete. That's all."

"Man, I wish I were home."

Sadie bristled. "Why, so you could talk me out of this?"

"So I could help keep you on the straight and narrow. Your

methods aren't always the most ethical, Sadie. That's all I'm saying."

Sadie was downright offended. "You make it sound like I'm some kind of vigilante. I've only ever helped people, Pete, and I'm not an idiot."

"No, you're not an idiot. You're very smart and very passionate, which sometimes come together as just enough skill to get you into a lot of trouble."

"Just enough skill?" Sadie repeated. "Do you have any idea how patronizing you are being right now?"

"I didn't mean it that way, I'm sorry. I just worry." His tone was sincere and apologetic, allowing Sadie to settle down. A bit.

"Apology accepted. Keep in mind that I'm dealing with missing Christmas ornaments stolen from a nursing home," Sadie reminded him. "The criminal element is pretty low, which keeps both the risks and the methods on the soft side." Compared to the sociopaths she'd encountered before, this was barely worth any concern at all, really. Except that Mary's ornaments felt as important as any other case she'd worked before. No one's life was on the line, but the peace Sadie wanted for the last part of Mary's life was.

"I would feel better if you would involve the police," Pete said.

There was just enough big-strong-man in his comment to ruffle Sadie's feathers all over again. "Of course, you do. You're one of the good ol' boys in that club, Pete, but I'm also trying to protect Mary. The police would come in, stomping their boots and making a fuss to the degree that there would be no way to keep Mary from knowing what's happened. Besides, the police don't care about old Christmas ornaments."

"The police care about crime, Sadie. It's our *job*, and we don't just stomp around and make a fuss. You're oversimplifying as a way to justify your desire to remain in control of this investigation."

Apparently, she'd hit a nerve too. "I only mean that I don't think this will draw the police's attention the way it's drawn mine. Mary is a dear friend, and I want her to have a calm, merry, and bright Christmas."

Pete let out a breath she chose to interpret as surrender. "You mentioned an incident report you could file through the facility."

"If it comes to that," Sadie clarified. She turned into the parking lot of Nicholas House and slid into an empty spot. She shifted into park but didn't turn off the car because—eleven degrees. "It would require talking to Mary, though, which I'm trying very hard to avoid."

"I think Mary could be a very small part of the report." His tone was more informative than judgmental, which kept Sadie listening. "Should this investigation get to the point where the police need to be called in, having had the report filed in a timely manner will protect you and the facility by proving you've followed the proper protocols. At the end of this investigation is a thief, Sadie. A criminal who will need to answer to justice. You need to move forward in a way that shows you weren't trying to circumvent the police, and I think you can do that without talking to Mary until you absolutely have to, but to have that report in progress will work in everyone's favor."

Sadie had thought about the fact that if she didn't find the ornaments, the police would have to step in. What she hadn't thought about so concretely was that if she *found* the ornaments, she would also find a bad guy. *That* would definitely necessitate the police. Ah, nutcracker.

"You think I should fill out the incident report?"

"Yes, as much as you can without talking to Mary. As soon as possible."

"Okay." She would fill out the incident report in exchange for Pete not freaking out about her doing this on her own.

"Promise?"

"Yes, Pete," Sadie said without hiding her irritation.

"I need to hear you say it," Pete pressed.

Sadie rolled her eyes and let out a heavy sigh. "Fine. I, Sadie Hoffmiller Cunningham, promise to fill out the official incident report with Nicholas House for Mary Hallmark's missing ornaments."

"Thank you," he said, sounding more victorious than Sadie liked. "Let me know if there's something I can help with from here, okay? We've got a final meeting with the local police in the morning, but plan to have that wrapped up by ten o'clock or so. We're getting to the airport early in case we can get an earlier flight, though that doesn't look promising. I can help look things up, run background checks, or maybe consult with you on how to avoid breaking any laws on your end of things which could jeopardize the entire investigation."

Sadie scoffed. "I will bear that in mind, Detective."

Pete's voice lost both the teasing and the irritation when he spoke next. "I really am worried about your safety above everything else, Sadie. I love you. I want you to be okay."

How did a girl not swoon when the man she loved said such pretty words? She turned off the car and got out, the phone still against her ear. "I love you too, Pete, and I'll be smart about this." She added a little sauce to her voice and closed the car door with her hip. "So, now that that's out of the way, do you want to know what I'm wearing?"

"Ooh," Pete said, gracefully picking up her lead. "If you're offering then I bet I do."

She started making her way toward the front doors of Nicholas House and patting the lacy mobcap still on her head. "Well, close your eyes so I can really paint a picture. First, there's lace."

"I like where this is going."

CHAPTER 21

🍬

The door to Mary's room was partially open and the lights were low inside, so Sadie entered without knocking. Mary was asleep, her hair having been taken out of its chignon and braided as it always was at night. She was dressed in a pink nightgown, her expression soft in the glow of the lamp beside her bed.

Fiona sat in the recliner beside the bed with headphones over her ears while she knitted the gray-and-navy-striped scarf of Ravenclaw House at breakneck speed while bobbing her head in time to whatever she was listening to. When Fiona looked up and saw Sadie, she smiled, put down her needles, and moved the headphones to hang around her neck.

"I'm sorry it's so late," Sadie said quietly.

"That's fine," Fiona whispered back, wrapping the partially finished scarf around her needles. "She fell asleep about half an hour ago, but we had a lot of fun tonight." She waved toward the hallway, and Sadie followed her out so they could talk without waking her.

"Did she need a breathing treatment while you were here?"

Fiona frowned. "Two. One around four o'clock when we got to

laughing over something ridiculous and then again after we came back from dinner—both times she just couldn't catch her breath. She responded well to both treatments, but . . . well, I know it's not a good sign."

Sadie reached for Fiona's hand. "Thank you so much for staying with her."

"I love it," Fiona said with sincerity. "I'm heading to my daughter's place in Houston on Christmas Day for two weeks and . . ." She paused to smile sadly and swallow. "I'm not going to have many more chances to just be with her, you know."

Sadie nodded. She did know. And it broke her heart.

Fiona shared Sadie's somber moment, then brightened. "Oh, did you know Ivy's coming for breakfast and the Christmas party tomorrow?"

"No," Sadie said. "I didn't know. Whose idea was that?"

"Ivy asked if she could join her for breakfast, and then Mary invited her to stay for the Christmas party." Fiona paused. "Mary told me what you said about not leaving Ivy with burden of their difficulties, and she's really taken that to heart."

"I'm not sure I'll ever understand why they have had such a hard time."

"Me neither," Fiona said. "And yet I have a son who I haven't talked to in fifteen years. Maybe I should make a bit more effort there, too. None of us live forever, do we?" She handed Sadie her knitting bag. "I'd better get my coat." She went back into the room, coming out a minute later while pushing her arms through the sleeves.

Sadie walked Fiona to the secured door, told her good night, and then returned to Mary's room. She watched Mary sleep for a few minutes before availing herself of Mary's sink so she could finally take off the mobcap and wash out the white hair spray. Only then did she realized that Fiona hadn't said anything about the old woman hat and hair—did that mean it looked normal to her?

Sadie ran some gel through her hair to make it easier to style in the morning and changed into the yoga pants and Aspen Colorado hoodie she'd brought to sleep in. A pair of red-and-green-striped fuzzy socks were her holiday token to an otherwise non-Christmassy outfit.

The day was certainly catching up to her, which would hopefully make the recliner a more comfortable bed than it might otherwise be if she wasn't so tired. Sadie got an extra quilt out of Mary's closet, a beautiful double-wedding-ring pattern that used to be on the bed in Mary's guest room. She turned off the bedside lamp so that only the Christmas tree lit the room and settled into the recliner, pushing it as far back as she could, which was almost flat.

The lights from the tree shimmered on the mirrored surfaces of the kugel ornaments. Sadie thought about Mary running her fingers over the ornaments just two days ago, pure joy on her face as she remembered each one, cherished them, and then handed them to Sadie to put on the tree. Were the ornaments safe, wherever they were? Had any of them been broken? She closed her eyes and prayed she could find them before they were lost forever.

CHAPTER 22

Sadie wasn't sure what awakened her, but when she squinted at her watch, she was shocked to see it was after seven o'clock. She'd expected a fitful night's sleep, tuned to any noise—one eye open, so to speak—and then to wake up early. So much for that. Mary was still asleep, and Sadie was glad for that.

As she lowered the footrest of the recliner, Sadie patted the arm as a thank you to the chair for a far better night's sleep than she expected. She folded the quilt, quietly returned it to the closet, and then inspected the tree to make sure all was as it should be. She didn't imagine anyone could have snuck in while she had been there, but she hadn't imagined she would sleep so deeply or so late either. Thankfully, all twenty-nine kugels and sixteen candy canes were accounted for and . . . fifteen, sixteen, seventeen Dresdens. Thank goodness.

She changed into the clothes she'd brought with her—jeans, Dansko clogs, and the green Christmas sweater with a cat tangled up in Christmas lights on it above the words "It wasn't me." She styled her hair, spikey since she didn't have a curling iron, and was finishing what little makeup she bothered with when she heard

Mary beginning to stir. She hurried to finish blending the creamy rose blush into her cheeks, then went into Mary's room.

"Hee-haw, Mary," she said quietly.

She was expecting a tired response, but Mary's voice was surprisingly alert from where she sat on the edge of the bed, her face turned toward Sadie, her braid draped over one shoulder. "Hee-haw, Sadie. You really did stay over, then?"

"I really did," Sadie said. "And I have to say I'm a little miffed you held out on me about how comfortable that recliner is."

Mary laughed and removed the elastic from the end of her braid. She held it out to Sadie. "Could you put this in the bathroom drawer on the right?"

Mary began undoing the weave with practiced fingers while Sadie put the elastic where it belonged. All the bathroom drawers were labeled with what they contained. Not for Mary's sake, but so the staff and family would always put things where Mary knew to find them.

"Don't blame me for the recliner," Mary said from her room. "I've never slept it. Joy's the one who's kept you in the dark. She and the recliner are well acquainted."

Joy, Sadie thought as she returned to Mary's bedside. The heaviness she'd felt when Joy had told her story returned. It was uncomfortable knowing more about Mary's granddaughter than Mary did, though she understood Joy's reasons. For Joy's sake, she hoped that she would confide in Mary. Sadie had no doubt the comfort and grace Mary would extend would be further balm to Joy's healing heart.

"Then I'll take it up with her," Sadie said decisively. "Mark my words."

A waterfall of wavy white hair cascaded over one shoulder when Mary finished undoing the braid, reflecting the lights of the Christmas tree and emphasizing the pink of Mary's nightgown, the flush of her cheeks, and the blue of her sightless eyes.

Sadie's breath caught in her throat. "Stay right there," she said.

Mary's fingers froze, still combing through the waves, and her eyes widened. "What? Is it a spider? That is the worst part of being blind: I can't see them!"

"No, not a spider," Sadie laughed, grabbing her phone from Mary's nightstand where she'd been charging it overnight.

Mary relaxed. "Then why do I have to stay still?"

"Just do what I say, woman," Sadie ordered as she hurried to frame up the picture. "You look so beautiful right now. I want to take a picture."

Mary laughed, but she sat up straight on the edge of her bed and put her hands in her lap. Part of the Christmas tree with her beloved ornaments showed in the background, but it was Mary who stood out with radiance and light. Sadie took three quick pictures. They were lovely, and she couldn't wait to share them with Ivy and Joy. "Okay, I'm done. How did you sleep?"

Mary's smile both softened and brightened, causing Sadie to sense something in the air she hadn't noticed before. "I dreamed about him," Mary said reverently.

"Him?"

"Doral." Mary said his name with such longing and joy that it brought tears to Sadie's eyes. "Goodness, it's like I'm right back there." With a hand on her chest, Mary closed her eyes and inhaled deeply. "He was waiting for me on the other side of the train tracks that ran behind the first home we bought in Cripple Creek. Oh, he was handsome." She put out her hand, and Sadie took it as she sat beside her on the bed.

"What did he look like?" Sadie asked. Dreams of the dying were sacred experiences.

Mary opened her eyes and looked ahead of her as though she were seeing the whole scene. Her smile got bigger. "Young, maybe thirty. He had a full head of hair and smooth skin. When he smiled, his green eyes flashed, making my knees go weak like always. He was wearing a suit—oh, but he was a sight to see in a nice suit, Sadie. Broad shoulders, straight back, long, lean legs. He was holding . . ." She paused to laugh and shake her head. "He was holding a loaf of my orange cranberry bread. He always loved that bread."

"It's one of my favorites, too," Sadie said with a nod.

"It's just like him to remind me that he hadn't had my bread for a while. Do you think they have ovens in heaven? And cranberries?"

"They better," Sadie said, only half playing along with the joke. She couldn't see how heaven would be heaven without cooking. And eating.

Mary sobered again, seeming to search her memory for the details. "Doral was waiting for me on the other side of the tracks because I was . . . packing."

Sadie blinked back tears. "You were getting ready to join him."

"Yes, but I wasn't quite ready," Mary said with a small shake of her head, though her smile lost none of its youthful radiance. "I was running here and there, throwing things in a suitcase set on an old stump we were always talking about removing but never did. And I kept telling him to hold on, I just needed a few more minutes." She paused. "No, I said I needed a little more *time* to make sure I didn't forget anything. Because I knew I couldn't come back once I left." She turned toward Sadie and blinked her watery eyes, unleashing a single tear that Sadie wiped away with her thumb. "He told me that it was fine, he would be there when I was ready. And . . . he said the boys would be there, too. Oh, Sadie, I miss them all so much."

"That's b-beautiful," Sadie said softly.

Mary was quiet for a few moments. "I need a little more time with Ivy," she said resolutely. "And I need to give my ornaments to Joy and tell her what she has meant to me these last few years. Then . . ." She let out a breath and the tension in her shoulders went with it. "And then I just want a few more days so that my family won't associate my passing with Christmas." She put her other hand over Sadie's and gave it a squeeze. "Oh, Sadie, even knowing how important these last things are for me to do, I could hardly stand to stay on my side of the tracks."

"A few more days," Sadie repeated. "That's heavy, Mary."

"No," she said, patting Sadie's hand. "It's light as a feather. There is a lifetime waiting for me there. A few more days and I get to *live* again. Dance. See my husband. Hold my boys."

They sat in silence for a full minute before Mary let go of Sadie's hand and pushed herself to her feet. She wobbled, and Sadie helped hold her steady, but then Mary waved her off.

"I'd like to dress up today, Sadie, for the party and to celebrate Christmas. There's a green dress in the closet, probably toward the back. It's got a flouncy hem and sweetheart neckline. I'll wear that with the black ankle boots, oh, and the diamond pendant that's in my jewelry box in the top drawer. Could you get those things ready for me?"

"Of course." Sadie stood and turned toward the closet, but then waited a moment in case Mary needed more help.

Mary felt with her feet for the thick tape-line on the floor. Once she'd found it, she followed it to the bathroom. Sadie almost ran forward and turned on the bathroom light when Mary began to close the door without having done so, but Mary had been living in the dark for a long time. The bathroom door shut, leaving Sadie surrounded by the feelings Mary's dream had settled in the room.

A few more days . . . Sadness tugged a few more tears from Sadie's eyes, but gratitude at being able to share this experience overtook the sorrow. Sadie did not wish for death, she had so much more living to do, but she didn't fear it either. That was probably why Mary had shared her dream, because she knew Sadie could hear it the way Mary had experienced it. Beautiful. Encouraging. Joyful, even.

Mary pulled the door open a few inches. "Sadie?"

Sadie wiped quickly at her eyes as though trying to hide tears Mary could not see anyway. "Yes, Mary."

"What time is it? I'm supposed to request help before eight or wait until after breakfast."

"It's 7:32," Sadie said, checking her watch.

"Oh, good. Would you see if one of the aides could help me shower? It is Tuesday, right? That's my shower day."

"Yes, it's Tuesday. It's Christmas Eve."

"That's right, Merry Christmas. Do you mind fetching an aide for me? I'll need to get my things ready first, so I don't need their help for another ten minutes."

No one was in the nurses' station when Sadie arrived. The "On

Staff" board showed that Harry was the nurse on shift, with Molly, Jose, and Xander as the day's aides. Harry and Molly were still people Sadie needed to talk to about Sunday night.

"Good morning."

Sadie spun around, startled, but then instantly relaxed when Molly stepped past her into the nurses' station. She pulled out a binder from a cubby beneath the countertop and opened it to a page where she started writing things down.

"Can I help you?" Molly asked, flashing Sadie a cheery smile that matched her snowman-shaped stud earrings.

"Yes, sorry. Mary would like help with a shower in about ten minutes. She said if she requested before eight o'clock that would be okay."

"Of course," Molly said, her plump cheeks further plumping as she smiled. She finished writing her note and closed the binder, then faced Sadie. "I'm Mary's aide today, and I was just about to check on her. You're the friend who stayed over last night?"

"Yes," Sadie said, falling into step beside Molly as they walked down the hall toward Mary's room. "I'm Sadie Cunningham."

"Nice to meet you, Sadie. How'd Mary do last night? We don't do our usual night checks when residents have company."

"She slept really well," Sadie said, feeling all soft when she remembered her friend's dream. "*Really* well."

"I'm glad to hear that."

They walked a few steps in silence, but Sadie was running out of distance before they reached Mary's room. She hoped her segue wouldn't be too abrupt. "You worked Sunday, didn't you, Molly? The float shift?"

"Yeah, I usually pick up one float in order to get a solid forty hours a week."

"How was Mary that night?"

"She needed a breathing treatment, but other than that, she was good. She had a lot of visitors, which is always great. Joy brought her sushi for dinner and on her way out told the nurse that Mary had eaten an entire California roll. We were pleased about that—and maybe a little jealous." She quirked a smile, and Sadie smiled back.

"Who else came to see her while you were here?"

"Ivy popped in, but didn't stay long, and then Joy's boyfriend came in just as I was leaving for the night."

That lined up with what Sadie had heard from the other people she'd talked to. "And did all the Sunday evening visits go okay?"

"Okay?" Molly repeated.

They had reached Mary's room, but Sadie turned to Molly, indicating she wanted to talk a little longer. "You said Ivy didn't stay very long. I just wondered if anything seemed . . . out of character."

"Well, actually, she was a little . . . skittery."

"Skittery?"

"Yeah, I came in to put away Mary's laundry and scared her, I guess. Ivy jumped like a mile and got all red-faced. It was weird, mostly because she's always so put together, ya know?" Molly lifted her chin and batted her eyelashes as though to demonstrate a debutante.

"I totally know," Sadie said with a laugh. Ivy was the poster child for the graceful golden years, but she'd been a bit "skittery" on the phone too, and she'd claimed not to know it was Molly who had brought in Mary's laundry while she was there. Was it so Sadie wouldn't know who to follow up with? "Ivy reacted that strongly when you came into the room?"

"Well, I didn't see her at first. She was on the other side of the open door, so when I came in and started singing 'God rest ye, Mary gentlewoman'—it's a spin I did just for Mary, ya know—it scared Ivy half to death. I mean, that's what she said. 'You scared me half to death, Molly.'"

Sadie had been picturing Mary's room while Molly told the story. "If Ivy was on the other side of the door then was she . . . by the tree?"

Molly considered that. "Yeah, at the foot of the bed, by the tree. That general area."

People were usually startled when they were concentrating on something else. "What was Mary doing?"

"I think she was asleep in her chair." Molly grimaced. "I felt bad about that. I hate waking her up, but I'd seen Ivy go into her room, like, five minutes before and assumed they were visiting. Plus, the door was wide open."

If Ivy had been by the tree, the open door would block her from view of anyone in the hallway. And if Mary had been asleep, Ivy could have been doing just about anything.

"This will sound strange," Sadie said, "but did Ivy have a box or maybe a shoulder bag with her?" She would have needed something fairly large to transport the ornaments out of Mary's room.

"No, she just had a regular purse—it was red, I remember that. When I surprised her, though, she had her hand inside her purse, and for a split second, I thought she was going to pull out a gun. My sister-in-law has her concealed-carry permit and keeps her gun in the side pocket of her purse. Freaks me out."

"Ivy had her hand *inside* her purse?"

Molly nodded. "But then she brought out her hand—without a gun," she grinned. "And she laughed awkwardly and I laughed awkwardly and Mary woke up and, so, ya know. We all carried on."

"How long did Ivy stay?"

"Not very long. I remember the call light went on just a couple of minutes after I'd left the room, but then Ivy met me in the hall before I could answer it, saying Mary was struggling to catch her breath. I wasn't involved in the breathing treatment or anything—that was Harry—but Ivy left pretty soon after that. She seemed upset; her neck was all flushed." Molly waggled her fingers around her neck to demonstrate. She looked past Sadie to the door to Mary's room. "She's probably ready for me, don't you think?"

"Oh, yes, of course," Sadie said, realizing she'd positioned herself in front of the door. She moved out of the way and then followed Molly in.

Molly went straight to the bathroom, knocked, then opened the door a couple of inches. The sound of the shower could be heard from inside the bathroom. "It's Molly, are you ready for me?"

"Just in time," Mary called out.

"I aim to please," Molly said as she stepped into the bathroom and closed the door behind her.

There was a tapping at the main door of Mary's room, and Sadie turned as Joy came in, looking around the room as she did so.

"Grandma's in the shower?" Joy asked.

"Just barely," Sadie said. "Molly's helping her."

"Oh, good. I have to be to work by nine so I don't have long but wanted to help her get ready." She moved to the dresser and with practiced efficiency retrieved a fresh set of underclothes and socks. Sadie had already laid out the dress and shoes, but hadn't thought of the other things.

"How did things go with Frank last night?" Sadie asked.

Joy gave her a relieved but slightly nervous smile that Sadie understood. Joy wasn't used to people knowing about her private struggles. "Really good. We both apologized and then talked about how we should have handled things." Her look changed slightly. "He said you asked him out."

Sadie's face caught fire. "I did *not* ask him out," she said, incredulous. "I was trying to determine if he was *your* Frank and asking a bunch of questions that, in hindsight, sounded a little . . ."

"Propositioning?"

"No!" Sadie said, but Joy was laughing, and Sadie couldn't help but smile despite her embarrassment.

"It's fine, we laughed about it too. He gets treated weird all the time. Like, this guy in his apartment keeps hitting him up for drugs. He just can't believe that Frank isn't a dealer, and then people will move to the other side of the street sometimes when they see him coming."

"That's too bad."

"Tattoo removal isn't as easy as people say it is. The skin is never back the way it was, and it's so expensive," Joy said, laying out the clothes in the order Mary would need them. "There's even ear surgery if he wanted to fix the gauges, but it's crazy expensive. He doesn't even own a car, so I can't imagine we'll fall into enough money for that any time soon."

Sadie thought about the money the ornaments could bring in. Not that earlobe repair should be a priority over tuition or a down payment on a house, but then again it might be if it improved the effect he made on people and opened new opportunities. "Is he willing to talk to me about his visit on Sunday?"

"Oh, yeah," Joy said, smoothing out the skirt of the dress even though Mary wouldn't be able to see her efforts. "Grandma is going to look so pretty in this. Frank and I both work until noon, but he'll come here as soon as he's ready. I'll pick Star up from the Everlights and bring her with me." Having finished her arrangement, she faced Sadie. "How are things going with finding the ornaments?"

"Slower than I would like. I've talked to a few people, but I need to get more information before I can bring everything together." It was tempting to grill Joy about Ivy. Did Joy think she could have taken the ornaments? Was there anything in her history that Joy might know that Sadie didn't? But Sadie thought better of it. If Ivy had taken the ornaments, Joy might have been part of the motive, and Sadie didn't want to complicate things between them. Plus, Sadie knew what purse Molly had seen; it was about the size of a loaf of bread. Ivy could have fit the candy cane ornament, and maybe a couple of the Dresdens in there—though that would be terribly irresponsible—but she couldn't have taken the kugels.

Ivy would be arriving for breakfast in half an hour, though, and that would be Sadie's chance to find out what had happened Sunday night when Molly had surprised her. Sadie looked at her watch—it was 7:58.

"I've got to talk to Jackie," she said quickly. "I'll check in on you later, though."

"Okay," Joy said, moving around the room to straighten it like she did every time she visited. "Good luck."

Orange Cranberry Bread

2 cups all-purpose flour
¾ cup sugar
1 ½ teaspoon baking powder
½ teaspoon salt
½ teaspoon baking soda
¼ cup butter, softened
1 tablespoon grated orange peel
¾ cup orange juice
1 egg
1 cup fresh or frozen cranberries, chopped
½ cup chopped nuts (optional)
Sugar to sprinkle on top

Preheat oven to 350 degrees F. Grease bottom of 1 standard-sized loaf pan.

In a mixing bowl, combine all dry ingredients together. Add butter and mix until crumbly. Add orange peel, orange juice, egg, cranberries, and nuts. Mix until just combined.

Spread into loaf pan. Sprinkle with a thin layer of sugar.

Bake 50 to 75 minutes, or until toothpick comes out clean from the center. Cool in pan 5 minutes, loosen sides, and turn bread out of pan to cool on a rack. Cool completely before slicing.

Note: This recipe can also make 3 mini-loaves, baked 35 to 40 minutes, or 18 muffins, baked 20 to 25 minutes.

Note: Shawn likes to add ½ cup of vanilla chips with the nuts and cranberries.

CHAPTER 23

Sadie was waiting outside the nurses' station when Jackie appeared on the foyer side of the security door a few minutes after eight o'clock. She had to transfer shopping bags from one hand to the other in order to wave her badge over the sensor. A soft buzzing indicated when the lock was disarmed.

"Can I help?" Sadie asked as she approached.

Jackie smiled as she transferred a few bags to Sadie's willing hands. Best Buy. Target. Bed, Bath & Beyond. "Thank you. Sorry I'm running late." She walked past Sadie into the nurses' station, where one of the aides—a tall young man with a ponytail halfway down his back and a tattoo of the Deathly Hallows on the side of his neck—was entering information from a small notebook to the computer. "Good morning, Xander," Jackie said. "Did the gingerbread cookies arrive?"

"Yep, night shift said the bakery delivered them at six. They're in the common room."

"Thank goodness for Christmas miracles," Jackie said as she crossed behind Xander and stopped at the door to her office. She turned to smile at Sadie. "I ordered five dozen miniature gingerbread men to be picked up at five yesterday, and they weren't ready. What if my party had been last night?" She shook her head as she turned her attention to the ring of keys she withdrew from her pocket. With her free hand, she jingled through the keys until she found the one she wanted, slid it into the lock, and pushed the door open. The overhead light in the office blinked to life once Jackie hit the switch. "Come on in, Sadie," Jackie said over her shoulder. She turned her head to look at the aide, who didn't seem to be paying them any attention at all. "Xander, I'll just be a few minutes."

"Okay," Xander said.

Sadie stepped into the office behind Jackie and closed the door. The office wasn't large and had the kind of commercial carpet that wasn't much thicker than the linoleum of the nurses' station on the other side of the threshold. A sturdy executive desk was against one wall and piled high with folders and papers and desk-organization paraphernalia. A bulletin board on the wall held a more personal collection of photos, thank-you cards, and comics cut from the newspaper.

Against the wall opposite the desk was a four-foot-wide filing cabinet, a reminder of how much paperwork was associated with Jackie's position. She'd told Sadie once that the trade-off for the raise and the position of authority was that she didn't get to be much of a nurse anymore. Documents had become her patients and details her methods of care. There was a Charlie Brown–type Christmas tree on the cabinet with a single red ornament bending the top over like it did in the cartoon. Sadie added watching the old Christmas cartoons to her list of things to do with the family; she hadn't seen those movies in years. It was strange to think that today was Christmas Eve. The Christmas spirit was becoming difficult to hold on to, and Sadie missed it.

Sadie put down her bags next to the ones Jackie slid off her arm.

"We're doing a drawing for the staff after the party," Jackie explained, waving toward the bags. "I was in charge of getting the prizes and totally forgot about it until last night after picking up my son, so we did some shopping on the way home. I figure I'll put a sticky bow on top of each item and call it good."

"Great idea." Being flexible was an important trait for anyone to have, but especially in regard to leadership.

"Have a seat," Jackie said as she waved to the folding chair set next to the desk. She pulled her rolling chair out from under the desk and sat, the chair lowering a few inches once her full weight was upon it.

Jackie was a heavyset woman with a round face and dark eyes further emphasized by permanent eyelash extensions that gave her a touch of the exotic. Her hair had been in a simple bob since Sadie had known her, always the same shade of light brown that had likely been her natural color twenty years ago. She wasn't wearing scrubs like she usually did, but instead had on wide-legged, black dress pants, a green sweater, and a necklace of tiny Christmas lights that matched her red Christmas-bulb earrings tied with little golden bows.

"I know it's not very festive of me, but when I hit this point, sometimes I just wish the holidays were over. The lead-up is exhausting."

"Don't I know it," Sadie agreed. It was exhausting without the pressure of trying to save Christmas for a dying friend.

Jackie turned to her computer and put her fingers on the keyboard. Her nails were the same shade of red as her earrings and glinted in the overhead light. "Okay, so you wanted a list of staff and visitors who were either working or visiting between, what, 6:00 Sunday night and 1:30 yesterday afternoon?"

"That would be great."

Jackie clicked and toggled, typed some things in, then clicked again. The printer set on the filing cabinet hummed to life. Sadie looked closer at the photos pinned above Jackie's desk while she waited for the lists.

"Are these your kids?" Sadie asked after noticing a photo of Jackie standing with three adult children—all of them taller than she was. Without a dad figure in the photo, Sadie wondered if Jackie was divorced. She didn't know her well enough to have asked before.

"Yes, my Three Musketeers," she said, glancing at the photo with a proud smile. "Or Stooges, depending on the day."

The next photo was of Jackie's daughter—deduced from the fact that she in the family photo—with two little boys and a girl standing in front of her. "And these are your grandbabies?"

Jackie stopped what she was doing to smile at the photo. "Aren't they the cutest things? Honestly, if someone had told me how wonderful it would be to be a grandma, I'd have skipped the first wave."

Sadie laughed, though she didn't agree. She loved all the grandkids she and Pete shared, but raising her own children remained the greatest joy of her life. "Do your sons have children?"

"If they did, I'd have the photos to prove it. They are both taking their time, but it's okay. They're working hard and staying out of trouble these days. I'm perfectly content with that."

Between the lines Sadie read that those two boys hadn't always stayed out of trouble, and she again thanked heaven that both of her children had been pretty decent teenagers and young adults. Shawn had done his share of dumb things—like dumping dish soap in the cemetery fountain and hiding an open can of sardines in his friend's car—but nothing criminal or with long-term consequences. "Your son flew in last night, right?"

"Yep. Glen has been in Springfield for, oh, four years now, I guess," Jackie said, going back to the computer. "Did you hear the update about the white Christmas we're expecting?"

Mentioning the fretful forecast sent a shiver through Sadie. "Not since last night. It's changed?"

Jackie nodded. "Supposed to start by three this afternoon and go through the twenty-sixth—that's when Glen was supposed to fly home." She gave a sneaky smile. "But I feel terrible that my prayers were answered when I know it will put so many other families out."

Sadie laughed, keeping to herself that her family was in the middle of that bull's-eye, but she didn't believe God answered prayers that way. "For your sake, I'm happy about that."

The printer spat out another document. Jackie pushed away from the desk, rolled halfway across the floor, and grabbed the documents from the printer tray with efficient ease. Sadie stood, and Jackie walked across the floor to meet her, holding the papers dramatically against her chest. "I trust you to guard these with your life and tell no one where you got them."

Sadie clicked her heels together and saluted. "Aye, aye,

captain." She relaxed and lowered her hand, speaking with sincerity now. "I can't thank you enough for the help."

"You're welcome. I just hope the ornaments turn up," Jackie said.

"Me too," Sadie said. "Oh, could I get a copy of the incident-report form you were telling me about?"

Jackie's eyebrows came together. "I thought we weren't going to go that route." She waved toward the lists in Sadie's hand, reminding her of the conversation they'd had about not treating this like an official investigation.

"We're not, but, well, I was talking to Pete, and he said it would be good to have it at least in process in case the police are brought in."

"Police?" Jackie said with a surprised laugh. When she lifted her eyebrows, the light caught her shimmery gold eye shadow just right. "I can't imagine this qualifies as a police matter, do you?"

"The severity of theft is defined by the value of the objects involved. Anything over two thousand dollars can be considered a felony in the state of Colorado."

The look of surprise remained on Jackie's face. "Two thousand dollars?"

"I'm more interested in the sentimental value, of course, but Mary's ornaments *are* rather valuable."

"How valuable?"

"I'm by no means an expert, but from my calculations, the missing ornaments are worth anywhere from four thousand to eight thousand dollars."

Jackie whistled under her breath. "Wow, I had no idea we were talking about that kind of money."

"You can understand why I don't want that information to go public." To put a value on the missing ornaments attached value to the rest of the ornaments still on the tree. And yet, someone else already knew what they were worth, which was why there had been a theft in the first place. "And I'd ask that, as we decided before, you not talk to anyone about this."

"Of course not," Jackie said. She clasped her hands in front of her. "But you'll keep me in the loop, right? You'll come to me before you call the police?"

"Oh, yes," Sadie assured her. "We'll want the incident report in place before we go to the police, which I am really hoping to avoid."

"Me too." Jackie turned to the filing cabinet and pulled open the second drawer, ticking through the tabs until she found the one she was looking for. She extracted a stapled set of papers and handed them to Sadie. "Make sure these come back to me."

"I will." Sadie added the report to the other papers Jackie had given her. "Thanks again for your help on such a busy day."

Sadie let herself out of the office—the nurses' station was empty now—and thumbed through the staff and visitor lists as she headed toward Mary's room. Each name on the list had a time next to it for when they checked in. The list of staff also had a check-out time, but the visitors list didn't, which was unfortunate.

Sadie was turning toward Mary's room when a flash of bright blonde hair on the other side of the secured door caught her attention.

Ivy.

Sadie mentally set the lists aside and faced the door. When Ivy saw Sadie through the glass, the hand she had raised to sign in froze. After two beats, she must have realized that changing her mind—which was what it looked like she was trying to decide to do—wasn't really an option. The lock disengaged with a buzz, and Ivy pulled open the door rather slowly.

Sadie rolled up the lists so they would be easier to hold; her shoulder bag was in Mary's room. She walked toward the front door so that when Ivy walked through, there was nothing to face but a politely smiling Sadie. And her own guilty conscience!

"Merry Christmas, Sadie," Ivy said after the door closed behind her. She adjusted her purse—the red, bread-loaf one Molly had described from Sunday.

"Merry Christmas, Ivy," Sadie said, then let her smile fall so Ivy would know she meant business. "We need to talk."

"I'm meeting Mom for breakfast. Can it wait?"

"Mary's getting ready, and, no, it can't."

CHAPTER 24

S adie would have loved to use Jackie's office for this conversation, but she didn't feel right about asking Jackie to leave when she still had work to do. She also would have liked to use Mary's room, but Mary was in there. Instead, Sadie and Ivy ended up in the dining room, sitting across from one another at a table in the far corner. From where she sat, Sadie could see part of Mary's door—the glass walls kept everything open and bright—allowing her to keep an eye on the comings and goings of the room while she and Ivy sorted things out.

Sadie hoped Joy was still with Mary, enjoying their time together, until she had to go to work and Mary was ready to go to breakfast. Mary usually ate closer to nine o'clock, though Sadie wondered if she'd want to eat early today since the Christmas party was at 10:30—roughly two hours away. Noise on the other side of the kitchen door testified that the staff was busy with both breakfast and party food.

Sadie turned her attention to Ivy, who settled herself in a plastic chair, crossed one leg over the other, reconsidered, then crossed the other leg before putting her purse on the table in front of her.

She was wearing black leggings, black, lace-up wedge booties, and a loose, red sweater under a black coat—AARP fashion model for sure. How did she get everything to coordinate so well all the time? *Focus.*

Sadie cleared her throat. "You said something yesterday on the phone that's stuck with me. When I mentioned the ornaments were missing, you said, 'Which ornaments'—why did you think only certain ornaments were missing?"

"I just assumed, I guess." She lifted her slim shoulders in a dismissive shrug.

"I don't think that's true."

Ivy raised her eyebrows a fraction of an inch, likely all that the Botox would allow. "Are you calling me a liar?"

Nice try, Sadie thought, recognizing the attempt to turn the tables. This wasn't Sadie's first holiday jamboree, thank you very much. "I think you took some of Mary's ornaments Sunday evening when you came to visit."

Ivy scoffed and crossed her arms over her chest into a posture that was meant to look incensed but looked defensive to Sadie's practiced eye.

"Here's what I think happened. Mary was asleep when you arrived, and you turned your attention to the Christmas tree, which has been a point of contention between the two of you. I think, despite Mary's opinion that you don't care about the ornaments, they do mean something to you—more than you've let on. You figured you could take a few of them, for sentimental reasons, and no one would be the wiser."

Ivy's mouth tightened, but her eyes held enough anxiety to convince Sadie she was on the right track.

"Now, given different relationship dynamics, it would make sense to just ask for them, but you and Mary have struggled for a long time, and so it would be difficult for you to trust that she would give you the ornaments as keepsakes if you asked. In order to avoid rejection, you took them instead."

Ivy's eyes got glassy, and she swallowed, boosting Sadie's confidence even more. She nodded toward Ivy's purse on the table between them. "You had the same purse Sunday, which means you couldn't have gotten the kugels out of the building without risking breakage, which would defeat the purpose, but you *could* fit a candy cane and maybe a few of the Dresdens in there. Maybe you came back for the kugels later that night—I haven't been able to finish going through the visitor lists."

Sadie crossed her arms on the table, staring down Ivy like Columbo, but without the squint. "So, how did I do?" Sadie asked.

Ivy swallowed again and sniffed. Sadie would have given her a tissue if the gesture wouldn't cost her the edge she'd managed to establish.

Ivy stared at her knees. "I only took the candy cane," she finally muttered.

"What was that?" Sadie had heard her, but wanted to make sure she hadn't missed an intonation or anything like that.

Ivy looked up. "The candy cane. We always called it 'Mary's Candy Cane' because of the story of how she chipped the end when she was little. I just . . ." Ivy looked aside as though studying the fake ficus tree in the corner while she collected her thoughts. After a few moments, she turned back. "As executor of Mom's estate— such as it is—I've seen what she's leaving to everyone, lots of sentimental and meaningful things that reflect something they've shared or whatever. Mom and I haven't . . . shared much, and there isn't a single thing she's bequeathed to me that includes her essence or whatever you want to call it. I just wanted something that was special *to* her and that reminded me *of* her.

"So I took the candy cane Sunday night, which was stupid, because of all the ornaments, that chipped candy cane is the one she would be most likely to notice was missing. It sticks out like a sore thumb on my tree—which is purple and bright green this year, for Mardi Gras. When I thought about how upset Mom would be when she learned it was gone, I planned to bring it back. But then you called and said a *bunch* of ornaments were missing. I was sure that if I told you I'd taken the candy cane, you would assume I'd taken the others, but I hadn't, so I just . . . did nothing."

"You should have told me, Ivy."

Ivy's eyes narrowed in irritation. "Except that, honestly, Sadie, this is none of your business, and I don't owe you anything."

"You're right," Sadie said, nodding. "You don't owe me anything, but this *is* my business. Mary asked me to help her enjoy her final Christmas, and I said I would do that. If you took more than that candy cane, please tell me right now so we can put an end to this."

Sadie's direct response softened Ivy's ire for a second time. She just needed a firm hand, was all. "Like I said, I only took the candy cane, and it would be a relief to give it back. I wish I'd brought it with me." She pushed her purse toward the middle of the table as though offering it up for Sadie's inspection, but Sadie didn't need to do that. She believed Ivy and was reminded again that face-to-face interviews were always so much more effective.

If only she'd gone to Ivy's work and confronted her there

yesterday instead of talking to her on the phone, they might be hours ahead by now. Like those kids who had confessed to Mrs. Claus, Ivy hadn't been able to sustain the lie in Sadie's presence.

"I could go get it now if you want."

"Isn't Mary expecting you for breakfast?"

"Oh, right. I could bring it after the party."

"That would be good," Sadie confirmed. She paused in hopes of creating a natural transition between the candy cane theft and a more conversational topic. "I'm glad you guys are having breakfast together."

Ivy brightened. "Me too. When we were kids, Mom always did a big Christmas Eve breakfast. She'd spend the rest of the day getting things ready for the big family dinner we'd do on Christmas Day, but I always loved the breakfast most. It was just our family, you know, our time together. I was nervous to ask her if we could have breakfast together today—she tells me 'no' a lot—but she actually said she wished she'd thought of it, and then she invited me to the party at 10:30." She talked like a teenage girl pleased to have been invited to a popular girl's birthday party, and it made Sadie's heart ache a bit.

"That's fantastic," Sadie said. "I'm so glad you two get this time together."

"So, now that you know I didn't take the other ornaments, are you going to look into Frank like I told you to?"

Ivy was not nearly as good at transitioning conversations as Sadie was, apparently, but Sadie went with it. "I've looked into Frank, and I don't think he took them."

"Sadie," Ivy said in a tone of disappointment while shaking her head. "You're dismissing him out of hand. If you had met him you would—"

"I have met him. I also ran a background check on him and had a long talk with Joy."

Her surprise morphed into frustration as she leaned forward across the table. "Of course, she would defend him. He's, like, the first guy who's ever looked twice at her."

Not the first, Sadie thought sadly, but of course she wouldn't say that and of course Ivy would only see the appearance aspects of Joy and Frank's relationships.

"I do think he's the first guy Joy has dared to trust in a very long time, but I have no reason to suspect him of doing anything that would endanger his relationship with Joy or the custody of his daughter. Not everyone is what they seem to be on the outside, Ivy."

Even Ivy, who sort of was exactly what she reflected on the outside—a woman concerned with appearances and a bit materialistic—was harboring a well of longing for a better relationship with her mother. Joy wasn't what she appeared either, and neither was Frank, at least he wasn't who he had been when he'd developed the presentation he now couldn't get away from.

Ivy shook her head. "I wouldn't dismiss him so easily, Sadie."

That was actually fair advice. Sadie had yet to talk to him personally about his visit Sunday night, and she might get a different impression than what Joy had given her last night, but Sadie didn't feel Frank deserved Ivy's suspicion. It was easy to make a quick judgment about outward aspects of a person. It was also lazy. Sadie would better know what kind of man Frank was after she talked to him this afternoon.

"I'll keep that in mind, Ivy," Sadie said, hoping her tone communicated that she was done discussing Frank. "Is there anything else you can tell me about your visit? Who came in, who Mary talked about, anything you saw that was suspect? I really want to find those other ornaments, but I can't do it alone."

Ivy relayed how Molly came in just as she'd put the candy cane in her purse, and then how Mary had needed the breathing treatment and Ivy had left to find the nurse.

"That nurse would have been . . ." Sadie searched her memory for the name. "Harry?"

Ivy nodded, and the smallest of smiles played on her unnaturally full lips, like she was enjoying a stolen candy.

"I don't think I've met Harry," Sadie said, though she knew his name from Carol's accounting of who had worked Sunday's night shift and today's "On Staff" board. She needed to find time to talk to him too.

"He's really nice," Ivy said, her face relaxing. "Mid-fifties, in really good shape, has white hair—the distinguished kind, not the old-fart kind. He moved here about six months ago after retiring from a hospital job in Florida. His wife died, like, a year ago, I think."

Sadie watched the way Ivy's eyes lit up as she talked about Harry, and she wondered if maybe he wasn't part of the reason Ivy had come back last night. She couldn't think of a subtle way to ask, however. "So, Harry came in and administered the breathing treatment?"

Ivy nodded. "I went out into the hall with him afterward, to ask him how she was doing in general. I had planned to stay longer but . . . it was hard to see the treatment—I hadn't ever been there for one before—and it kind of upset me. Afterwards, I gave Mom a quick kiss good night, then took the ice cream to the freezer in the employee lounge for later. Harry said he'd make sure no one else ate it; he's really sweet that way." She paused and the Harry-induced smile fell. "She's getting weaker every day now it seems."

Sadie felt the same thickness in her throat that Ivy seemed to be trying to swallow. It was difficult to face that Mary was failing; even worse when you managed to avoid thinking about it and then something reminded you.

Sadie leaned forward and lowered her voice. "Can I tell you something, Ivy, and trust that you won't tell Mary I told you?"

Ivy leaned in and nodded eagerly, hungry to share in a secret.

"Mary and I talked about the struggles you two have had. She knows she's to blame for some of the difficulty and doesn't want you to be left with the weight of that."

Ivy's eyes filled with tears. "She said that?"

Sadie nodded. "I get the sense you're trying to improve things too. You've come to see her almost every day since she's been in Nicholas House, even when she hasn't been particularly gracious about those visits."

"I am trying hard to make things better," Ivy said, putting her hand to her chest magnanimously. "But sometimes it just feels like it doesn't go anywhere—like her not accepting the robe and being so weird about an extra pair of socks. Yet she lights up when Joy walks into the room. I mean, I had plans to get green smoothies with my Jazzercise gals after our ten o'clock class today, but I totally cancelled that so I could come to this nursing-home party. I did all of that for her, for us."

So self-sacrificing, Sadie thought, hoping Ivy didn't explain things this way to Mary. "That's really great you accepted the invitation."

"Right?" She sat back, smiling contentedly.

"I believe that if you're both trying, then things can only get better, and I wanted you to know how proud I am of you." It felt ridiculous to say that to a woman of her own generation, but she wanted to encourage both Mary and Ivy to keep trying. There would surely still be bumps in the road, but that road was getting shorter every day, and if they could both let the annoyances roll off them instead of using them as weapons against the other, it could make all the difference.

Ivy looked past Sadie and straightened. At the same time, her chin came down, her head turned slightly, and her smile changed. Sadie looked to the side and saw an older man with white hair—the distinguished kind, not the old-fart kind—wave at Ivy from the other side of the glass that separated the dining room from where the Christmas party was being set up. The common room held a few dozen chairs, the facility Christmas tree with wrapped gifts beneath it, and a long table covered with a red cloth that Sadie assumed would be the food buffet. A swag of garland hung along the back wall.

Nurse Harry wore navy-blue scrubs, but even the relatively shapeless clothes accentuated his upper body in very flattering ways, attesting to his charms that Ivy had explained earlier.

"I'm going to say hi to Harry really quick," Ivy said, standing up like she was on camera, keeping her neck up and her back straight.

"Okay," Sadie said, holding back the desire to roll her eyes. "I'll see if Mary's ready for breakfast yet."

She watched Ivy cross the short distance to the common room

door as though walking the runway. She kind of was, though, judging from the way Harry's eyes didn't leave her for even a second.

Sadie also kept her back straight as she stood from the table but doubted anyone was paying attention to her. She headed for Mary's room, a little annoyed with Ivy, but not too much. Love was a beautiful thing, and Ivy deserved beauty like everyone else did. Sadie just hoped Ivy would spend the time she had left with Mary, and not flirting with Mary's nurse.

CHAPTER 25

M ary was festive and bright-eyed in her emerald-green dress
with the diamond pin when Sadie came back into her room.

"You look amazing, Mary," Sadie said.

Mary waved it away with exaggerated humility. "Oh, stop it."

"I've got to get going, Grandma," Joy said, leaning in to kiss her
on the cheek. "But we'll be back by one o'clock so we can get to
Mass early, okay?"

"Wonderful, sweetheart," Mary said, feeling around for Joy's
cheek so she could pat it affectionately. "Have a great day."

"It started with you, so it's already great," Joy said in that easy
way the two of them shared.

"Oh, Joy," Sadie said, suddenly remembering the mobcap she'd
worn home from the mall last night. "Could you return something
to Holly for me?" She hurried into the bathroom and returned with
the cap.

"Sure," Joy said, taking the cap and folding it carefully in her
hands. "You'll be missed today."

"Oh, I'm sure," Sadie said with a laugh.

"No, really. Holly texted me an hour ago asking if you'd reconsider doing the morning shift."

"Don't tell me the scheduled Mrs. Claus called in sick."

"No, she's just not very good, and Holly would love to tell her to take the last shift off."

"What are you two talking about?" Mary asked from her recliner.

Joy raised her eyebrows at Sadie, but spoke to Mary. "Sadie didn't tell you about her moonlighting last night?"

"Moonlighting? She slept in my chair." Mary jabbed her finger into the arm of the recliner.

Sadie narrowed her eyes at Joy, warning her not to do it, but Joy only grinned wider. After revealing her history last night, Joy seemed to have lost the discomfort and anxiety that had been such a part of her bearing before. Maybe everyone was like that; once they were honest, they could be calm.

"Oh, she's got a story for you, Grandma. Make sure she tells you everything. See you this afternoon."

Sadie was still scowling as Joy let herself out of the room.

"Now what is this about?" Mary said.

"That granddaughter of yours," Sadie said in a playfully stern voice, but then she proceeded to tell Mary the story, only leaving out the reason she'd gone to the mall in the first place. While she told the story, she helped Mary into the ankle boots she would wear for the day. Mary laughed at Karishna's confession, and asked Sadie to describe the Mrs. Claus costume in detail. Sadie did so as she escorted Mary from the room since Ivy hadn't come for her.

"Oh, Sadie, I wish I could have seen you. You were a natural, of course."

"Other than I'm too young and spry to play such an old woman," Sadie said.

Mary patted Sadie's hand holding her elbow. "Well, of course."

When Sadie and Mary entered the dining room, Ivy excused herself from what looked like a cozy conversation with Nurse Harry and hurried over to meet them.

"Mom, you look amazing," Ivy said, looking Mary up and down. "I haven't seen you wear this dress in years."

"Well, it hasn't fit for years, but it was always your dad's favorite color on me."

Sadie stepped aside so Ivy could take over as escort and then excused herself, eager to return to Mary's room, where she could finally go over the lists Jackie had given her.

The staff list revealed nothing new—other than the fact that Shep had been five minutes late, tsk-tsk—but it was good to have everything she'd been told confirmed with an official document.

The visitor list was trickier. A total of forty-seven people had visited during the twenty-hour time period covered by the list. Sadie found Joy's name for the sushi visit, but Star hadn't signed in separately, leading Sadie to make a note that when people visited, only one of them had to sign in. That any number of unaccounted-for people could be roaming the facility at any given time was not encouraging news. A thief would try to be covert, and therefore could have come in with someone else without leaving any record of it.

Ivy had arrived at 8:05, and then Frank had arrived at 9:13. Sadie made a note to ask him how Mary had been feeling while he visited. She hadn't woken up well Monday morning, and Sadie wondered if he'd have noticed anything the night before.

A few other names on the list stood out to Sadie. She recognized the name of a woman from the hospital board who had visited Phillip Parker in room 18, and Melissa Granger—Rachel Haskin's daughter she'd seen yesterday. Melissa had checked in at both 9:04 and 12:45 yesterday, as well as 6:17 on Sunday night. Rachel was in the room next to Mary's, the fourth door down the hall, and had been a resident for a couple of years.

Mary had told Sadie that she and Rachel had once been in a quilting circle together back in the 80s, until Ronald Reagan obtaining the presidency had divided the group and they had disbanded. Rachel no longer recognized Mary, though, and Sadie sensed there was no love lost between the women, even after all these years. Was it a stretch to find out if Melissa had seen anything out of the ordinary on Sunday?

Sadie circled Melissa's name, then reviewed all her notes, rewriting some of them in her notebook, reminding herself who she still needed to talk to, and trying to plan out the day as best she could. It was discouraging to see how very little she'd actually accomplished once she'd condensed all her notes. It felt as though she'd been working so hard—going nonstop for half the day yesterday and up and running again today. Yet what did she have to show for it other than a better understanding of those who *hadn't* taken the five kugels and five Dresdens—Frank, Joy, and Ivy.

Her strongest lead was Carol, but the only actual reason for that was because of Carol's licensing situation. Sadie had no evidence, no conflicting information that pointed toward Carol at all. Sadie had been quick to drop her suspicions toward Frank because Joy had explained his past in a sympathetic way, yet Sadie wasn't willing to give Carol the same consideration even though Jackie had been positive about the changes the woman had made in her life and career since losing her license almost five years ago.

The growing frustration led Sadie to look at her list as parts of a whole instead of the whole itself, which seemed impossible to scale. She needed to choose one thing she could do and then cross that off her list once she'd completed it. She went over who she still needed to talk to and decided on Nurse Harry. Like Molly, he had worked Sunday night and was working today. Molly's information had led to Ivy and the recovery of Mary's Candy Cane. Maybe Harry would give Sadie something just as valuable.

Sadie put her notes and lists in her shoulder bag and hid it in Mary's closet, behind the laundry hamper just to be safe. Then she went looking for Harry, hoping the unattended ornaments would be safe for a few minutes. Luckily, the facility was getting busier by the hour as families arrived for holiday visits; many of them would be staying for the Christmas party that would start in less than an hour. Crowds could be both good and bad, but in this case, Sadie thought it was good. The thief wouldn't want to risk being seen going into Mary's room, which was visible from the nurses' station, the dining room, and the common room. Although, if the thief thought no one knew about the missing ornaments, he or she might try again. Sadie determined to stay in view of Mary's room herself just to make sure.

Ivy and Mary were at a table with another resident enjoying breakfast—well, sort of. Ivy only had some fruit and half a hard-boiled egg on her plate. Mary was working through a plate of biscuits and gravy. Several members of the staff, including Jackie and Carol, were setting things up for the party in the common room. Harry wasn't there, so Sadie started toward the nurses' station but was almost knocked over when Harry came out of a patient's room.

"Whoa!" Harry said, stepping quickly to the left to avoid running her down. Sadie also stepped to her left to get out of his way. "Sorry about that. You okay?" he asked, transferring the bundle of laundry he held into one arm so he could put a free hand on Sadie's shoulder to steady her.

"I'm fine," Sadie said, finding his hand on her arm rather distracting. He had very nice arms. "My fault, really."

"Nah, I'm always moving too fast. You're sure you're okay?"

Sadie nodded, then cocked her head to the side slightly. "You're Harry, right?"

"Sure am, but not the wizarding kind."

Sadie laughed. "I wanted to talk to you, if I could." She looked at the laundry. "Can we walk and talk? I don't want to keep you."

"I'm just running this to laundry, but sure, I can chat for a minute. It's just this way." He nodded toward the top curve of the oblong hallway, and Sadie fell into step beside him. She had to hustle to keep up; he was a fast walker.

"I had some questions about Sunday night. You were the nurse on staff, right?"

He confirmed, and she asked him the same questions she'd asked Molly. He gave the same answers. Ivy arrived around eight o'clock, breathing treatment about fifteen minutes later. Frank came to fix something in her room, stayed until about ten. The aides checked on her every three hours, per her care plan, and she slept like a baby. She'd still been asleep when they did rounds Monday morning, and then he hadn't been back to work until today.

They reached the laundry room, and Harry pushed open the door and dropped the bundle of sheets and towels into a canvas bin. Sadie got a quick view of three washers and four dryers facing one another in the room. The back wall was covered in shelves stacked high with linens.

"Is that everything?" Harry asked as he turned to face her in the hall. The laundry room door swung shut.

Sadie tried, and failed, to think of anything else to ask him. "No, that's all. Thanks very much."

"No problem."

Harry stopped at the door next to the laundry room that was labeled "Employees Only."

"I'm just grabbing a protein shake," Harry said over his shoulder as he entered the room, which was clearly an employee break room. In the time it took for the door to close behind Harry, Sadie noted a table set in the middle of the room with a blue countertop running along one wall and a bank of lockers against the opposite one.

Harry pulled the door open a split second after it had closed, twisting the cap off a pre-made protein shake, cappuccino-flavored, as he returned to the hall.

Sadie quickly scanned the room for what she might have missed with the first glimpse. She saw a fridge on the back wall next to a bulletin board filled with documents and official employee notices. She moved her eyes to the bank of lockers, watching them until the door closed and cut her off.

"I need to make sure I don't overdo it on the sweets at the party." He winked at her and took a sip. Maybe he and Ivy would make a good match after all. "Was there anything else you needed?" Harry asked.

She met his eyes and smiled. "You've been a great help, thank you. So, I hear you just moved here from Florida?"

"About six months ago," he said with a nod as they began walking back toward the nurses' station.

As they talked about his relocating, Sadie noted the holiday energy as employees buzzed from patient to common room. Family members and visitors conversed with one another, some of who were already holding cups of wassail. Sadie's mouth watered; she hadn't eaten all morning, and she was a sucker for good wassail.

Sadie recognized Bella, one of the other nurses, dressed in casual clothing. She hadn't realized that the off-duty staff was attending the party. There was Shep, too. He was dressed in acid-washed jeans and a zippered pullover. When she saw Carol helping to set up the table, she felt her focus zoom in, noting how easily Carol laughed with Bella as they straightened the tablecloth.

Carol was dressed in a black top, dark-wash jeans, and red flats. Her hair was pulled into a knot of curls on top of her head, presenting a very different picture from the frazzled woman Sadie had met yesterday. Was that because she now thought she'd gotten away with the theft?

Sadie started looking for additional staff specifically, counting off the ones she knew, and surmised that most, if not all, were there. Maybe they'd been asked to arrive early and help finish setting up? The kitchen was busy, the staff was at ease, and the guests were already enjoying themselves even though the party hadn't started yet. Everyone, it seemed, had purpose.

Purpose made for excellent distraction. The opportunity to do more than simply interview people fizzed in Sadie's veins. Nothing remedied discouragement in a case like taking action.

Ivy and Mary rose from their table in the dining room, which meant they would be heading back to the room. Which meant they could protect the tree. Sadie hadn't done a great job of watching Mary's door, though she'd tried.

Perfect.

Sadie hurried to Mary's room ahead of them, retrieved her lockpick set from her bag, slid it into the back pocket of her jeans, and was back in the hallway before Ivy and Mary had reached the doorway of the dining room. Ivy caught Sadie's eyes, and Sadie lifted a finger, indicating she would be back in one minute, though it would certainly take longer than that.

Easy as you please, Sadie made her way to the back of the building, smiling and nodding when she made eye contact with anyone in the hall, complimenting one of the residents on her Christmas cardigan, which was red shot with gold that matched her big, gold, clip-on earrings. Melissa was walking Rachel around the hallway, as she often did, and Sadie made a mental note to talk to her about Sunday night. She passed the common room, where even more people were holding cups of wassail. Sadie kept her sights focused and withstood the temptation.

When she arrived at the "Employees Only" door, she looked both ways, waited for one man to go around the corner, and then slid into the room. She paused a moment to make sure no one followed her with a "Hey, you're not allowed in there!"

When no one issued an objection, Sadie wedged one of the chairs under the door handle to prevent her from being interrupted and then turned to face the room.

Pete's interrogations regarding breaking the law came to mind, but sometimes you had to take risks to meet your goals and, quite frankly, Sadie was running out of things to do. Mass was four hours away. There was no time to be cautious.

Wassail

2 ¼ cups sugar
4 cups water
2 cinnamon sticks
8 allspice berries
10 cloves
½-inch piece ginger
4 cups orange juice
2 cups lemon juice
2 quarts apple juice

In a large pot, combine sugar and water. Bring to a boil for 5 minutes. Remove from heat and add spices. Cover and keep warm for 1 hour. Strain liquid. Before serving, add juices and return to a boil. Remove from heat and serve. Makes 18 servings.

CHAPTER 26

One thing Sadie hadn't noticed in her glimpses into the room with Harry a few minutes earlier was the restroom door tucked next to the lockers. Thankfully it was empty. It would have been awkward for Sadie to explain both her presence and the door wedged to lock them in if a staff member had been here. There were also two rows of hooks on the wall, filled with coats and a few purses belonging to the brave, though ignorant, staff who didn't feel the need to lock up their personal effects.

Sadie searched the purses first—nothing relevant and none of them belonged to Carol. Then she turned her attention to the lockers. Of the twelve lockers, four had personal locks likely supplied by the employees themselves. The first two were dial-type combination locks and the third was a key lock. The fourth was a barrel lock—the type of lock where the tumblers were stamped with numbers that opened when the combination was physically lined up.

Sadie felt for her pick set in her back pocket—still there—but decided to start with the barrel lock. The default factory setting was "1-2-3," and approximately seventy-five percent of people never changed it after purchase. Sadie dialed in the numbers and then shook her head at the folly of people when it popped open. She also celebrated her successful first try. It was nice when choosing easy worked out. Heaven knew that wasn't usually the way things went.

Inside the locker were a pair of snow boots—empty—a Tapout T-shirt that smelled like the gym, and a wallet that belonged to one Mike Shephard—or Shep as she knew him. There were a few credit cards, twenty-two dollars cash, and a Mickey Mouse temporary tattoo inside the wallet. The locker also held a pack of cigarettes and two Red Bulls. Sadie was tempted to leave an anonymous note inside the locker, suggesting Shep consider making his health a priority in the coming New Year and change the code on his lock, but she didn't have time to play life coach.

The keyed lock was next, and Sadie picked it in under a minute. Not too shabby, if she did say so herself. Picking locks was pretty much like riding a bike, it seemed.

Inside that locker she found a wadded-up set of navy-blue scrubs, which meant this belonged to one of the nurses. The scrubs were a size medium, so they wouldn't be Harry's or Jackie's, but that was the only information she could deduce. She found an insulated coffee mug that needed to be washed out and a bag that only held makeup. Nothing exactly incriminating.

Sadie had to look up instructions on how to crack a dialed combination lock. She'd never broken into one of those before, but it wasn't hard to figure out thanks to her years of experience. It took almost three minutes to pop the lock, but she still felt the thrill of success when it opened.

She felt another thrill when the locker revealed a photo of Carol and a teenage boy taped next to the magnetic name tag Carol had worn on her scrubs yesterday. In the picture, Carol was wearing a tank top and a visor—her shoulders were sunburned—and there were trees and a mountaintop in the background. The teenage boy was about her same height, with braces and acne sprinkled across his forehead. He was wearing a Braves hat and squinting one eye. Was Carol a single mom?

Sadie had been a single mom for most of her children's lives and had a natural sensitivity for people in similar situations. But she also understood the desperation that many single moms faced as they tried to meet the needs of their children. Sadie had been financially secure thanks to her career as a teacher and an excellent life insurance policy Neil had left behind, but many women in similar circumstances—perhaps even most women in similar circumstances—did not.

Carol had lost her nursing license and was now working as an aide, which would have a much lower pay rate. Even if Carol was paid better than a typical aide, it was surely nowhere near what she'd made as a nurse.

She returned her attention to Carol's locker and was immediately disappointed to find no ornaments. She'd dared hope for just a moment that they'd be inside. There was instead a rolled-up set of burgundy scrubs, a pair of black clogs, and a purse hanging from one of the hooks. Inside the purse was a protein bar, some cinnamon-flavored gum, multiple wadded-up receipts, a half-empty pack of pocket tissues, floss, nail clippers, some bobby pins—but no hairband—and a set of business cards for Marley's Antiques bound together with a rubber band.

She felt a rush of adrenaline go through her as she stared at the cards. Not only had she driven past the store's black-and-gold sign a hundred times, but she'd also seen the name on receipts

she'd found at Mary's after Marley had purchased some of her antiques last summer. He had not purchased her ornaments, however,
though he'd given a bid. Why would Carol have one of their business cards, let alone two dozen?

Knowing she needed to examine everything in detail, Sadie
moved the purse to the table and dumped out the contents. In a
separate zipped pocket that she hadn't noticed on her first search
she found a purse-sized planner, ChapStick, coins, three pens, and
a lighter.

She lined up the contents in three separate lines, then took a
picture. As soon as her phone was back in her pocket, she picked
up the six-by-three-inch planner, undid the snap that held it closed,
and opened it. Two folded papers fell out onto the table. One
was the letter Sadie had read yesterday from the Department of
Regulatory Licenses. The other was a paycheck stub from Marley's
Antiques.

Carol worked there? Sadie looked between the banded business cards and the paystub that showed Carol had worked sixteen
hours at fourteen dollars an hour plus a five-percent commission,
which had come to forty-seven dollars. The "Year to Date" column
showed that this was not a new enterprise. Over the course of the
year, she'd earned nearly eight thousand dollars in wages and sixty-
five hundred dollars in commissions.

Sadie read and reread every detail, then moved her gaze to
Carol's name—Carol M. Benson.

M.

Marley?

The sound of voices in the hall startled her and then the door rattled as someone tried to open it. Sadie's heart leaped to her throat as she froze.

"It's locked?" someone said from the hallway.

"I didn't think it did that." Sadie recognized the second voice as Shep's.

"Jackie will have a key."

Working double time, Sadie put everything back in the purse, except for the planner, quickly checked the pockets of the rolled-up scrubs, and then popped the final lock on the final locker in under a minute. The only thing in there was a CNA training manual and a silicone bracelet that said "Be the good you want to see in the world." She considered putting that bracelet in Carol's purse—she could use the reminder—but instead shut the locker and checked the unsecured lockers. Other than an empty Diet Coke can in one and a stray pair of socks in another, Sadie found nothing.

Her heart was hammering, telling her she needed to leave immediately. She put her picks back into her pocket, hid the planner under her shirt, said a little prayer—eyes closed and everything—and removed the chair from beneath the doorknob. She listened carefully and realized she could hear singing. Had the party started already? She checked her watch—10:32. Apparently it had. Good. Hopefully that meant Jackie was unavailable to get a non-existent key to let people into the break room.

Sadie opened the door an inch at a time, pausing between each increment until she could clearly see the hallway in front of her. Hearing nothing but the singing, she eased herself out of the room, checking every direction to make sure she was alone. No one was there, which allowed her to breathe almost normally. She cursed the glass walls of the common room as she waited just out of sight.

After a full minute had passed, she realized that she had no choice but to strike a casual attitude and walk down the hall.

No one noticed her. In fact, everyone was facing the other way, toward the piano, where someone was playing "Santa Claus Is Coming to Town." Yet another Christmas miracle. Sadie picked up her pace, desperate to reach Mary's room before anyone could wonder where she was coming from.

The first thing Sadie did when she arrived back in Mary's room was search for Marley's Antiques on her phone, then click on "Images." She didn't find Carol in any of the pictures collected on the internet over the years, but she did find some photos of Jedidiah Marley—red hair, though not as bright as Carol's, same brown eyes. Carol wasn't just familiar with antiques, she wasn't just an employee at the antique shop that had bid on Mary's ornaments, she was family to the owner who was the only person, other than Sadie, who knew exactly how much Mary's ornaments were worth.

Holy. Nutcracker.

Sadie was ready to jump in her car and speed over to Marley's Antiques right that minute, but knew she needed to go through Carol's planner first. She settled herself into one of Mary's dining chairs and started on the front page. She couldn't give each page the attention it deserved, but she was an excellent skimmer.

The month-at-a-glance calendars at the start of each section only showed a smattering of appointments in the tiny squares, but the daily pages, however, had to-do lists, appointments, and her work schedule—three twelve-hour shifts, mostly days, and one or two float shifts every week. Now and then she worked an additional shift, and in August, she had worked eight twelve-hour shifts in a row. The hours she worked at Marley's were also accounted for, taking place mostly outside regular business hours.

There were also notes about specific items on certain days.

- brush and comb—Etsy. Ship a.m.
- 20's hat sold—eBay. Express shipping
- Pink glass vase sold—eBay. Ship Monday.

There were several similar notes every month—not necessarily on days she worked at Marley's—and Sadie thought about how Mary had told Sadie to make sure Joy looked into selling the ornaments on eBay. She also thought about that five-percent commission detail on Carol's paystub that proved Carol was involved in sales somehow. Yet most of the hours she worked weren't business hours.

Sadie put the planner aside long enough to text Pete, finally ready to take him up on his offer of help.

Sadie: Are you at the airport?

Pete: In line at TSA. What's up?

Sadie: Are you still willing to help with this case?

Pete: Within the limits of the law, yes.

Sadie rolled her eyes. Limits schlimits.

Sadie: Could you look into Marley's Antiques? Specifically their online sales? Carol Benson works there part-time and gets commissions.

Pete: The shop on College Street?

Sadie: You know it?

Pete: Brooke has bought some things there over the years. Remember that armoire we helped her move last summer? That was from Marley's.

Sadie: Well, they might also be a fence!

Pete: I'm on it.

Relieved to have a second set of hands and eyes on this case, Sadie finished skimming the daily pages and came upon a section labeled "Notes." Carol seemed to use these pages for a variety of lists, something Sadie grudgingly admired since she too was a determined list maker.

There was a list for tracking weight loss that had been started in January but not added to after March. Carol was average-sized, so did that mean she'd achieved her goals or given up? A quick calculation showed she'd lost three pounds, so either reason she stopped tracking could still apply.

There was a list for birthday gifts with names and dates written to the side, including Jed's birthday—April 14. There were lists about decorative items Carol wanted for her apartment, things to do with Ty, who, Sadie deduced after consulting the calendar and some other lists, was Carol's son. All the activities on the list were summer ones. Did he not live with her full-time, then?

There were recipes possibly copied from a magazine, and random bits of information Sadie imagined Carol writing while she was on the phone with someone—an address for P&G returns, a phone number for Allstate Insurance, a Social Security number without any name attached to it. And then the lists and notes ran out, leaving half an inch of blank pages between the last list—for Christmas cards, though there was no indication she'd sent any—and the end of the planner.

Sadie flipped through the blank pages just to make sure she hadn't missed anything. A page in the middle of the section caught her eye, and she flipped back to it. There was no title for the list.

- Cabragle86
- Harold Tanner—Georg Jensen tea set—10/21/16
- Genevieve Coolidge—tennis bracelet, broken catch—2/12/17
- Rachel Haskin—cameo brooch—8/3/17
- Constance Bagley—diamond earrings—2/28/18
- Bill Fry—autographed copy of first-edition *Huckleberry Finn*—4/10/18
- Lewis Merrill—emerald tiepin—1/12/19
- Barbara Peterson—pearl necklace and drop earrings—3/2/19

Below that was a second list:

- ~~Phoebe—quit 2/19~~
- Molly
- Bella
- ~~Shep—started 12/16~~

Sadie recognized Rachel Haskin's name, of course, but she'd never heard of the other people. Could they be former residents of Nicholas House? Had Carol sold a brooch for Rachel and these other people?

Sadie flipped back to the calendar, but there was nothing on the 2019 dates themselves that coordinated with this list. She looked over the notations about eBay and Etsy sales around those dates, but none of those coincided with the items listed either. If Carol was stealing from the residents, she'd want to keep any written information to a minimum, right?

The list of staff was equally perplexing and, at first glance, looked like a hit list, though Sadie knew Shep was currently alive and drinking wassail across the hall. Plus, it wasn't a complete list of the staff.

She jumped when the door to Mary's room opened, and quickly put Carol's planner in her purse and grabbed her phone so it would look like she was catching up her email while she waited for them.

"We're back," Ivy said.

Sadie looked up with a smile she hoped hid her surprise. Was it 11:30 already?

"Who's here?" Mary asked.

"Hee-haw, Mary," Sadie said.

Mary relaxed. "Oh, hello, Sadie." She patted Ivy's hand. "Ivy, dear, could you help me into the recliner? I'm afraid I'm a bit tired."

Sadie stood out of the way while Ivy helped Mary get settled, feeling both guilty and grateful that she wouldn't have to stay to visit. She'd found some momentum, and she didn't want to lose it now. Mary immediately closed her eyes once nestled in the recliner.

"Ivy, are you staying?" Sadie whispered after Mary's shoulders relaxed in sleep.

"I was going to stay until Harry takes his lunch break at noon. We're going to grab a kombucha before I head home and get ready for Mass."

Sadie's eyebrows lifted in surprise. "You're going to Mass with your mom? That's wonderful. I didn't know you were religious."

"I'm not," Ivy said quickly and with a laugh, as though wanting to make that very clear. "It's been a source of contention over the years, but that kind of makes it an even bigger deal that she invited me, right? And equally big that I said yes, considering how boring Mass is." She smiled with no trace of how indelicate her comment was, then continued. "I'll bring the candy cane ornament when I come back."

"Great idea," Sadie confirmed. "I should be back before you leave."

"Okay, cool. I'm just going to catch up on Insta until Harry's ready." Sometimes Ivy was sixty-something going on fifteen.

Sadie let herself into the hall, which was still full of people visiting and laughing together—one of the very best parts of Christmas. Then she turned and headed one door down to Rachel Haskin's room.

CHAPTER 27

Sadie knocked on the door to Rachel's room and waited for a voice to say "Come in" before she entered.

Rachel was sitting on the bed, her white hair puffy like dandelion fuzz around her head, while Melissa helped her take off a sensible pair of black pumps. The black skirt Rachel wore didn't quite cover the top of her knee-high nylons, but when she stood it was probably fine. She also wore a black top and Christmas cardigan, bright greens and reds making a variety of Christmas pictures—Santa, Frosty, Rudolph, a Christmas wreath.

Melissa looked up at Sadie as she removed the second shoe and set it aside. "Hi."

"Hi," Sadie said, feeling awkward now that she was there. Sometimes her determination to solve a case blocked the social acceptability of her decisions until she found herself in the middle of them. "I'm Sadie Cunningham—Mary Hallmark's friend."

"I know who you are." Melissa stood and smiled excitedly. "I love your books."

"Oh," Sadie said, not having expected that. "Thank you so much."

"Mom and I read them together," she said, waving at Rachel, who was fiddling with the sleeve of her sweater. "Don't we, Mom?"

"What?" Rachel said, a blank look on her face as she glanced between them.

"This is Sadie Cunningham," Melissa said louder. "The writer. Remember her books that we like so much? The mysteries with the cute covers and yummy recipes. I made the Snowball Cake for your birthday last year."

Rachel's face softened, and she put her hands demurely in her lap. "Oh, isn't reading such a gift? 'Take a look, it's in a book.'"

Melissa's smile fell briefly, but then lifted again. "That's right, Mom. Books are the best."

Melissa turned to Sadie and gave an embarrassed shrug. "Sorry, I thought she'd remember. She really has enjoyed the books, though. She laughs and laughs at some of the crazy stuff in the stories."

"I'm very glad to hear it, thank you." Knowing that people enjoyed what Sadie toiled and twisted into a story was incredibly validating.

"Mom was a librarian for an elementary school for more than twenty years, you know."

"That's wonderful," Sadie said, smiling at Rachel, who was distracted by her sweater again. "I wondered if I could ask you a few questions."

"Um, sure," Melissa said, her face brightening. "Is it research for a book?"

"No, not really."

Melissa's face visibly fell, but then she shrugged a shoulder as though accepting her fate. "Oh, okay."

"It's about a brooch—a cameo—"

"My brooch!"

Sadie and Melissa both startled, snapping to look at Rachel, who was patting her skirt and sweater as though checking her non-existent pockets. She looked around the bed and began pushing herself to her feet. Melissa hurried to her.

"No, stay there, Mom. We're going to get changed before we go to my house for the family party, remember?"

Rachel tried to push her away, then pulled the pillow off her bed. "Where's my brooch?" She looked at Sadie with narrowed eyes. The blank look she'd had before had been replaced with one of accusation. "You took it!"

"No," Sadie said, her stomach sinking to realize what she'd set off.

"It's okay, Mom," Melissa said, putting the pillow back in place. "Remember, I took the brooch home for safekeeping."

"You took my brooch!" Rachel said, then pursed her lips. "Where is it? Why do people keep taking my things?" She tried to slap Melissa's hand, but Melissa managed to grab her wrist.

"I'll bring it back tomorrow," Melissa said, unable to hide the tension in her voice.

Wanting to help, Sadie walked to the foot of Rachel's bed. "Did you make this, Rachel?" Sadie interrupted, running her hand over the quilt folded there, an intricate pattern of greens and reds and golds. It was very Christmassy, in fact.

Rachel turned her attention from Melissa to Sadie, but her eyebrows were pulled together and her lips were tight.

"Is this a pinwheel pattern?" Sadie asked.

Rachel blinked at Sadie, then looked at the quilt. "It's a

Christmas-star pattern," she snapped. "There are fifteen different fabrics used in each star."

"And you made this?"

"Stop touching it!" Rachel said, swatting toward Sadie's hand though she was out of reach.

Sadie put her hands behind her back. "I'm sorry. It's beautiful."

"Yes, it is. I made it myself." Her tone was still sharp, but her expression changed as though she knew she was angry but wasn't sure what she was angry about.

Rachel smoothed her hand over the top of the quilt. "There are two hundred and thirty-four blocks in this quilt. I did one block every day for two hundred and thirty-four days. I made it myself."

Sadie asked about the colors, which fabrics were Rachel's favorites, and where she'd gotten the idea. The details Rachel could remember about making the quilt were astounding, and although Sadie had started the conversation in hopes of distracting her from the brooch, she found herself quite taken by Rachel's passion for her craft. It reminded Sadie of the conversations she and Mary had shared in the early years of their friendship. What creators these women had been, dedicated to growing their talents and bringing beautiful things into the world.

Rachel turned during a lull in the conversation, saw her daughter, and smiled. "Oh, there you are, Melissa. Is David here?"

"Not yet," Melissa said, her voice sad. She cleared her throat. "Soon, I hope."

"I haven't seen him in ages, you know."

"Why don't you sit in your chair for a bit before we change your clothes," Melissa said, putting her arm under her mom's shoulder to help her stand and walk the few steps to the upholstered chair. She handed her mom a magazine. "Would you like to read?"

"Oh, *Better Homes and Gardens*. I love their articles on gardening."

Rachel began turning the pages one at a time. Melissa watched her for a moment, then caught Sadie's eye and nodded toward the hall. Sadie followed her out of the room.

"I'm so sorry," Sadie said.

"You didn't know, and, honestly, I'm surprised Mom even remembers. The brooch has been gone for almost two years. She hasn't talked about it in months."

"Gone?"

Melissa frowned. "It's my fault. They told me to take it home, but Mom loved it and remembered the stories about it. It had been her grandmother's, and her mother had brought it over when she came from Norway. Mom wore it to church every week when we were growing up, and then started wearing it almost every day a few years ago." Melissa smiled. "At first, she was great about always putting it back in her jewelry box at night, but as she got more and more confused, she started putting it in strange places.

"Sometimes we'd find it after just a few minutes—she'd put it in the bathroom drawer or it was still pinned to the blouse she'd worn the night before. Then it would be gone for hours, and we'd turn her room over only to find it in a shoe or the pocket of a coat she hadn't worn in months. Each time it went missing, Mom was beside herself, calling herself names and feeling like she'd let down her mother and grandmother. It was awful. Then we'd find it, and she'd calm down.

"When I suggested taking it home for safekeeping, she'd cry

and beg me not to. So I didn't, and then one day it was just gone. We looked everywhere, the staff looked everywhere, but it never turned up."

"She must have been so upset."

"She was a complete wreck," Melissa said, shaking her head sadly. "After a week or so, she stopped asking about it multiple times a day. Then it would be a few days between her remembering, and then eventually she stopped asking about it altogether. Like I said, it's been months since she's said anything."

"What a tragedy that it was lost," Sadie said.

Melissa nodded. "I keep hoping we'll find it in some crazy place we haven't checked yet, but we think she might have thrown it in the dining room trash or maybe even flushed it down the toilet." She took a heavy breath. "We're going to have to move her into a long-term care facility in the New Year. She requires too much care to stay in Nicholas House, and I'm hoping we'll find it when we pack everything up."

"I'm so sorry she has to leave here," Sadie said, putting her hand on Melissa's arm.

"It's just life, I guess, right?" She forced a smile and stood a bit straighter.

Sadie took a breath. "You mentioned the brooch had been missing for almost two years?"

"Well, more like a year and a half. Why?"

The list in Carol's planner had August 2017 next to Rachel's brooch—about a year and a half ago. "I'm worried that some of the residents' things have gone missing. That, perhaps, some things might have been . . . stolen."

Melissa's eyebrows shot up her forehead. "Stolen?"

Sadie hesitated, but then explained. "Some of the vintage orna-ments on Mary's tree are missing, and, well, they aren't the kind of thing that would simply be misplaced."

"You're kidding," Melissa said, dropping her hands to her side.

"It happened Sunday night, and Mary doesn't know yet. I'm trying to figure out what happened to them before she does *and* make sure no more ornaments disappear from her tree. It's a tricky balance, as I know you understand—surrounding her with the things she loves, but also protecting those things at the same time."

Sadie's phone vibrated in her back pocket, signaling an incom-ing text message.

"I get that," Melissa said. "I never worried about Mom's brooch having been stolen, though, because she'd lost it so many times before. Jackie talked to the staff as part of the incident report I filed, but nothing came of it, other than determining when it was last seen, which was when one of the aides put it in the jewelry box the night before we found it missing. I talked to that aide myself—just to figure out when exactly she'd seen it and where ex-actly she'd put it—but I don't think she had anything to do with its disappearance—she worked harder than anyone to find it and kept following up with me for a long time afterward."

"Which aide was it?"

"Carol. Do you know her?"

"Yeah, I know Carol," Sadie said evenly. Interesting that she was the last one to have seen Rachel's brooch. "Your mom has been here a long time, hasn't she?"

"Three years next month," Melissa confirmed. "I think she's the longest resident here now that Barbara passed away."

"Barbara Peterson?" That was one of the names on the list in Carol's planner.

"Yeah, she was great. Younger than the other residents, suffered from muscular dystrophy, which was why she came here even though she was in her forties. She passed away last June."

Three months before Mary had moved in, which explained why Sadie hadn't recognized the name. "Do you know if anything of hers was reported missing?"

Melissa pondered that, but then shook her head. "No. Do you know something I don't?"

"Not necessarily. I'm just trying to figure out if there are any patterns." It was an answer full of holes, so Sadie prepared her next question quickly, before Melissa could think too much about what she hadn't explained. "Are you aware of any other things going missing?"

Another text-message alert vibrated her phone, and Sadie swallowed. It was hard not to whip out her phone to see who was texting her. What if it was Pete with information she needed?

Melissa scrunched up her face again, then shook her head. "I don't think so—oh, wait, there was a tiepin." She looked up and to the left as though searching for the details in the recesses of her memory. "It belonged to a former resident, Lewis—I can't remember his last name. He moved in, gosh, last January, I think, but was gone a month later. He was always lodging complaints about something—the food, the bath schedule, the activities, you name it—and his daughter was just like him. She complained to Jackie every other day about one thing or another. In fact, the reason he left was because he said Shep couldn't take care of him. You know Shep?"

"Yes, he's a fantastic aide."

"He is," Melissa agreed, nodding. "He's also the only African American on staff. I'd heard Lewis had been rude to Shep a few times, but then one night he called Shep the N-word and that was the last straw with Jackie. She told Lewis to find a new place. It got ugly. Lewis's family threatened a lawsuit. Jackie tried to get him out in three days, but had to give them ten, by law. There was something about a missing tiepin when his kids were packing up his stuff, which they blamed on Shep, as you would expect people like that to do. No one took it seriously. I wouldn't put it past Lewis to have hidden it himself just so he could land another blow on his way out. Poor Shep. He was embarrassed but, you know, kept smiling like he does."

"Do you know if the family filed an incident report about it?"

"They probably called the *police* about it. I don't know, but . . . do you think someone could have stolen it?"

"I don't know," Sadie said honestly. "Anything else you can remember?" She was tempted to ask about the tea set specifically, or Barbara's pearl necklace and earrings, but didn't want to give out too many details.

"No," Melissa said as a third text message came through on Sadie's phone. "I'm just sick about Mary's ornaments, though. I mean, we've been here three years and have had nothing but good experiences. They have the best staff, and Mom has loved their food, though they do tend to overcook the vegetables."

"You've never had a bad interaction with a staff member?"

"No, not really. I mean we get the wrong laundry sometimes, and there was an aide last year, Phoebe, who would say she'd changed the bed but hadn't really. She was older and had worked here forever, but once she was written up a couple of times she quit on her own."

Phoebe was one of the names on the staff list below the items Sadie now assumed to all be resident's items that had gone missing. But Phoebe was crossed out—because she didn't work here anymore? Shep's name was crossed out too, though.

"How long has Shep worked here?"

"You must not have been at the party."

Sadie shook her head; she'd been breaking into employee lockers.

"Jackie had gifts to celebrate different staff members, including Shep, who has officially been here three years now. They gave him a pair of Apple AirPods; I can't believe you didn't hear him whoop about it. Carol will have been here three years in January; she got a pair of big headphones, the kind that fit over your ears." She cupped her hands next to her head to demonstrate. "Xander hit his one-year mark, and he got a three-months' Xbox subscription, whatever that is."

"I'm sad I missed the awards," Sadie said. "Do you know off the top of your head which staff members have been here since your mom first moved in?"

Melissa scrunched up her face in thought. "Um, Jackie, of course, then Shep and Molly. Maybe Jose, too? Bella? I can't remember if she was here when we got here or if she was hired a few months after that. I think that's all. There's a lot of turnover in places like this. It's really a gift to have so many long-term employees."

"Agreed."

Feeling like it would be too abrupt to leave the conversation at that, Sadie asked after their plans for Christmas. Rachel was coming home for the day, but not staying the night since Melissa didn't have a bedroom on the main level of her house and stairs were hard for her mother.

Melissa asked about Sadie's next book, and Sadie explained she'd turned one in before the holidays, which Melissa then wanted to hear all about. Finally, the conversation wound down. Sadie thanked Melissa for her help and wished her a Merry Christmas.

Sadie turned toward Mary's room but pulled out her phone before she went inside. She had to check those text messages!

Pete: Marley's sells through eBay, Etsy, and a few vintage retailers, but owner comes in clean. Former military, no record.

Pete: Carol also comes up clean, other than her license issue.

Pete: Her ex-husband, though, has an interesting history AND has custody of their son—no other kids. Lives in Colorado Springs.

Sadie hurried to reply.

Sadie: Thank you! I found a list of items I think have been stolen from residents of Nicholas House over the last few years. I'll send you a picture. Can you see if they match up to any of the online sales?

Pete: Yep.

Sadie knocked lightly on the door to Mary's room before letting herself in. Mary was asleep in her chair, and Ivy was texting on her phone, one slim leg over the other one. She glanced up but otherwise didn't move.

"Hey, Sadie, I'm out of here in five minutes, just gotta comment on this post."

"No problem." Sadie went to the closet where she'd stowed her shoulder bag and purse. She pulled out Carol's planner and sat on one of the dining chairs so she could open the planner on her thighs.

"You do a bullet journal?"

Sadie, phone poised to take a picture of the list, looked up at Ivy. "A what?"

"A bullet journal—a notebook where you make charts and put in pictures and things."

"Sounds dangerous."

Ivy laughed, startling Mary.

They both went silent, but after a moment, Mary settled back to sleep.

"No, this is just a regular planner," Sadie said, softer this time.

"Oh, that is so cute."

Cute?

"I love all that old-school stuff."

It was on the tip of Sadie's tongue to remind Ivy that she was older than Sadie was, but she didn't because she was a professional. At least for today. "Yeah, I love that *old-school stuff*, too." She lined up the frame and snapped a picture for Pete.

She wasn't sure what to make of what she'd learned from Melissa. The list of items had to be things from Nicholas House and the dates next to them must be when they went missing. She knew the jewelry was valuable, as were Mary's ornaments, and a first-edition Mark Twain, but a tea set? Sadie had bought a nice one at the mall last year for eighty bucks.

And what did the staff list mean? She'd determined it must be a list of staff who had worked during the same time frame that the items went missing. Phoebe was crossed out because she had quit before some of the items disappeared, and Shep was crossed out because he had started after the thefts began.

The color of pen used for the list suggested that Carol had copied all the details prior to this year into this new planner. Had she been tracking these items since she started working here almost three years ago? Yet she knew of missing items prior to her hire date. She'd also started after Shep, which explained why she'd have assumed he had worked there over the course of the thefts too.

She sent the picture to Pete's phone.

Pete: I'll let you know what I find out. Everything okay?

Sadie: I think so.

Pete: Have you broken any laws yet?

Sadie: Oh, stop it. 😑 How much longer until your flight?

Pete: You HAVE!!!

Sadie: Sorry, bad reception. I'm going through a tunnel.

Pete: SADIE!

Sadie silenced her phone, and though she wished there were two of her so that someone could stay with Mary and the ornaments, there was only one. She had to make a choice, and she chose Marley's Antiques.

CHAPTER 28

She was only a few steps down the hall when she heard the buzz of the lock disarming and looked up to see Frank coming through the door. She stopped in the middle of the hallway and checked her watch. It was 11:46—hadn't Joy said Frank worked until noon? She wondered if this was yet one more miracle Christmas had sent her way.

He spotted Sadie, too, and in the next instant, their first meeting yesterday flooded Sadie's mind and sent fire to her cheeks. He looked wary, and she took full responsibility for him feeling that way. Which meant it was her responsibility to help both of them get through this awkwardness.

She squared her shoulders, swallowed her embarrassment, and headed toward him. He was still dressed in his work clothes—a blue-and-white-striped, button-down shirt with his name tag peeking out beneath the black coat he wore. His knit hat was pulled low over his gauges, and his red cheeks and nose attested to the cold front leading in the storm she was trying desperately to ignore.

When Sadie reached him, she beckoned him to the side of the hallway between two of the residents' rooms so they would be out of the way. There were still a lot of family members coming and going. Oddly enough, that many people gave them a degree of privacy. Plus, with their history, Sadie thought it better not to be alone with him. She didn't want to give him the wrong idea. Again.

"Hi, Frank," Sadie said, hoping her smile didn't seem false. Or lecherous. "You're early."

"Uh, yeah," he said, unable to hold her gaze for more than a second at a time. He shoved his hands into the pockets of his jeans. "I've already got six hours overtime this week, so Clint let me go early. Store wasn't too busy. Joy said I should talk to you as soon as possible, so I came straight here."

She was relieved that he didn't seem interested in rehashing their earlier encounter. "Right, thanks for coming. I was actually just leaving, so I'm really glad you came when you did. Do you remember what time you arrived here Sunday night?"

It was a trick question because Sadie knew what time he'd arrived. His answer would go a long way toward his reliability as a witness, however.

"I think it was about 9:15 or something. I came straight from work." He explained how he'd fixed the nightstand, tightening the bolts with the Allen wrench he'd brought from home. "Then I talked to Mary for a while."

"What time did you leave?"

"Man." He squinted toward the ceiling. "Ten, maybe?"

"Did anyone come in while you were there?"

"Like, visitors? Nah. I think the whole rest of the building was asleep. I was surprised Mary was still up, but she was chatty and I was, like, cool. She's a kick to talk to. She told me all about World

War II and living in Cripple Creek." He smiled. "I could talk to her for hours."

Sadie smiled as well, loving how talking about Mary softened the lines of Frank's otherwise tight jaw and neck. "What about the staff?"

Suddenly he was tight again. "What do you mean?"

Was it a difficult question to understand? "Did any staff come into the room while you were there?"

He hesitated, and Sadie started counting Rudolphs in her head so she wouldn't break the silence. With the knit cap pulled low and his coat covering his sleeves, he looked like a regular, nerdy kid. There were a few tattoos visible on his neck, but even they weren't too noticeable with the coat's collar in the way. It struck Sadie that this was who he really was. Like someone with facial scars or a disability, though, people struggled to see *him* beyond gauges and tattoos.

Frank shifted his weight and scratched at his one arm. "I didn't talk to nobody."

That wasn't what Sadie had asked. "But a staff member *did* come into the room?"

"Mary said it was okay if I used her toilet, and as I was finishing up, I heard someone in the room talking to her. I kinda freak people out sometimes, especially if they don't expect me, and I felt weird about having used her toilet and all that so I didn't come out of the bathroom until she left."

She. Harry and Shep had been on duty that night. Molly had only been there until ten. "Who was it?"

"Dunno," Frank said, shrugging his skinny shoulders. "I didn't come out until the door closed."

"Mary didn't say who it was?"

"I didn't ask her or anything," Frank said.

Sadie held back a sigh. Because why would Frank have asked? He didn't have the same natural curiosity that Sadie did.

"And do you know why *she* was there?"

"I think she was giving Mary some medicine. There was one of those little plastic cups on Mary's tray next to some water in a bigger cup. She asked me to dump out the water 'cause if she drinks too much before bed, she has to pee. I mean, she said 'use the ladies' room.'" Frank quirked a smile. "She's always real fancy like that."

He looked past Sadie and straightened from where he'd slumped against the wall. Sadie looked up and saw Ivy and Harry talking in the hallway outside of Mary's room. Harry said something and Ivy laughed loudly. Ivy put her arm through Harry's, and they headed toward the common room. Was that where they were going for the kombucha? Maybe Harry kept some cans of the nasty stuff in the employee break room with his protein drinks.

"She don't like me," Frank said.

Sadie faced him again. "She just doesn't know you. But don't give up on her just yet."

Frank shook his head. "Nah, chicks like that never like me. Think I'm gonna steal their purses and stuff."

"That sounds like stereotyping to assume that's what she thinks, Frank." Even though it *was* what Ivy thought.

He met her eyes, surprised. "What?"

"Have you ever had a conversation with Ivy?" From what Sadie knew, the two of them had only met once, and it hadn't been a lengthy visit since Joy had tried to get him out of there as quickly as she could.

"Well, no."

"And yet you have her all figured out." Sadie smiled when she said it so he wouldn't feel like she was being accusatory or judgmental. "We often make up our minds about someone before we've gotten to know them."

"You're saying I done the same thing she did—decided about her before I knew her."

Sadie didn't need to put a bow on what she'd already said. She smiled and steered things back to the topic at hand. "Is there anything else about that visit you can think of?"

Frank crossed his arms over his chest and looked at the floor. After a minute, he raised his head. "Nah, everything else was good. Mary finally got sleepy, so I helped her into bed and then I left. That's it."

"You helped her into bed?"

"She was kind of dizzy."

And he hadn't thought that counted as a detail to share? "Really?"

"Yeah, like, she was all ready for bed when I got there, ya know, and, like I said, in the mood to talk, but then, as I as leaving, she stood to use the toilet—oh, sorry, ladies' room." He quirked a smile again. "And she's usually so steady, ya know, but she was kind of wobbly, so I asked if I should help her to the bathroom and she said yeah, so I did. Didn't go inside or nothin'." He waved his hands in front of himself as though warning Sadie away from jumping to conclusions. "I guess she did okay, but I think she was like holding on to the counters and stuff. I waited and then walked her back to bed and helped her lay back like I seen Joy do—a hand behind her back and the other arm under her knees so she pivots, ya know? Once I had her all tucked in, I turned off the lights and left. I think she was asleep before I even got out of the room."

Sadie pondered that. She'd never seen Mary unable to get herself into bed or struggle with her balance. Not even during this last week when she'd needed more breathing treatments and naps every afternoon.

"How long was it between that staff woman coming in while you were in the bathroom and Mary having a hard time with her balance?"

"Fifteen, twenty minutes."

Five years ago, after their disastrous wedding, Pete had had to take sleeping pills for a few weeks while he recovered from his injuries. She remembered that it took about twenty minutes from when he took the pill to when he was slurring his speech and asking for pickles—he craved salt when he took them, for some strange reason. It hadn't been in the paperwork about possible side effects. Had Mary been given a sleeping pill?

"That it, then?" Frank asked, half-turning toward the door. "I gotta get ready before Joy picks me up for Mass."

"Picks you up? Don't the two of you share her car?"

"Sometimes, yeah, but I got off early so she wasn't able to pick me up or nothin'."

Sadie did some quick calculations in her head. His work was a solid four miles from Nicholas House, and his apartment was somewhere between his work and the mall, which was three miles from here at least. "Did you *walk* here?"

"In this cold?" He smiled a full smile that showed at least part of why Joy had fallen in love with him. His teeth weren't perfectly straight, but they were white and bright, and his smile was rather dazzling. She almost said as much, but stopped herself just in time. "Nah, I'd have froze to death. The only way to survive in this cold is to run." He moved his arms like someone jogging.

"You *ran* here?" She glanced at his jeans and steel-toed boots.

"Wasn't nothin'," he said. "Good for me. Anyways, I better get going."

"Whoa, no way am I letting you run back home. I can drive you."

"Oh, you ain't gotta do that," Frank said, shaking his head. "I'm good."

"You're getting a ride. From me. I won't take no for an answer."

His smile fell. She stared at him and knew he was remembering their meeting yesterday. She thought of all the women who had been taken advantage of by pushy men over the years. Pushy, older men.

"I mean, it's totally up to you," she amended, "but I'd be glad to take you home. It will save you half an hour."

He watched her, and though she was embarrassed that he had to think so hard between running in subzero temperatures and riding alone in a car with her for five minutes, she tried not to show it.

After several seconds, he shrugged. "If you don't mind, that'd be nice."

CHAPTER 29

Frank was back to his awkward self once he was in the front seat of Sadie's Prius. He only spoke enough to tell her how to get to his apartment. His hand was on the door before she'd even come to a stop outside his eightplex with a cracked parking lot and limited green space. The wind had picked up, bending the trees that lined the back of the lot. She shivered even though she was inside the car.

"Thanks, Mrs. C.," he said quickly as he hopped out of the car. He pushed the door shut and ran with long, lanky strides to one of the basement apartments, the wind tugging at the open sides of his coat he hadn't zipped up.

Sadie pulled back onto the street, heading toward Marley's. She passed the auto parts store where Frank worked a few blocks later—in walking distance just like Joy had said. It was hard to imagine a single dad working full-time could get by without a car.

At the next light, Sadie spotted the Quick Copy Center and thought of Carol's planner. She wanted to spend more time studying it, but she worried Carol would need it for something nonnefarious and panic when she realized it was gone.

The gal at the counter didn't grill Sadie about the ownership of the planner, though Sadie had made up a convincing story, just in case, and told Sadie it would be pricey since she had to copy every single page. Sadie wished she had thought to mark the pages she wanted copies of ahead of time. Then again, there might be additional information on other pages that would be helpful.

"It's fine," Sadie said.

The girl shrugged as though to say, "Some people have more money than sense." Sadie didn't necessarily disagree, but she didn't agree either. Not in this instance, at least.

A few cars parked out front of Marley's Antiques proved there was still vintage shopping being done this late in the day, and a handwritten sign on the door said the store would be open until three o'clock.

When Sadie pushed the door open, it jingled an old-fashioned bell hanging from the ceiling. Sadie hoped a deserving angel would get his wings . . . but then hover nearby to help Sadie with this investigation. Time was getting short, and yet she dared believe that luck, or the very angel she was wishing wings for, would be on her side.

Marley's Antiques smelled of lemon polish, old wood, and copper. The shoppers spoke softly to one another as though in reverence of the items now resting after their days of fashion. Large furniture items such as bookcases and armoires displayed smaller treasures like teacups, toys, and statues.

A display of vintage Christmas items sat upon a velvet-covered table just inside the front door. There was a bronze reindeer in the center surrounded by a variety of dolls, dishes, and Christmas-themed décor that filled the rest of the table. Sadie's eyes were drawn to a tree by the table covered in vintage ornaments. There were beaded wreaths, crystal icicles, fake candles clipped to the branches, and some glittery balls. There were also a few kugels and two Dresdens—though, sadly, none were Mary's. The condition of those on display made Mary's look even better—and more valuable—by comparison.

The shop wasn't large, but the space was well used without feeling claustrophobic. An old-fashioned soda counter acted as the checkout, and the man from the Google Images Sadie had searched for was helping wrap a set of plates in paper for an older woman who was telling him about the oyster stew her mother always made for Christmas Eve dinner. Sadie decided to browse until she could get Jedidiah alone.

After wandering through a few aisles, Sadie came upon a shelf full of tea sets—three of which were silver. One of the items on the list in Carol's planner was a Georg Jensen silver tea set with the name Harold Tanner next to it. How valuable could a tea set be?

"Can I help you?"

Sadie turned with a start. The laugh lines around Jedidiah Marley's eyes attested to a happy disposition Sadie hoped would be to her benefit. "Oh, good morning."

"Afternoon, actually, but it is a *good* one." He nodded toward the tea sets. "Interested in a service?"

Sadie had a British son-in-law, so she knew that "service" was another name for tea set. "Oh, um, perhaps." She cleared her throat and hoped she sounded confident. "Do you, by chance, have a Georg Jensen set?"

Jedidiah whistled under his breath and shook his head. "I wish I did. Those are pretty hard to come by."

"Yeah," Sadie said as though she understood the context

enough to be disappointed. "Any idea what you might sell it for, if you had one on hand?"

"Well, depending on the model and the size of the set, a complete service could be anywhere from five to fifty thousand dollars."

Sadie felt her eyes bug slightly. "Fifty thousand dollars?"

"Georg Jensen quality is hard to beat and highly sought-after by collectors. This Reed & Barton set is of a similar quality, however." He stepped past her and lifted the pot that looked more like a water pitcher to Sadie's American eyes. "From 1932, and with both the sugar bowl and the cream dish, though the spoons are not original."

"It's lovely, but I really had my heart set on a Georg Jensen."

"You'll probably need to go to a picker for such a specific item," he said, replacing the pitcher on the oval tray.

"A picker?"

"An antique expert who searches for specific items. I could put you in contact with a guy out of Denver who specializes in silver."

Sadie wasn't interested in a picker, and yet if he were an expert and knew how to find exact items, he might have information that could be helpful to a novice like Sadie as she tried to learn the fate of the items from Carol's list. "That would be great."

Jedidiah nodded toward the counter. "I've got his card up front. Just make sure you tell him I sent you. I want to get the credit even if I don't get the sale." He winked at Sadie and headed back to the counter. She followed.

An elderly man with a dented milk can was already waiting to check out, so Sadie browsed the items hanging near the counter while she waited for the men to finish discussing the dairies of Colorado in the 1950s. Sadie had never had a passion for antiques, probably because she didn't know how to put them together in a home. The stories behind heirlooms were always intriguing, though. If she was right about the items on the list in Carol's planner having been stolen from residents, those were stories that had come to an end. The new owners wouldn't know how the brooch had been a gift from a mother to a daughter who brought it from Norway. They wouldn't know for what occasion Barbara Peterson had owned a pearl necklace with matching drop earrings or how much the tea service had meant to Harold Tanner.

The old man finally took his handwritten receipt and headed out the door with his milk can.

"I've got the card for that picker right here," Jedidiah said as Sadie stepped up. He pulled out a long wooden drawer from beneath the counter filled with business cards and began ticking through them like a horizontal Rolodex.

"You have a lovely variety of, uh, wares," Sadie said, waving her hand toward the displays.

"Thank you. We try to keep things fresh."

Sadie smiled at the irony of fresh antiques. "Where do you get the items you sell?"

"Estate sales, mostly. In the summer, my wife and I travel all over the Midwest."

"You must have staff to cover the shop, then," Sadie said as casually as she could manage.

There was a basket filled with antique drawer pulls and handles on the counter, and to keep from seeming too intent on his answer, Sadie picked up a cut-crystal pull just like the ones on her grandmother's china cabinet, the bronze having darkened to a charcoal-gray patina. Holding it in her hand brought back the sensation of touching those pulls as a child—she'd thought they were diamonds back then—and the memory made her smile. Maybe that was what drew people to antiques.

Jedidiah pulled a card from his drawer with a triumphant flourish. "My sister, Carol, helps cover the store when we're gone. And we have a woman who winters in Southern Utah, then lives here in Fort Collins from May to October. They are the reason my wife and I can travel as much as we do—which we love to do. We reset the shop every October."

"What do you do with the things that no longer have a place after the reset?" Sadie asked, putting the drawer pull on the counter and searching the basket for a matching one. Wouldn't it be cute to have these on just a couple of her kitchen cabinets? They were eighteen dollars apiece, but if seeing them made her think of her grandma's diamond cabinet, it felt like a bargain.

"We always have more than we can fit," Jedidiah said with a chuckle. "We'll put some things in storage—there are trends in antique sales just like in retail—but we keep a current listing on the computer in case people come looking for something we might not have set out. We also sell a lot of past stock online."

"You have an online store?"

"Not my own website or anything like that. The marketing it takes to be successful at that is ridiculous. My sister runs an eBay store that does pretty well, though, and we do individual listings on places like Etsy," he said. "Online sales help us stay busy when the foot traffic slows down, so it's a win-win. I couldn't keep my doors open without it."

"Your sister seems to have quite a hand in the shop." So Carol could have sold the ornaments online without Jedidiah even knowing. Maybe there hadn't been time to complete the sale, though.

Sadie glanced at a door behind the soda-counter checkout covered in old Coca-Cola signs and posters. What if the ornaments were back there right now?

"Carol worked for me full-time after she moved back to Fort Collins a few years ago. She learned the ropes pretty quick."

That lined up with what Sadie had learned—that Carol had already been living in Fort Collins when she asked Jackie for help finding a job once her license was reinstated, but still probationary. "Oh, yeah?"

He nodded. "She's back in the medical field for the most part these days. Here's the card for the picker—Jacob Cray."

She took the card, still unsure if it would be an asset to her investigation. But every little bit helped.

"Thank you." Sadie glanced at the Christmas table, where two white-haired women were talking to one another about the items on display. She turned back to Jedidiah. "I noticed you have a few kugels on your tree." She watched his reaction carefully to see if he gave anything away.

Jedidiah glanced at the tree. "A few," he said. "I thought I'd be sold out by today, though the ones that are left aren't the best representatives. Are you in the market?"

Sadie eagerly picked up the thread. "Possibly."

He picked up a pen and paper from beside the old-fashioned cash register. "I might have a sizable lot of kugels coming available in the next few months. If you want to put your name and number down, I can contact you if they come in."

Sadie picked up the pen and wondered what she should write. It didn't seem wise to put her own name. "You can anticipate things like that?"

"I gave a bid on a large set of kugels last summer—mint condition, truly some of the best I've seen. The woman didn't want to sell right then but asked me to hold the bid. I'm hopeful she'll want to sell once Christmas is over."

He didn't know Mary was dying? Or was he trying to throw Sadie off the scent?

He handed her the paper. "There's a collector out of Salt Lake who's also interested. He bought ten of the kugels I had at the start of the season. Locals always get first priority with me, though. I'll put your name at the top of the list."

"That's generous of you," Sadie said. "What can you tell me about this set you're hoping to get?"

"Well, there are thirty-three kugel ornaments, every color, including three in orange—I could hardly believe it. There's also a yellow gourd, and if you know anything about kugels, you know how remarkable a find any gourd is, but especially a yellow one."

"Right," Sadie said, though she had not known that. Gourds were a top seller? Not grapes or pine cones or that beautiful teardrop that looked like liquid silver? She did, however, know that one of the missing ornaments was a yellow gourd from Mary's tree. Was Jedidiah's comment a coincidence or a confession? "They're one of the more valuable ones, aren't they?"

"Oh, yeah," Jedidiah said, nodding. "I saw a pink gourd last summer at an estate sale, and they were asking four grand for it. Just the one ornament."

Sadie's eyes went wide before she could school her expression, which she was sure was exactly as it had been when he'd told her the price range of a Georg Jensen tea service. "Four thousand dollars?"

"And that was a good deal," Jedidiah said. "But I didn't have that kind of capital. I should warn you that this set I'm waiting for will sell for a pretty penny, if I'm lucky enough to get it at all."

"I imagine it would, if one of the ornaments is worth four thousand dollars."

Jedidiah laughed and shook his head as he corrected her. "It's *worth* upwards of eight thousand dollars in the condition it's in. It was selling for four—I can only buy stuff I know will make me a profit."

"Goodness." Sadie could see Mary's yellow gourd in her mind's eye, halfway down the tree and in full view of anyone who came into the room—perhaps too much temptation for someone who knew what it was worth.

"I know. It's crazy sometimes." He nodded toward the blank paper still in Sadie's hand.

Sadie was flattered that he thought her capable of paying fifty thousand dollars or more for a set of ornaments and wrote down the name and number of her friend Gayle. The ringing bell indicated a new customer, and Jedidiah looked past Sadie and gave a nod of his chin in recognition before turning his attention back to Sadie.

"I'll call you if the ornaments come in and give you, say, twenty-four hours to decide before I contact the Salt Lake collector. Does that work for you?"

"Um, yes, thank you." Gayle had recently started dating Sadie's brother, Jack, back in Garrison, which Sadie thought was completely adorable. Gayle would go along with it should Jedidiah call her for some reason.

Someone approached from behind. "Sorry I'm late, Jed, I had to help clean up after the party and—" The words stopped at the same time the footsteps did.

Sadie turned to see Carol standing a few feet away, dressed in the black sweater and red shoes she'd worn to the party.

"What are you doing here?" Carol asked, her tone a mixture of anxiety and surprise.

"Um, shopping?"

CHAPTER 30

Jedidiah looked between them with curiosity. "You guys know each other?"

Carol let out a breath and adjusted her purse on her shoulder— a purse Sadie had gone through forty minutes earlier. Had Carol noticed her planner was missing yet? Sadie would pick up her copy of it in another hour but wasn't sure how she'd get the original back to Carol. Maybe she'd pick the lock of the locker again and put it in there.

"Um, yeah, sort of," Carol said, though she sounded uncomfortable with the admission.

"She's looking for some kugels," Jedidiah said, making Sadie want to scowl at him.

"Kugels?" Carol paused, looking at Sadie as if she were a tricky math problem.

"Yeah, I told her about that lot I bid out last summer. Dang, I sure hope that lady decides to sell."

That lady?

Carol frowned at Sadie. "Could I talk to Mrs. Cunningham in the back room for a few minutes, Jed?"

He looked between them, his kind shopkeeper expression turning to polite concern. "Of course."

Carol walked around the soda counter, and Sadie followed her through the door covered in old Coca-Cola signs. Most of the walls of the back room held shelves crammed with items and boxes labeled in marker. Big pieces of furniture were pushed against the far wall, and a long worktable was set in the center of the room, piled with tools—both vintage and modern—along with a rocking chair in three separate pieces. There was no box of ornaments waiting to be mailed to Australia.

One shelf near the worktable was filled with packing supplies, including flattened Priority Mail boxes and rolls of bubble wrap.

Carol walked to the worktable, then faced Sadie and folded her arms over her chest. "What are you doing here?"

Sadie didn't want to give anything away, and yet this was her prime suspect and she'd been caught investigating. She had to take a chance, and she didn't have time to be evasive. "I'm trying to find some Christmas ornaments that went missing from Mary Hallmark's tree so I can put them back before she realizes what's happened. I learned of your connection to this antique store, and I came to check it out."

"Because you think I took them?"

Sadie didn't want to say that straight out, even if it were true. "Because *someone* took them, and this is one of a half dozen leads I'm investigating."

"Because, what, you're a detective or something?"

Sadie didn't appreciate Carol's sarcasm. "Yes," she said simply. "I'm a private investigator, and I'm working this case." She didn't even squirm as she misrepresented her situation. She hadn't had an active investigator's license for years.

Carol's expression fell. "You really *are* a private investigator?"

Shoot, she was being forced to lie again. Or could this one count under the umbrella of that first lie? "Yes, and I'm a good friend of Mary's. You have a connection to an antique shop that bid out Mary's ornaments last summer, which means you know how much they're worth."

She could see by the slight widening of Carol's eyes that she was surprised about how much Sadie knew.

"I didn't take them."

"Forgive me if I don't take your word for that, Carol. I also know you were the last person to handle Rachel Haskin's brooch."

Carol's neck turned red, and her eyes took on a hint of panic. "I didn't take Rachel's brooch, and I certainly didn't take Mary's ornaments. I wasn't even on shift when they disappeared."

"The timeline I've developed says they disappeared sometime between 6:00 Sunday night and 1:30 Monday afternoon. You worked both of those days."

"They were there when I left Sunday, and—" She cut herself off.

The words hovered in the room between them for the space of breath. "What do you mean they were there when you left? Do you mean they *weren't* there when you came back to work on Monday? How do you know that?"

Carol let out a breath that sounded like . . . surrender. Or resignation. "I get nervous when residents have valuables in their rooms, so I try to keep an eye out."

Keep an eye out! Holy nutcracker, the woman was practically

confessing. Why hadn't Sadie thought to record this conversation on her phone?

"To protect them," Carol said as though reading Sadie's mind, dropping her arms to her sides. "I didn't want anything else to go missing, so when I see something of value come in, I try to convince the family to take it home. That's why I told Rachel's daughter to take the brooch—a late-nineteenth-century coral cameo from Norway? It should never have come to Nicholas House in the first place, and I did everything I could to convince her to remove it. I even tried hiding it in Rachel's room once, but Rachel freaked, so I helped them find it and hoped that would be the lesson they needed, and then a few weeks later it was gone.

"I didn't think anyone else would know how much Mary's ornaments were worth. I wouldn't have if I didn't work in my brother's store." She waved a hand to indicate the storage room. "I chatted casually with Mary about her ornaments, and she didn't reveal anything about how valuable they were, which led me to believe she wouldn't tell other people either. And then she said she'd be taking them down Christmas Eve. I thought surely they would be safe for forty-eight hours—it was such a short period of time. The other things that were taken had obvious value, but the ornaments? Well, I didn't think they would be noticed. I really didn't."

Sadie's head spun. She hadn't expected to get so much information from Carol, and she struggled to distill it in her mind. "You know an awful lot about this." She'd meant the words to sound neutral, maybe even a little complimentary, but they sounded like an accusation, and she watched Carol realize the same thing.

Sadie tried again. "What I meant was—"

"I don't think I should talk to you anymore. I had nothing to do with Mary's ornaments, and I would never steal from a resident."

So help her, Sadie believed her, but she needed more information. "But you know there have been crimes committed against residents of Nicholas House, and you've done nothing . . ." It was superfluous to finish the sentence.

"It's not like that," Carol said, shaking her head and looking at the floor. "I need you to leave."

Sadie took a stab, hoping to get something before she was forced to go. "What about Cabragle68?"

Carol's eyes went wide, and her head came up again. "You know about the eBay store?"

Sadie nodded and forced herself to maintain eye contact so as not to give away the exaggeration of what she actually knew.

Carol threw her hands up in another flash of defensiveness. "Then why are you here?" She paused and lifted her eyebrows in realization. "Wait, you think I'm behind Cabragle68." It wasn't a question.

"Give me somewhere else to look, Carol," Sadie said, spreading her hands. "You know someone is stealing from the residents at Nicholas House—" Sadie nearly bit her tongue to keep from saying that she had a list of staff Carol was trying to vet as that list was currently being copied—along with the records of the last year of Carol's life.

Carol covered her face, and Sadie thought she might cry until Carol took a deep breath and rubbed her face instead. After a few seconds, she lowered her hands, looked squarely at Sadie, and lifted her chin.

"I want to talk to a lawyer."

"I'm not arresting you," Sadie said. "I'm just trying to return heirloom ornaments to a dying woman."

"I'm not talking to you anymore." Carol started walking toward the door that led back to the antique shop. She stopped when she reached it and turned back. "If you really want to find Mary's ornaments, you're wasting your time here."

"Do you know who the thief is? You can tell me, and I'll leave you alone."

For a moment she thought Carol might give in, then Carol shook her head. "I'll talk to an attorney and make sure I'm protected before I say anything else. I'm sorry, I know that makes me seem guilty, but . . . sorry."

Carol put her hand on the doorknob, and Sadie's mind whirled, trying to think of a new solution. Carol pulled the door open and stood back so Sadie could leave first. Sadie walked out of the storage room.

She could hear Jedidiah talking to a customer somewhere in the store and saw the crystal handle she'd put on the counter earlier. It wouldn't create much of a delay, but she needed to extend this opportunity to talk to Carol for as long as she could. Was there some way she could convince Carol to tell her what she knew? Was the missing information in the planner Sadie hadn't been able to read in detail yet?

"Can I buy this?" Sadie asked, pointing to the drawer pull.

Carol hesitated, but then nodded. She did work here after all.

Sadie went around to the customer side of the counter. The card for the picker Jed had recommended was there, and she tucked it into her wallet. She'd wanted a second pull, but she didn't want to get distracted digging through the basket.

That Carol knew something that might be helpful burned in Sadie's chest. If she'd approached it differently, could there have been a different outcome? And yet, she *had* learned a lot: there was a pattern of thefts from the residents at Nicholas House, Carol had been looking into different staff members and crossing out the ones she'd cleared, and Cabragle68 was an eBay store—did that mean the stolen items had all been sold there? The ornaments?

While Carol wrote out a receipt, Sadie texted Pete.

Sadie: Cabragle68 is an eBay store that might have sold the stolen items.

Pete: On it. Just boarding plane, take off in 15

"That will be $19.36," Carol said, using a pad of paper and a calculator to factor the sale.

Sadie opened her purse and pulled a twenty-dollar bill from her wallet. She tried to catch Carol's eye as she handed over the money, but Carol avoided her gaze. In two weeks, Carol was supposed to get her license reinstated after three years of working as hard as ever for far less pay. It was foolish to dismiss her as a suspect—especially when Sadie didn't have anyone else in the running—but it was just as foolish to assume Carol was the thief without looking at other options. There was just so little time.

Carol took the money, then opened a cash drawer and began counting out Sadie's change. As she did, Sadie thought back to the things Jedidiah had said about the ornaments he hoped would come up for sale.

"Your brother doesn't know Mary's a resident at Nicholas House or that she'd dying or that you know about the missing ornaments, does he?" He wouldn't have talked so freely about the ornaments he hoped to sell to Sadie if he had known to protect the information for his sister's sake.

"Of course not," Carol said, picking out the pennies from the compartment. "She's a resident, and her information is private."

"Did you know about the bid he did for her?" Sadie held her breath, thinking Carol might say, again, that she needed to talk to a lawyer first.

Carol paused, considering the question, then nodded. "When Mary moved into Nicholas House, I recognized her name from a home visit Jed did last summer, but I didn't know the *ornaments* Jed was so excited about were hers until after work Sunday when I put two and two together and came over here to look it up."

She was opening up, and Sadie wanted as much advantage as she could get from that. "Tell me who I should be looking into," Sadie begged, her voice just over a whisper. "Help me find these ornaments before they're gone forever."

Carol held out her hand with Sadie's change, but kept her eyes glued to the countertop. "I can't." Her voice was ragged with sincere regret. "I'm sorry, I really am, but . . ." She paused. "I just can't . . . trust you."

There was heartbreak in those words. What if the nurse who refused to participate in the medication disposal with Carol had lied about it when people started asking questions? What if she was a lazy nurse, difficult to work with and unconcerned with protocols, until those broken protocols put her at risk? How hard was it for her to say Carol was lying in order to protect herself? Would Carol have assumed that justice would prevail and therefore not protected herself the way she could have? Was having a lawyer even an option when a case was brought before the board of regulatory licenses?

There was no way for Sadie to know the answers to those questions, but maybe there was something she could do to help Carol feel safe enough to tell what she knew before it was too late.

Sadie cleared her throat. "I have a friend who's a lawyer, Bob Bailey," she said, keeping her voice even and compassionate. "He was a litigator in Denver for most of his career, then retired here in Fort Collins with his wife not long after my husband and I moved here." Sadie skipped explaining their monthly dinners together and the shared trips to Mexico and Edmonton. "He's mostly retired, but I know he would give you good advice, and if I asked him to, I think he would talk to you this afternoon."

Sadie reached for the same pen and paper she'd written Gayle's contact information on earlier. The top sheet was gone, and she wondered if it was in the file with Mary's bid on the ornaments. She pulled her phone out of her purse and found Bob's number.

"I'm not going to talk to *your* attorney," Carol said, but she watched as Sadie wrote down his information.

"He's not *my* attorney," Sadie said. "And anything you tell him will be protected by client privilege." She pushed the paper toward Carol, but when Carol reached for it, Sadie didn't let go. Carol met her eyes, still suspicious and uncertain. "I'm going to ask him to make you his top priority if you call him."

"It's Christmas Eve," Carol said, sounding scared. "He won't talk to me on Christmas Eve."

"He will," Sadie said with confidence. Bob loved Sadie's Cinnamon Pie, and she would offer to make him one every month for the next year if he'd do this. "You need to protect yourself,

Carol, I get that, but I need to find Mary's ornaments. Bob can help you navigate your situation, hopefully quickly enough that you'll feel safe sharing what you know in time to help Mary. If that doesn't happen, at least you'll have someone to help you through the process when the police show up, asking you the same questions I'm asking." She let the words fall like sleet before she added, "And they won't take no for an answer."

Cinnamon Pie

Pie Crust
1 ¼ cups all-purpose flour
½ teaspoon salt
½ cup unsalted butter, chilled
2 to 4 tablespoons ice water

Filling
1 (8-ounce) package cream cheese, softened
1 cup sugar, sifted
¼ teaspoon salt
1 egg, plus 2 egg yolks, slightly beaten (retain egg whites for
   crust egg wash)
1 cup half-and-half
1 teaspoon vanilla extract
¼ cup melted butter
3 to 4 tablespoons ground cinnamon
2 tablespoons flour, sifted

Whipped Cream Topping
1 quart heavy whipping cream
1 (3.4-ounce) box instant Jell-O pudding, cheesecake flavored
⅓ cup powdered sugar

To make pie crust

Combine flour and salt in a large bowl. Cut in butter with a pastry cutter, working in one tablespoon of water at a time until smooth dough forms. Roll dough out to about ¼-inch thickness, a few inches larger than your pie plate.

Put crust in 9-inch pie plate. Trim, fold, and pinch crust edges as desired. Freeze 1 hour.

To make filling

Preheat oven to 350 degrees F.

In a large mixing bowl, beat cream cheese and sugar until light and smooth. Add salt, eggs, half-and-half, vanilla, and melted butter; beat until combined. Once fully incorporated, add the cinnamon and flour, a bit at a time, making sure it is well combined before adding the next portion.

Brush frozen pie crust with egg wash. Bake crust for 5 minutes to cook the egg wash.

Pour the filling into the prebaked pie crust and bake at 350 degrees F. for 40 to 50 minutes or until a toothpick inserted into the center comes out clean.

Allow pie to cool to room temperature before slicing.

To make whipped cream topping

Using a hand mixer or stand mixer, beat cream, Jell-O, and sugar on low, increasing speed a little at a time until medium-high speed is achieved. Continue beating until stiff peaks form.

Note: This makes more whipped topping than you need. You can half the recipe, or you can use the topping for other desserts. Topping will keep for up to ten days in the fridge.

CHAPTER 31

From her parking spot in front of Marley's Antiques, Sadie texted Bob to tell him that a woman named Carol Benson might call—she needed advice ASAP—and that if he'd do this he'd get a year's supply of Cinnamon Pie. He responded immediately.

> *Bob:* I get one pie regardless of whether or not she calls for my help. If she does call, I'll meet with her immediately and get the year supply. Deal?
>
> *Sadie:* Deal.
>
> *Bob:* Oh, and you have to explain to Barb if talking to this woman means I have to miss her sister's horrible Christmas Eve dinner. Or is it her horrible sister's dinner?
>
> *Sadie:* Worth it.
>
> *Bob:* 👍

Bless her wonderful friends. She took a breath, opened up a fresh message, and texted Pete.

> *Sadie:* Talked to Carol but she clammed up on me, said she wanted a lawyer. I referred her to Bob.

Pete: Good idea. Tell him that if he wants to contact Detective Arrington at the department, he'll take a statement.

Pete: Also, I don't think it's Carol.

Sadie didn't either, but wanted to understand Pete's reasoning and was willing to play devil's advocate to get his full opinion.

Sadie: Why not?

Pete: Everything Marley's has sold online is legit, great reviews and high ratings.

Sadie: That only means she's good at what she does.

Pete: True, but Cabragle68 is an eBay store that has sold seven items over the last four years, all from the list you sent and all in the months specified.

Sadie: Carol has only worked at the store for three years.

Pete: She likely put the list together from the Cabragle68 site.

Three dots appeared and danced on her screen while Pete wrote a new message.

Pete: I have bad news.

Sadie held her breath.

Pete: The last item Cabragle68 sold was a lot of 5 Dresdens. They were priced low and sold in under half an hour.

The air pushed out of Sadie's lungs, and she had to swallow around the instant lump in her throat. It was several seconds before she could respond.

Sadie: When did they sell?

Pete: Sunday, just before midnight. They are marked as shipped. You know what that means, don't you?

Sadie: I'm not going to get them back for Mary ☹

Pete: Yes. And this is clearly theft, over state lines, and a violation of all kinds of ecommerce laws and regulations. Cabragle68 has also taken down the store, which means they must know someone's looking into this, which puts you in danger. We need to involve the police, and we need to do it quickly. We can file a Stolen Property Report with eBay and possibly get the ornaments back if we move quickly enough. The kugals were listed at the same time, but they were taken down before they sold. The whole store was taken down, but that doesn't remove sales history from eBay's database, which is how I found him.

Sadie: Any idea who Cabragle68 is?

Pete: No, the store only exists on eBay. There's nothing else about him on the web. I'll keep looking—but my flight is about to take off.

Sadie: Send me what you get before you have to turn off your phone. I'll let you know when I'm ready to involve the police.

Pete: We're running out of time.

Sadie: I know.

CHAPTER 32

Sadie stopped by the copy store, but they hadn't even started copying the planner. She asked the girl to call her as soon as it was ready to be picked up and left without it. She signed into Nicholas House at 12:55 and could feel the change in mood as soon she stepped into the unit. It was quieter than usual, even though there was Christmas music playing softly over the speakers, and there was no one in the halls. The nurses' station was empty, and the window into Jackie's office was dark.

Sadie was having a hard time determining her next move as the knowledge that Mary's ornaments had been sold thudded in her head like an offbeat bass line. It wasn't supposed to have happened this way. Sadie was supposed to have found the ornaments and restored them to Mary's tree. She was supposed to have saved Christmas.

And yet, the kugels hadn't sold, which meant there was a chance of recovering them. But if she involved the police, Mary would be pulled into this. Sadie looked at the dark window to Jackie's office and knew what she had to do, but she didn't want to do it. Jackie wasn't on Carol's list, but she should have been since she had been employed during the time all the thefts had happened.

"Hee-haw, Mary," Sadie said as she came into the room.

Mary lifted the remote to pause the movie she was listening to—*Scrooge*. "Hee-haw, Sadie. You're back."

"I'm back," Sadie said simply, wiping her palms on her black jeans. She hadn't felt nervous, aside from the anxiety of possibly being caught when she was breaking into the lockers, but this was different. Jackie's office held confidential documents, and if she were caught there . . .

She decided she wouldn't break in until Mary and her family had left for Mass.

"I have a question for you." Sadie kept her tone light as she sat in the chair next to Mary's recliner. "Have you been prescribed a sleeping pill? Did you take something Sunday night?"

Mary put out her hand automatically, and Sadie took it. "Not *prescribed*," she said easily. "But Jackie suggested I take some of that over-the-counter stuff. I can't remember what it's called—E-something."

Jackie.

"Are you taking it every night?"

"Now, Sadie, don't start going mother hen on me. It's perfectly safe. You can buy it at any grocery store."

"I'm all for you getting a good night's sleep. I'm just curious. You said months ago that you were going off all your meds except for pain medication as needed, but then Frank said you got really sleepy really fast on Sunday night. He had to help you to bed?"

"He did not," Mary scoffed, shaking her head. "He walked me

back from the bathroom, I remember that, but I'm sure I got into bed all by myself like I always do."

She didn't remember?

"It wasn't really *medicine*, anyway," Mary continued. "It's not going to prolong a life I'm nearly finished with. It just helped me sleep. Besides, I talked to my doctor about a sleeping pill last month, and he'd said that he hesitated to prescribe anything because of my respiratory issues. He said it could cause problems, which is why I only agreed to take an over-the-counter one."

Mary had had breathing issues the last few weeks, but she'd had three on Monday. She'd never needed three treatments in a single day before.

"And Jackie gave the pill to you?"

"Yes, she's such a sweetheart. She visits me every day, tells me about her kids and grandkids, asks me how I'm feeling. She came in Sunday night—popped in real quick and then popped out. I knew it was late, so I didn't ask her to stay and visit, besides I had Frank to talk to. And it worked, I slept really well, though I don't think I'll try it again. Do you think that's why I was so sluggish yesterday? From an over-the-counter pill like that? Maybe I've become more sensitive or something."

"Possibly," Sadie said, ready to change the subject now that she'd gotten the information she needed. Her stomach felt like a stone. How ironic that she'd talked to everyone except Mary, who had the missing piece all along. Sadie didn't think she'd given Mary an over-the-counter anything. That Jackie had given Mary medication that had affected her breathing made Sadie burn inside. She needed other thoughts to dilute the anger and sadness building up in her mind. "So, I heard you invited Ivy to Mass?"

"Honestly, I didn't think she'd come, but I'm pleased that she accepted, even if it's only to make me happy."

"Doing things for the sole purpose of making the people we love happy isn't a bad thing."

"Agreed," Mary said. "Which is why I put up with her flirting with Harry through the whole Christmas party."

"She did?" Sadie said, frowning. "I was afraid that might happen."

"It's fine," Mary said. "I like Harry, and it would be good for Ivy to marry for love now that she's married so many other men for money and gotten out of those marriages with more than her fair share."

Sadie laughed, but it was an intriguing detail. She'd assumed Ivy had financial pressures, which was why Mary didn't want her to know the value of the ornaments. "Ivy has money?"

Mary nodded. "If she ends up marrying Harry, make sure you tell her to do a prenup. Her ex-husbands sure wish they'd have done one. If I bring it up, we'll fight about it. And I'm trying really hard not to fight with her, so I need your help."

"She's a grown woman, Mary, and—"

"And," Mary cut in, "*you're* the one who convinced me to try to mend our relationship, which I'm grateful for, but that means someone has to do the heavy lifting around here. Just promise me you'll mention it to her, that's all. Didn't you get a prenup when you and Pete got married?"

"Yes, to protect our children's interests and make sure there wouldn't be discord between them later on, but—"

"There you go," Mary said, sitting back in her chair. "Just tell her that."

There was a light knock at the door. "Hi, Mom, it's me. I'm back."

"Speak of the devil," Mary said softly enough that only Sadie could hear it over the tapping of Ivy's high heels as she came into the room.

Sadie swatted Mary's arm playfully, remembering that Ivy was here to return the candy cane ornament. At least that one would be back on the tree in time.

"I'm glad you got here early," Mary said.

"I'm glad you invited me." Ivy wore a flowing red dress, with a black overcoat and black, heeled boots. Diamond snowflakes hung from her ears and matched the diamond pendant at her throat. Ivy would turn heads when she walked into St. Joseph's.

Instead of crossing to Mary immediately, Ivy moved to the tree and then pulled something wrapped in bubble wrap from her black-and-gold purse that probably cost more than all of Sadie's Christmas sweaters combined. Carefully and quietly, Ivy pulled back the bubble wrap to reveal Mary's chipped candy cane. She put it on the tree, a little farther down than where it had been originally. Sadie would fix it later.

"What are you doing, dear?" Mary asked.

"Just adjusting the tree a little," Ivy said, turning back to Mary, who had put out her hand as she always did when someone came to visit. When she was holding their hand, she knew right where they were.

Sadie stood from her chair so Ivy could sit by her mother.

"The tree is really pretty, Mom. It makes this place look like home."

"Thank you, dear, but I know it's not your style. That's alright."

"It's *your* style, and it's beautiful," Ivy said without reacting in offense.

"Thank you. I wanted to talk to you for a minute before Frank and Joy arrive."

Sadie couldn't tell if Ivy tensed at mention of their names, but decided to believe that she didn't.

Mary didn't wait for Ivy to respond. "After Mass, I'm going to give Joy my ornaments."

To her credit, Ivy did not react, though it took Mary a few moments to realize it. When she did, her shoulders relaxed.

"I'm sure she'll be very grateful to have something that meant so much to you," Ivy said.

"Does it upset you?"

"It doesn't upset me, Mom. I know how important Joy has been to you these last years, and I'm glad for all she's done. I've known the ornaments were designated to go to her from your will, remember?"

"And I didn't think I'd get a chance to give them to her myself. Now that I can, though, I worry you'll feel left out."

"I won't feel left out," Ivy said. "I'm glad you get to give them to her yourself. They will mean that much more to her because of it."

"Before I give them to her, I wanted to give you something from the collection. As I said, I know they aren't your style, dear, and I don't want you to accept it just to please me, but, well, if you wanted the candy cane—the one with the chip—I would like you to have it. I promise it won't hurt my feelings if you don't want it though."

Ivy was quiet for a few moments, and when she spoke, it was with reverence and emotion. "You're giving me your candy cane?"

"Somehow you and I missed the mark in regards to our relationship. I'm not sure if I'll ever understand why, but I know I had
a part. My greatest hope, now, is that when I'm gone, you will remember me without hurt and sorrow. I love you, Ivy, and I wish I'd
done a better job of showing it. I hope you'll forgive me. The candy
cane has always meant so much to me, and maybe you can see it as
a symbol of us—different women twisted together, side by side, into
a whole."

Ivy blinked quickly though her face barely moved. She let go of
one of Mary's hands in order to dab at her eyes with her manicured
fingers. Sadie crossed to the nightstand and handed Ivy a tissue.
"I'm sorry, too, Mom. For everything. I've always been such a pain
in the neck."

"True," Mary said, causing Ivy to laugh. "But I love you, and
I'm glad to be your mother. I know you're not religious, but I believe there's more after this. I believe we'll have the chance to be a
family again, and I plan to do a much better job of it there."

Mary moved her hands to Ivy's cheeks, then leaned forward
and kissed her on the forehead, letting the kiss linger. She pulled
back, lowered her hands, and waved at the tree. "Go ahead and
take it now, so there's no confusion later. It should fit in your
purse—maybe you can wrap it up in that extra pair of socks or
something to protect it."

Ivy stood and walked to the tree. She glanced over her shoulder,
giving Sadie a questioning look. "Did you tell her?" she mouthed.

Sadie shook her head and mimicked zipping her lips closed.

Ivy looked relieved. "Are you sure, Mom? You don't want Joy
to have it?"

"I want *you* to have it, if it will mean something to you."

"It will mean the world to me, Mom." Ivy reached forward and removed the candy cane she had replaced minutes earlier. "I can't think of a keepsake I would want more than this. Thank you."

"Oh, good," Mary said with a slight sniffle, then turned toward Sadie. "Is there something we could wrap it in, Sadie, so it won't get broken?"

"Um, actually," Sadie said, lifting her eyebrows toward Ivy and nodding toward her purse. "I've got some bubble wrap that would probably work."

"You have bubble wrap?" Mary asked, incredulous.

"Well, you never know when it might come in handy."

Ivy removed the bubble wrap from her own purse, not trying to keep it quiet this time.

"Could I hold it before you put it away, Ivy?" Mary said, holding out her hand.

"Of course," Ivy said. She lifted the ornament from the branch and brought it back to Mary. Just as when she and Sadie had been decorating the tree, Mary took the candy cane and ran her fingers over the curve and down the shaft until she reached the chip at the bottom. "Actually, Mom, I think I'd like to keep it on the tree until you give Joy her ornaments. I'd like to be there for that, if it's okay and you don't think it will upset Joy."

"Of course it's okay," Mary said, her voice bright with Ivy's desire to be a part of Mary and Joy's relationship instead of outside it. Ivy smiled and put the bubble wrap away.

"You remember the story?" Mary asked, looking toward Ivy when she returned to sit beside her.

"I would love to hear it again," Ivy said.

Sadie's phone in her back pocket vibrated with a text message.

Mary beamed. "Well, I was about two years old, and—"

"I'm going to step into the hall," Sadie interrupted in a gentle voice.

Sadie closed the door softly behind her before sliding her phone out of her pocket.

Pete: One eBay feedback comment mentioned that the store said it was out of Texas but postage came from Fort Collins. It's not a BIG deal, but is additional fraud, according to eBay's terms of service.

Sadie: The names of the employees on Carol's list of who could be behind the thefts left one out—Jackie.

Pete: You think Jackie could be behind all this?

Sadie: I think she's at least involved. Not sure how.

Jackie was good at her job but had never struck Sadie as internet savvy. She was certainly the best paid of the staff, so she had less motive, and Sadie had seen her with the residents over these last months. Her care for them was genuine and sincere. Yet she'd given Mary a contraindicated medication. Jackie also didn't show up on either of the sign-in lists she'd given Sadie that morning.

Sadie: Can I get Detective Arrington's contact information? I assume he's the person you've been talking to at the department.

Pete: Talking to?

Sadie: I know you've been talking to someone just like you know I've been bending some legalities. You're going to be on a plane, and I'm going to need to coordinate with someone.

A moment later a "new contact" message showed up on Sadie's phone. She wasn't ready to call the detective yet, but she saved the information into her phone.

> *Sadie:* Thanks.
>
> *Pete:* Be safe, Sadie.
>
> *Sadie:* Of course.
>
> *Pete:* And don't break any more laws!
>
> *Sadie:* Would you look at that? Another tunnel . . .

CHAPTER 33

Sadie was looking up "cities named Springfield" on her phone when Joy, Frank, and his daughter came through the security door. Sadie hadn't met Star, but smiled at her as the three of them walked toward her. Star's mother must have been African American, giving her daughter tightly curled hair and dark skin. Her eyes, however, were as blue as her daddy's.

Sadie followed them into Mary's room, where there was more visiting while Mary got her coat and scarf, refusing everyone's offers to help. Sadie was glad to see Ivy interact politely with Frank, and almost effusively with Star, complimenting her blue velvet dress and black, sparkly dress shoes. Joy was wearing a red sweater and black skirt that could have come from Mary's closet. She wasn't a typical twenty-five-year-old woman, probably never would be typical anything, but she was happy and coming to believe such happiness could continue as her life unfolded. That was yet another miracle, though it would hopefully extend far past Christmas.

"I'm ready," Mary finally said. She put one arm out, and Frank stepped up, taking her elbow. Then she put one hand down at her side, and Star took it in her much-smaller one. Joy and Ivy fell into step beside each other as the five of them left the room. Reconciled. Together. A family.

Sadie hurried ahead of them to open the door that led out of the secured portion of the facility. "You have a good service," she said as they passed by.

"Every service is a good one," Mary said, patting Frank's arm. "Especially when I have such wonderful company."

Sadie waited around in the hallway, pretending to do some last-minute research on her phone but really staking out the area. After five minutes had passed with no staff appearing, she headed toward Jackie's office door. The nurses' station was as empty as the rest of the building felt now that the Christmas party was over and half the residents had gone home to celebrate with their families.

Moving fast in case one of the staff did return, Sadie took her lockpick set out of her pocket and slid the independent tension tool out of its separate compartment before choosing her go-to pick—the three-ridged rake she'd already used on the lockers. A door lock was more difficult to pick than a padlock, however, to say nothing about feeling like she was out in the open.

She inserted the tension tool and got to work on the first pin. When it reset, her confidence improved. The last pin was sticky, but she applied more torque, and it finally gave way. She quickly removed her tools and let herself into the office, which was dark thanks to the closed blinds of the small window that looked into the nurses' station.

There was no exterior window, seeing as how the office was set in the center of the building, and Sadie couldn't turn on the light without risking someone in the nurses' station seeing the light around the edges of the door or window. She folded the pick back into the casing, replaced the tension tool, and then exchanged the pick set for the tiny penlight she normally kept on her key ring but had slipped into her pocket just in case. She held the light in her teeth so she could use both hands. What she wouldn't do for a headlamp!

Jackie had pulled the blank incident report from the middle drawer that morning, so Sadie started there. She found the file for blank reports—there were five copies—and then looked at the files surrounding that folder, which she assumed would contain completed forms, including the one for Lewis Merrill's tiepin and Barbara Peterson's pearls.

There was a file for "Incident Report—Staff Injury," filled with completed forms that included a stamped date and a signature— Jackie's presumably—that confirmed each report had been filed with the corporate office.

The next folder was titled "Incident Report—Resident Injury," which included a dozen different forms filled out with information about things like falls, harassment of one resident toward another, and one report of a resident hitting one of the aides with a shoe.

By then Sadie felt like she understood the nature of these files, so she skipped over the incident reports for "other injury, other staff," but then pulled out the file for "Incident Report—Other Resident." She assumed this was for incident reports regarding residents but not specific to physical injury.

She laid the file open on Jackie's desk and, still holding the penlight in her teeth, scanned the papers. The first form was from January concerning a record player that a staff member had knocked off a resident's nightstand, breaking the arm. The paper was stamped and signed, as the other reports had been, but it also included an explanation that the record player had been repaired at the facility's expense a week following the breakage. The next report was for a pair of missing eyeglasses reported in March, also stamped, but without any explanation of how it was resolved. The third form was for Barbara Peterson's pearls. Reported in April, there was no stamp, no signature. The next paper was for Lewis Merrill's emerald tiepin, stamped and signed.

Sadie looked between the forms, puzzled at why one would be stamped and one wouldn't be. Had one been filed with corporate and the other not? Was this a clue, or simply proof that Jackie wasn't as detailed in her paperwork as she could be? It did seem that the file only held information for the current year.

Sadie pulled out her phone and looked over the list from Carol's planner—specifically noting the items from prior years. Sadie went back to the filing cabinet, looking for archived files that might have information about the other items.

The bottom drawer of the cabinet held forms from the last five years, each year represented by a dozen or so files in a specific color—year-end reports that Sadie quickly realized gave a summary of the staff, residents, expenses, and income for that year. There were separate files for Monthly Census, Staff/non-continuing, Resident/non-continuing, and then one for Incident Reports.

Sadie pulled the incident reports from the previous year and laid it on top of the other files still open on Jackie's desk and sorted them into types that matched the different incident report files. According to Carol's list, there had been two thefts of resident valuables last year, but no report had been filed for either of them. There were half a dozen reports similar to those Sadie had found in the current year's file regarding items of insignificant value—a top set of dentures, towels, a pair of slippers. All of those forms were stamped and filed.

Sadie considered this for a few moments, and then pulled the resident file for Bill Fry from the archives, owner of the autographed copy of *Huckleberry Finn*. She quickly determined that Mr. Fry had passed away in September of last year, five months after the theft date listed in Carol's planner. There was a lease agreement, a contact information page, a hospice agreement, some medical forms, and then an inventory sheet that Sadie looked at in more detail.

To serve as a control for her study, Sadie pulled Mary's chart. All the same general information was in her file as had been in Bill Fry's. Every piece of furniture Mary had brought with her was on her list, as well as things like her pewter jewelry box and its contents.

- 1 diamond pendant
- 1 pair gold hoop earrings
- 1 pair silver hoop earrings
- 1 pair cubic zirconia studs
- 1 gold watch—FOSSIL brand
- 1 gold cross on gold chain
- 1 ebony rosary
- 1 gold wedding band with 1/3 carat diamond (usually worn by resident)

The list seemed to be a pretty detailed accounting of the things Mary had brought with her. It didn't list the ornaments, of course, because those had been brought later. At the bottom of the page were both Mary and Ivy's signatures, agreeing that this was a complete list.

Sadie went back to Bill's inventory list. No first-edition book was listed, yet there was a blank line near the middle of the list. She brought the page closer to the light, thinking the only way to remove items from the list would be to redo the list—tricky since it required signatures—or use Wite-Out. There was no correction fluid on the page.

She set Mary's list beside Bill's, looking between them several times until she felt fairly confident that Mary's was an original and Bill's was a copy. She couldn't be certain in this light, but the paper of his report was a bit brighter, the lines a bit blacker, and the variation in that one empty line in the middle of his report could be the result of the original document having been altered. Making a copy and then destroying the original would hide the correction fluid, and while the blank line in the middle looked odd, it wasn't evidence of theft.

Sadie put Bill's file back and pulled out Genevieve Coolidge's file—another resident on Carol's list that Sadie had found no additional information about. There was no diamond tennis bracelet on her inventory sheet either, but there was a blank line near the top of the page, and, like Bill's, the paper was a brighter white than the other admission forms. There were no incident reports in the archives for either of the items that had gone missing, and yet Cabragle68 had sold those items. Carol's list served as a secondary record.

Jackie was responsible for filing incident reports, keeping patient files up-to-date, and closing out each year's files for archival storage. It seemed, however, that when Jackie closed out files from one year to the next, the incident reports for the items sold through Cabragle68 didn't make the transition.

Sadie carefully closed the folders she'd gone through and returned them to their places in the drawers. She went to Jackie's desk and moved her penlight over the picture of Jackie's children. Using her phone, she went to Instagram, found @JackieGrand and scrolled through her pictures, clicking on the first one of her grandchildren she came to.

An Instagram user by the name of @Carebearybear was tagged in the photo. Sadie clicked on the handle and quickly determined she was the girl in the picture on Jackie's desk—Carley Peterson, Jackie's daughter and the mother of Jackie's grandchildren. A bit farther down Jackie's feed was one of her sons, Brandon, and around Christmas of last year, she found a picture of her other son, Glen. He lived in Springfield, which Sadie had thought was Springfield, Colorado, except it didn't make sense for him to have flown here from such a short distance. But there was also a Springfield, Texas, south of San Antonio.

C-A for Carley. B-R-A for Brandon. G-L-E for Glen. Sadie wasn't sure what the 68 stood for, but if Jackie and Carol were the same age, and Carol had graduated with her nursing degree twenty-eight years ago, Jackie could have been born in 1968.

Sadie turned off her penlight and stood in the darkness of Jackie's office. Jackie had worked at Nicholas House since it had opened sixteen years ago, and she'd been the director of nursing for seven years. She was a mother, a grandmother, and a respected member of the community. When she walked into the room, the residents smiled, glad to see the woman they thought of as their friend, as well as their caretaker. No one thought of her as a thief, and yet somehow, for some reason Sadie couldn't even guess at, she'd preyed upon the very people she cared for.

Sadie hadn't found the ornaments, but she had found proof of who knew where to find them. She pulled out her phone and called Detective Arrington.

He answered on the second ring.

CHAPTER 34

Sadie looked at the tree—Mary's last Christmas tree—and let out a heavy-laden breath. She could hear the Tabernacle Choir at Temple Square singing "Away in a Manger" from the overhead speakers somewhere in the facility and thought about Mary sitting in the pews at St. Joseph, communing with God while surrounded by her family. She stepped closer to the tree and ran her finger along the smooth surface of Mary's candy cane ornament.

Mary had compared herself and her daughter to the candy cane, and Sadie thought of her own understanding of its symbols: white for His peace, red for His sacrifice, the shape of the crook a reminder that He will bring His children safely home if they will but listen to His voice the way a sheep knows the voice of its shepherd.

Perhaps people could never appreciate the beautiful things in life, like peace and home and comfort, if they didn't also face the struggles of loss and disappointment and fear. Maybe those things needed to be twisted together in order for anyone to even want a shepherd to call for them.

The thoughts did not lessen the weight in Sadie's stomach for what had to be done, but it did give her hope that all of them could rise above what Jackie had done—even Jackie, if she chose.

Pete had been barraged with text messages for the last forty minutes since his plane had landed, but he'd caught up quickly and convinced the Fort Collins Police Department to humor her on this case—yet one more Christmas miracle. He was on his way back from Denver but couldn't guarantee he'd arrive before Mary returned from Mass. Sadie was on her own. Sort of.

She checked her watch. Jackie should be there any minute. Detective Arrington, currently hiding in Mary's bathroom, had arrived at Nicholas House within fifteen minutes of Sadie's call. He explained everything to Harry, who then called Jackie about an emergency with Mary Hallmark and could she come over right away? When Jackie arrived, Harry simply would not be at the nurses' station, which would bring Jackie directly to Mary's room. Ironically, it was Jackie's commitment to her patients that would make this confrontation work.

Hurried footsteps from the hall caught Sadie's attention, and she faced the door while straightening her Christmas sweater around her hips and lifting her chin in preparation for what was to come.

There was a light knock at the door, and then Jackie stepped into the room. "It's me, Mary," she said as she pushed open the door. "I came as quickly as I could. What's happened?" Jackie stepped fully into the room, her eyes scanning the otherwise empty room until they landed on Sadie. She pulled her eyebrows together. "Sadie? Harry called and said that Mary's breathing treatment wasn't working and—"

"Mary's fine," Sadie said. "She's at Mass. But the situation *is* urgent. I need to talk to you."

"Wh-what?" Jackie looked toward the door. "Harry said there was an emergency—"

"Jackie."

Jackie faced Sadie, two bright spots of pink blooming on her apple cheeks. "What is going on? I left my family Christmas party because I thought Mary was in trouble."

"I found the ornaments."

Jackie froze, her eyes wide. She seemed to realize the expression she was making and immediately softened her face into a look of surprise. "You did?"

"Well, some of them. The five missing Dresdens are on their way to a buyer in New York. The Fort Collins Police Department will be working with police there to intercept them. There's a whole procedure for stolen items sold on eBay, and though the holidays might impact it to some extent, it looks like Mary should get them back. The kugels on the other hand . . ." Sadie shrugged. "I'm hoping that since you took down the listing that means you still have them. I'd very much like to get them on the tree tonight, if possible, and your cooperation will go a long way with the police as your case moves forward."

The room went silent, and Sadie stared at Jackie, who looked away first, then forced a humorless laugh.

"Look, Sadie, I don't know what you're talking about, but—"

"You *do* know what I'm talking about, Jackie." Sadie's tone was soft. There was no point in being angry anymore. "For what it's worth, I don't believe you meant to hurt anyone. I think you felt what you were doing was a victimless crime, but you were wrong. People *were* hurt, Jackie, and mercy can't rob justice."

"I'm leaving," Jackie said, her voice suddenly firm as she turned toward the door of Mary's room. She stopped when the bathroom door opened, and Detective Arrington stepped into the room. He was six foot four and built like a linebacker—in fact, he had been a linebacker at one time.

Jackie's eyes went wide, then she swung back around to face Sadie. The pretense was gone, leaving nothing but fear.

Arrington cleared his throat. "Jacqueline Potter, you are under arrest. You have the right to remain silent. Anything you say can and will—"

"Wait," Jackie said, looking between Sadie and the officer, but then leveled her eyes on Sadie. "Can we talk, just you and me?"

Arrington, who had paused, started up again. "Anything you say can and will be used against you in a court of law. You have the right to have an attorney. If you cannot afford an attorney, one will be provided for you. Do you understand these rights?" As he moved toward her, he reached into the inside pocket of his coat.

Jackie stared at the handcuffs he withdrew, her face losing all color.

Arrington took one of her hands, and she squeaked and pulled away from him. The detective tensed, and Sadie hurried forward to stand between them, her face toward Jackie.

"Jackie, do you understand the charges against you?"

"No!" Jackie said, looking terrified.

Sadie took a breath. "We know you stole numerous items from residents of this facility over the course of approximately five years. We know you falsified admission paperwork to make it look as though those items were never here. We know you did not properly file incident reports with corporate regarding those missing items, and we know that you then sold those items on eBay, with a total revenue of roughly fourteen thousand dollars over the last few years. Carol has verified the information we've already found and—"

"Carol?" Jackie said, and some of the fire in her eyes dimmed.

"She's been trying to find out who was behind the thefts since she first suspected there was something going on. Most of the items were misplaced more than once prior to their disappearance, and they were rather evenly spaced throughout the year. When she realized it was you, a few months ago, she didn't come forward because not only were you her friend, but you'd hired her when few people would have, and you were responsible for her final assessment that would determine whether or not her license was returned. She is currently at the police station with her attorney, distraught over what she has no choice but to do—which is to tell the truth about what you've done. I hope you can appreciate the position she's in."

Tears finally welled up in Jackie's eyes. "She turned me in?"

"*I* turned you in," Sadie said, taking full responsibility. "Carol is telling what she knows, which is the right thing to do even if it's painful. She should have done it when she first realized who was behind the thefts. I only hope that they don't make things too hard for her because of her hesitation."

Jackie looked at the ground for several seconds. "I didn't take the tea set. Harold gave it to me."

"Don't say anything," Sadie said, shaking her head quickly. "You've been Mirandized. Everything you say will be used in your trial."

"I read your books, Sadie, I know how this works, but I want you to understand. I'm not a bad person." Her voice broke, and she sniffled.

Sadie gave Arrington a pleading look, and he nodded before stepping out into the hall. Sadie hoped he wouldn't get in trouble for leaving them alone, but she appreciated the opportunity to talk to Jackie alone.

"What happened?" Sadie asked after the door closed. "How did it get this far?"

Jackie sniffled again, and Sadie fetched her a tissue from the box on Mary's nightstand. "That tea set had been in Mr. Tanner's closet, wrapped in newspapers for months and months. I knew he had it because of the inventory sheet, and so one day I brought in some silver polish, took it out, and shined it up. He didn't have much family and they never came to visit, but he was so grateful for my care of the tea set. For a few weeks he kept it on a table in front of the window in his room, and then one day he told me he wanted me to have it as a gift. I refused, of course, I'm not . . . I'm not supposed to accept gifts, but it meant so much to him to give it to me, so I took it. I kept it for a few weeks, but I didn't really have a place for it, and then my water heater went out so I asked my son to help me sell it."

"Glen, from Texas?" That's where Cabragle was located.

"It wouldn't look good if a seller based in Colorado was selling the same item I was given in the state of Colorado. Mr. Tanner died a couple of months later, and his family asked about the service. I had to do something to keep them from knowing what had happened and asking for it back, so I went through the incident report process but I didn't file it with corporate. I kept thinking the family would come back after the funeral to follow up, but they never did." She dabbed at her eyes.

"So when you closed out the files for the year, you just left the incident report out and altered his incoming-inventory list?"

Jackie stared at her. "How do you know that?"

Sadie wasn't about to answer. "And Rachel Haskin's brooch?"

Jackie sighed. "Rachel had lost that brooch a dozen times as her dementia became worse." Her voice lost some of its humility. "She would cry each time she found it gone, and we would go through her room and find it in a shoe or wrapped up in a pair of underwear in the laundry basket. One night, when I went in to check on her, it was on the floor under her bed, like a piece of garbage. I picked it up and realized the clasp had broken, not surprising with the way she'd been taking care of it. I slid it into my pocket. I had every intention to give it to her daughter and insist she keep it at home, but then I found myself researching how much it was worth."

"You sold it for half its value," Sadie said, repeating something Pete had passed on to her after his plane had landed.

"Things sell faster if they're well priced," Jackie said. "And even at half price, the sale caught up some bills and allowed me to visit my son, who I hadn't seen for a year. Everyone assumed Rachel had truly lost it, which would have happened eventually. We tell the families over and over again not to bring valuables."

Sadie bit her tongue to keep from saying that it wasn't the victim's fault. She didn't need to because Jackie paused and shook her head. "It was just so . . . easy, and there was always something I didn't have enough money for—my car needed new tires, my daughter's husband was laid off so they couldn't pay rent. After each one, I told myself it was the last, but a few weeks or months would go by, and I'd do it all over again, swearing again that it was the last time." She blinked, and tears slid down her cheeks.

"And Mary's ornaments," Sadie said. "With your badge, your comings and goings are tracked differently than the staff or the visitors so you could give me those lists without revealing that you'd come in Sunday night. You gave Mary a sleeping pill to make sure she wouldn't wake up, and then you picked off ten ornaments, five of each. We've already found the Dresdens you sold; a fraud report has been issued. Where are the kugels?"

Jackie folded her arms tight around herself and dropped her chin. "In my office," she said. "There's a locked drawer in my desk. They hadn't sold before you started asking questions, so I pulled them. I can get them." She hung her head and put her hands over her face. "I'm sorry," she said through a sob.

Sadie crossed to her and pulled her into an embrace. Jackie resisted for a moment and then fell against her shoulder and cried, regret and sorrow pouring from her as she apologized for taking from people who had so little left. From people she cared about. People she was legally, as well as ethically, bound to protect.

Sadie let her cry until there was a tapping on the door. The detective poked his head in. "We've got to go, Mrs. Cunningham."

Jackie pulled back, wiping at the mascara smeared on her puffy cheeks. Sadie realized the makeup must be all over the shoulder of her sweater too, but that could be easily fixed. What Jackie had done? Not so much.

"What's going to happen to me?" she whispered, looking at Sadie with pleading eyes.

"First, you're going to get the ornaments so I can replace them on the tree. Then Detective Arrington is going to take you to the police department, where you'll be booked and able to make a statement. In a couple of hours, Pete and I will come down and secure your bail. You should be able to spend Christmas Day with your family. The more you cooperate with this process, the better things will go."

"I'll cooperate," Jackie said, wiping at her eyes. "But . . . the residents?"

"Harry will manage things here until corporate decides how to replace you. He's worked as a director before, which helps. The licensing board will decide what to do with your license."

Jackie's chin trembled. "I'll never be a nurse again."

"No, you probably won't. You've committed multiple felonies, Jackie. It's not going to go away."

Jackie started to cry again.

Detective Arrington stepped forward, still holding a pair of handcuffs.

"You . . . w-won't need those," Jackie said between sobs.

Detective Arrington looked at Sadie, and she nodded her opinion that Jackie wouldn't give him any trouble. He hesitated, but returned the handcuffs to his pocket and opened the door before waving Jackie out so that he could follow.

Jackie sniffed and looked at Sadie, then the tree. "Please tell Mary how sorry I am."

"I'm hoping I won't have to tell her any of this," Sadie said. "But she'd be the first person to tell you that most of the happiness and unhappiness we experience in life is based on the choices we make."

Jackie nodded once, then headed out of the room. Detective Arrington gave Sadie a quick nod and followed Jackie.

Sadie turned to look at the Christmas tree and wrapped her arms around herself.

Mary, Ivy, Frank, Joy, and Star would be back from Mass in half an hour. Most of the ornaments would be back on the tree, and Sadie took comfort in the fact that, while she felt unsettled and regretful about all that had happened, Mary did not have to.

There was another tap at the door, and Sadie wondered if Mass had finished early. The door opened, and Pete poked his head in, then stepped into the room, holding what looked like a bakery box in his hands.

It took a moment to comprehend what she was seeing, then she raised both hands to cover her mouth.

Pete smiled and, without saying a word, crossed the distance between them, put the box on Mary's bed, and gathered Sadie into his arms. She should ask about his flight and the road conditions—had the snow started yet? She should thank him for all his background work and convincing the police to do things her way, but instead she held on tight and sobbed into his shoulder much as Jackie had sobbed into her shoulder a few minutes before, but for very different reasons.

"Hey," he said, turning his head to kiss her temple. "Everything's okay." He nodded toward the box. "I saw Arrington as they were coming out of Jackie's office. These are the kugels."

She nodded and shook her head at the same time, looking between the box and the tree and her sweetheart while she tried to get ahold of herself. She could be strong and determined and tough as nails, but with Pete, she could be everything else. He put his hands on the sides of her face and used his thumbs to wipe her wet cheeks. "You did it, Sadie. You saved Mary's Christmas."

It was all Sadie needed to fall apart all over again.

CHAPTER 35

🍬

Christmas morning, Sadie sprinkled the crushed candy canes over the top of the Cunningham Candy Cane Cake and smiled. It had turned out perfectly. She probably should have kept the layers in the freezer until she knew when the family party would be happening, but after everything, Sadie thought Pete deserved something special. She'd make another one later.

She covered the cake with plastic wrap and put it back in the fridge, put a kettle on the stove, then went to the window and watched the falling snow while Michael Bublé sang "Let it Snow" on the radio mounted under the counter in Sadie's kitchen. The snow had started yesterday evening and hadn't stopped. There were already fourteen inches on the ground and eighteen more in the forecast.

She and Pete hadn't stayed to watch Mary give the ornaments to Joy yesterday afternoon, but both Joy and Ivy had texted her the details and thanked Sadie for all she'd done. Best of all, they'd managed to keep Mary from realizing five Dresdens were missing.

Jackie's kids arranged her bail before Pete and Sadie had to, which allowed the couple to go home and enjoy some take-out

Chinese food. It tasted okay, but Sadie was too tired to cook or complain.

It was midnight before they crawled into bed for a long winter's nap. With heads on their pillows, Sadie told Pete about Mary's dream of her husband, and they'd both cried. For Ivy and Joy. For their own loves lost. For gratitude to have found love again with each other. They'd slept in until almost nine o'clock Christmas morning, waking up to Merry Christmas text messages from their kids hunkered down all across the country, waiting for travel conditions to improve.

Breanna, Liam, and her grandsons had sent a picture of all of them blowing her a Christmas kiss from a hotel in Chicago, probably. Eight major airports had suspended all flights until further notice, and the Department of Transportation was begging people to stay off the roads until December 26. Sadie was behind on making the food for the dinner anyway, so it was alright that things had been pushed back as long as she knew everyone was safe.

The kettle on the stove whistled, and Sadie turned away from the window to pour herself and Pete a stiff mug of cocoa—mint, to keep things snappy.

Sadie stirred until the cocoa was smooth and rich, then plopped a snowman-shaped marshmallow on top. With a mug in each hand, she headed for the living room, where Pete was smiling while texting on his phone.

Pete put his phone aside in order to take the mug she held out. "Thanks," he said.

"You're welcome." She sat next to him on the love seat, and they stared into the fire and sipped their cocoa in wonderful companionship. "The cake is finished. Should we have it after dinner? I forgot to pick up the clams for the cioppino, but I have everything else, and I think it will still turn out. We just have to be committed to eat a ton even if I only make half a batch. It doesn't keep well, you know."

"I was thinking that maybe we should take that cake to the new neighbors," Pete said, completely derailing Sadie's train of thought.

She turned and faced him. "Give it away? I made it special for you."

"And I appreciate it very much, but we will hate ourselves tomorrow if we eat a whole cake today. I'll help you make the next one for the family party."

Sadie dug for an additional excuse. She didn't feel ready to meet the people who had moved in and might change Mary's house into something modern and . . . not her. "It's eleven o'clock in the morning on Christmas Day. Hardly the best time to meet new neighbors."

Pete leaned forward and put his mug—still half full—on the coffee table with a resounding thud as though he were in a pub. He took hers out of her hand and put it down as well before standing. "Ah, come on—what else do we have to do today?" He reached a hand down to her, and when she took it, he pulled her smartly to her feet, then kissed the tip of her nose, which made her smile despite her confusion. She was usually the one pulling him around to anything remotely social. "Besides, we want to get over there before the storm gets worse."

Sadie gave in. "It *would* be a good idea to give them our number as well as the local emergency resources in case the power goes out. They might be from a state that doesn't experience weather like this and therefore be uninformed about the perils."

Pete grinned. "See, it's thinking that way that keeps you on the nice list year after year, Sadie."

Five minutes later, they crossed the street in their boots and coats and hats and gloves, Pete holding Sadie's arm with one hand and the cake set on a glass plate with his other. So help her, if he dropped that cake . . .

Under the snow was a perilous sheet of ice that made Sadie even more grateful that none of their kids were driving right now. What a relief that the new neighbors had shoveled Mary's walks—and recently too. There was only the slightest dusting of snow on the sidewalk leading to the front door. Sadie *was* glad there would be new people to love this house, but she didn't know if she'd ever think of it as anything other than Mary's.

They were halfway up the walk when the Christmas lights strung along the eves suddenly turned on. It was nearly noon, but the lights were bright amid the falling snow, and Sadie pulled Pete to a stop. That the lights had turned on so suddenly felt strange. Were they on a motion sensor? She looked from the lights to the number of cars covered in snow in the driveway and began pulling Pete back the way they'd come.

"They have company," Sadie said, wishing she'd thought of that excuse before they'd left the house. "We don't want to interrupt the party."

"If they're having a party, they might appreciate another dessert," Pete said, moving forward again and squeezing his arm close against his side so that her hand was trapped and she was forced to walk with him.

"Pete," she said, firmer. "This is a really bad idea. We'll just come back a diff—"

A chorus of voices began singing "We Wish You a Merry Christmas," which happened to be one of Sadie's favorite Christmas songs. She'd taught it to her second-graders every year back when she'd been teaching full-time. Sadie planted her feet and pulled her arm out of Pete's grasp, refusing to be dragged—literally—into someone else's family party.

"There is no way I'm going to interrupt Christmas carols, Peter Cunningham." She put her gloved hands on her hips to further make her point as Pete turned to look at her. He held the cake plate with both hands now that he wasn't holding on to her.

"Come on," Pete said, a laugh in his voice that only further ignited her stubbornness. "We're almost there. We'll just knock and see what happens."

"See what happens? This isn't right."

He looked at her, still grinning, and then, of all things, winked at her! "Suit yourself." He turned toward the front door, leaving Sadie standing on the sidewalk halfway between the street and the house. He was going to deliver the cake to the new neighbors without her? Well, that wouldn't do. They'd give him all the credit.

She tried to catch up without slipping on the shoveled, but still slick, walkway. The front door opened, and she felt heat flush through her cheeks when the singing got louder. Pete hadn't even waited for them to finish the verse!

There was nothing to do but make the best of an awkward situation, so Sadie planted a smile on her face and promised herself that she would apologize to them later, when they knew her and Pete well enough to understand how out of character this was for them. Sadie made eye contact with the man in the doorway and froze like Frosty himself.

"Shawn?" she said in disbelief. She swung her eyes from her mountain of a son to the woman standing beside him in the doorway. "Breanna?"

Sadie's children, still singing, beamed back at her and then stepped onto the porch. Rather than coming to her, they moved to the sides so that the other people inside the house could come out and fill up Mary's long porch.

Liam had Phillip on his hip and Eddie by the hand. Maggie followed Shawn, and behind them came Pete's son, Jared, his wife, Heather, and their three children, including Fig, who waved at Sadie excitedly even though he was ten years old now; they'd always had a special bond. Pete's daughters, Brooke and Michelle, along with their husbands and children, came out, too.

Soon every one of Pete and Sadie's children and grandchildren filled the wide porch where Mary and Sadie used to sit and crochet together while they solved all the world's problems. Bringing up the rear was Jack, Sadie's brother, his son, Trevor, now a teenager, and Gayle.

"I . . . I . . . What?" Sadie fumbled for words when the singing stopped.

They all laughed as Sadie looked from one sweet face to another. Minnie, Jared's three-year-old daughter, broke from the crowd first and ran down the steps to Sadie, hugging her tight around the legs. Eddie followed his step-cousin's lead and soon all the grandchildren were giving Grandma Sadie hugs. Sadie laughed through her tears and hugged each of them back.

"I think you pulled off the surprise, Pete," Jack said with a laugh.

Sadie looked from her brother to her triumphantly grinning husband.

"I don't understand," she said, wiping at her tears. Her family was all here. Ahead of the storm she thought was going to ruin everything. In Mary's house. Is this where Breanna and Liam had taken the family photo they'd sent this morning? When Sadie got back to her phone, she would look at the background more closely.

"I talked to Mary as soon as she said she was going to sell," Pete said. "She absolutely loved the idea."

"We can't afford it," Sadie said, remembering late-night conversations over the last few years about getting a bigger place. It always came down to the fact that the town house had plenty of space for the two of them, and it didn't make sense to buy something bigger when they didn't need the space very often.

"Fort Collins is woefully lacking in large-capacity rentals capable of accommodating family reunions and other group events," Liam said, drawing Sadie's attention. "It was a worthwhile investment on our part and will pay for itself if we can rent it out for sixty nights of the year. Projections deem that a conservative estimate." His British accent was more pronounced now that he was living in jolly ol' England most of the time.

It took Sadie a few moments to catch up with what he'd said. "Rental? *You* bought this?"

Breanna explained. "You've done such a great job managing our cabin in the months we're not in the country, we didn't think you would mind managing another house that our families could use when we need the space. We'll call it 'Mary's Place,' a cozy home away from home for you and all you hold dear."

Sadie was trying to keep up but felt like she needed to call a time-out so everything could download in her mind. Preferably in list form.

"The girls have been helping me get it ready for weeks now," Pete said, smiling at his daughters. "We didn't do much remodeling—other than some new carpet—but we've spruced everything up and made sure things were in working order. We coordinated the furniture deliveries and workers around your schedule, which, thanks to your wonderful planning skills, is color coded on our household calendar.

"Jack and Trevor did a lot of the painting over Thanksgiving when we were in New Mexico, and the out-of-town kids have been trickling in the last few days to help with the final details while I was finishing up in Arizona. A lot of the furniture is Mary's—things her family didn't want—and each bedroom has a queen bed; most of them have a bunk bed, too. We put a bunch of bunks in the downstairs family room. You can sleep almost forty people in Mary's Place, Sadie—isn't that something?"

"Forty," Sadie breathed.

"Maggie and I are going to be contributors to the occupancy limits," Shawn said. "A birth mother picked us two weeks ago. She's due in February—a little girl." He gave Maggie a side hug, and she leaned into his embrace.

Sadie's chin began to tremble. Mary's Place and a granddaughter?

"We'll be adding one more, too," Jared's wife, Heather, added, a hand on her rounded belly Sadie hadn't noticed.

Sadie put her hands over her face to cover the full-on ugly cry she could not hold back anymore. She felt Pete's arm snake around her shoulders, turning her into him.

"We'll see you guys inside," Brooke said. "The cioppino is

almost ready. I just need Sadie to make sure I got the spices right. Dad, I'll take Mom's cake. It looks perfect!"

When the door closed behind the last of her family members, Sadie gave in and sobbed into the front of Pete's coat, her tears freezing even as they fell. After nearly a minute, she lifted her face and looked up at him. "I can't believe this," she whispered.

"You *have* to believe, Sadie, or Santa doesn't bring you any presents."

"All this coordination, and I never suspected a thing."

"It wasn't easy," he said, his smile softening as he wiped at her freezing tears with one of his gloved hands. "But do you remember what you've said each time I asked what you wanted for Christmas?"

"Everyone I loved in the same room together," Sadie whispered, fresh tears springing up with the recollection. Were his eyes a little glassy, too?

"I know there is nothing more precious to you than our families, Sadie, and I have watched you do everything you can to forge strong relationships with each one of them. Merry Christmas." He leaned down to seal the best gift ever with a kiss that chased away the winter chill. "You taught me to believe in miracles, Sadie. I don't have the words to describe what it was like to be part of one for you."

Cioppino

1 teaspoon minced garlic
3 tablespoons minced onion
1 teaspoon oregano
1 teaspoon red pepper flakes

1 ½ teaspoon salt
1 ½ teaspoon pepper
¼ cup olive oil
2 tablespoons tomato paste
1 ½ cup dry red wine, cooking (beef consommé can be used in place)
1 (28- to 32-ounce) can crushed tomatoes
2 cups chicken broth
18 small clams or mussels (optional)
1 pound any white fish, cut into 1-inch pieces, lightly salted
1 pound shrimp, raw and shelled, lightly salted
1 pound scallops, lightly salted
1 (6-ounce) can crab meat

Combine garlic, onion, oregano, red pepper flakes, salt, pepper, and olive oil in a large soup pot over medium heat. Sauté for 5 minutes, stirring constantly.

Add tomato paste and red wine. Bring to a boil; boil for 6 minutes, stirring constantly.

Add crushed tomatoes and chicken broth. Bring to a boil. Reduce heat and simmer on low for 30 minutes, covered, stirring every few minutes.

If adding clams, boil clams 10 minutes, uncovered, and then remove from pot with slotted spoon. If any shells are unopened, discard. Set opened shells aside.

Add white fish, shrimp, scallops, and crab meat. Simmer, covered, for 10 minutes, stirring every few minutes. Add cooked clams. Serve immediately. Garnish with parsley or basil.

Serves 12.

Note: Reheat on stove, not microwave, and only until heated through. Shrimp and clams get rubbery when overcooked.

Epilogue

Sadie and Pete enjoyed every minute of the days their families were in town, but did not complain when they dropped into bed exhausted the night they had all finally left. It had been a magical holiday season, but Sadie was reminded that part of the magic was because it didn't last forever.

On December 31, Mary slipped—light as a feather—from this life to the next. Five days later, she was laid to rest next to Doral and their sons. It was a lovely service and a fitting tribute to a woman who had lived a simple, quiet life, and yet had made a lasting impact on the lives of so many.

Afterward, everyone came back to Mary's Place for a luncheon that Sadie, Brooke, Michelle, Carol, and Harry had spent two days getting ready. Harry, as it turned out, was an excellent cook and a remarkably good director of nursing too. Ivy felt sure Nicholas House would offer him the position. Corporate had approved Carol's excellent assessment as soon as things had settled; once her license was reinstated, she'd been offered a full-time nursing position at Nicholas House. The Snow Flurry cookies were everyone's favorite item on the buffet as they gathered to share memories of receiving them from Mary at Christmas for so many years.

Sadie smiled every time she saw Mary's wedding ring on Joy's finger during the luncheon. On Christmas Day, after Joy had told Mary all the things she hadn't told her before, Mary had slipped the ring to Frank for when he was ready, which had turned out to be the day before Mary passed away.

Joy hadn't talked about selling the ornaments yet, but the ones Jackie had sold on eBay had been returned so the collection was complete. Carol had offered to help sell them on eBay if they preferred to take that route, while Jedidiah Marley had renewed his interest in purchasing the entire collection. He didn't know yet that the buyer he had on file, Gayle, didn't know anything about the ornaments, but there had been a great deal going on, and Sadie would get that ironed out eventually. The funeral had only been a week ago.

"Well, I think that's it," Pete said, standing up from the computer desk and stretching his arms over his head with a satisfying groan. The cold case he'd been working for months had been solved, and he'd just sent off the final report. That meant they would have a month or so before he took on the next case. Maybe they'd see if the Baileys were up for a trip to San Diego. Sadie wasn't sure she remembered what it felt like to have the sun warm her face. Sadie gave Pete a celebratory kiss.

"Well done," she said proudly.

He draped his arms around her hips and waggled his eyebrows. "What do I get for finishing?"

"Other than my heartfelt congratulations?" she asked, innocently. "I can make you a sandwich."

He pulled her tightly to him and was nuzzling her neck when the doorbell rang.

"Impeccable timing," he grumbled as Sadie wriggled away and hurried toward the door. Sadie was laughing when she pulled the door open, then sobered quickly as she stared at the blue tub with her and Pete's names on it. She'd seen it before in Mary's storage unit. Her eyes moved from the tub to the person holding it.

"Hi, Frank," she said, opening the door wide enough to let him in.

"I'm just dropping it off," he said, coming in and putting the tub in the entryway. "I promised Joy we'd get the storage unit cleared out before Ivy has to make another payment from what's left in the estate." He was already on his way out, but waved over his shoulder when he saw Pete. "Hey, Mr. C."

"Hey, Frank," Pete returned.

Frank waved again and then jumped into the passenger seat of Joy's car. Joy waved from the driver's seat, and Sadie and Pete waved back until the car had pulled away from the curb.

"I'm not sure I like being called 'Mr. C.' It sounds so gangster."

"I believe the correct term is 'gang-stah,'" Sadie said. "And it's a sign of affection for him to talk to you like a homeboy."

Pete laughed as Sadie closed the door, then they both turned to the tub Sadie was hesitant to open.

"I guess this is our inheritance," Pete said, looking from the tub to Sadie and back again.

Sadie took a breath and knelt down so she could pull off the lid. A layer of tissue paper covered everything except a note written on pink paper lying on top. The paper had embossed lines, almost impossible to see, that helped guide Mary's hand so she could still write letters, though sometimes the handwriting was hard to read. The handwriting wasn't the problem in this case, though. Sadie's tears prevented her from getting past "Dear Sadie and Pete."

Pete left the room, quickly returning with a box of tissues. After half a dozen attempts of Sadie trying to read the note, Pete took the paper from her hands, lowered himself to the floor beside her, and cleared his throat.

Dear Sadie and Pete,

Watching you two together always did my heart good, and I decided to leave you the quilt that Sadie helped me make a few years ago—the last quilt I ever completed. The pattern is one of my favorites, X's and O's, and one I made for each of my children when they married. I hope that as you lie beneath it, you remember how much I love you both, how grateful I am to have known you, and that I wish you all the love and happiness you can possibly find. You have been a balm to me these last years.

If I can leave you with a bit of advice, it is to never stop living and growing and learning, both together and separately. Life comes with only one guarantee—it will not last forever. Embrace every day and know that there is never a shadow so dark that some joy can't find its way through if you let it. Like a quilt, life comes together one piece at a time, and it takes some patience before you can stand back and proclaim it a masterpiece.

All my love,

Mary

Cunningham Candy Cane Cake

Chocolate Cake
2 cups flour
2 cups sugar
¾ cup cocoa powder
2 teaspoon baking soda
1 teaspoon salt
2 large eggs
1 cup buttermilk
1 cup vegetable oil
1 teaspoon vanilla
1 cup boiling water

Frosting
1½ cups salted butter
1½ cups vegetable shortening
10 to 11 cups powdered sugar, divided
1 tablespoon peppermint extract
¾ cup water or milk, divided
red food coloring
¾ cup cocoa

Chocolate Ganache
1 (6-ounce) bag semisweet chocolate chips
½ cup heavy whipping cream

Additional Ingredients
2 to 3 candy canes, chopped

To make the chocolate cake layers

Prepare three 8-inch cake pans with parchment paper circles in the bottom, and grease the sides. Preheat oven to 300 degrees F.

Add all dry ingredients to a large bowl and combine. Add eggs, buttermilk, vegetable oil, and vanilla to the dry ingredients and mix well.

Slowly add water (use a ladle to make sure batter doesn't splash as water is added). Mix well.

Divide batter evenly between cake pans and bake for 30 to 33 minutes, or until a toothpick comes out with a few crumbs. Remove cakes from oven and allow to cool in the pans for 10 minutes. Remove cakes from pans and set on cooling racks to cool completely.

To make the icing

In a large bowl, beat together butter and shortening until smooth. Slowly add 4 cups (1 pound) powdered sugar. Mix until smooth. Add peppermint extract and ½ cup of milk or water. Mix until smooth.

Add another 4 cups (1 pound) powdered sugar and mix until smooth. Add additional powdered sugar until proper consistency is reached. Add remaining ¼ cup of water or milk and mix until smooth.

Remove 1 ½ cups of icing and dye it red with red food coloring.

To assemble the cake

When the cakes are cool, remove the tops of the cakes with a large serrated knife so they are flat. Place the first layer of cake on serving plate. Spread the red icing into an even layer on top of the cake.

Place the second layer of cake on top of the red icing and spread with white frosting.

Top cake with third layer of cake.

Add cocoa to remaining icing, and mix until well combined. (You may need to add another 2 to 3 tablespoons of water or milk to get the icing to a nice, spreadable consistency.)

Frost the outside of the cake with the chocolate buttercream.

To make the ganache

Note: Don't make until cake is frosted. The ganache sets up fast.

Place chocolate chips in a medium-sized bowl. In a separate bowl, microwave heavy cream until it just begins to boil.

Pour heated cream over chocolate chips and cover bowl with clear wrap. Allow to sit for 5 to 7 minutes, then whisk until smooth.

Pour ganache on top of the cake, then use an offset spatula to spread it to the outer edges of the cake, pushing it over the edges in some spots to make drips of ganache down the sides.

Top the cake with chopped candy canes. Allow ganache to set, then refrigerate cake until ready to serve.

Acknowledgments

It was so much fun to revisit Sadie in this story. I'm grateful that Shadow Mountain supported the idea and, specifically, Lisa Mangum, who took the time to help me plot it out. Thanks to Heidi Taylor Gordon, Chris Schoebinger, Richard Erickson, and Malina Grigg for making it happen. Thanks to Lane Heymont for taking care of the business aspects and always championing my work, and to Becki Nelson for her help in keeping the facts consistent with the rest of the series. Jenny Proctor (*Wrong for You*, Covenant Communications 2017) was an excellent beta reader for this story—thank you so much for everything.

Big thanks to Jennifer Moore (*Charlotte's Promise*, Covenant 2019) and Nancy Campbell Allen (*The Lady in the Coppergate Tower*, Shadow Mountain 2019) for the brainstorming and cheerleading, and the Test Kitchen Bakers who jumped on board for another book: Danyelle Ferguson (*Origami Girl*, Wonderstruck Books 2019), Annie Funk, Laree Ipson, Whit Larson, Sandra Sorenson, Lisa Swinton (*Love in Bloom*, Amazon 2019), and Katie Wilson for all their incredible help with the recipes.

Thank you to the ladies who let me use their recipes for this book: Kathrine Faust of Faustbakes.com for Cinnamon Pie, Krista Jensen for Orange Cranberry Bread, Annie Funk for Soup in a Jar, Crystal White for Cunningham Cheeseball, and Danyelle Ferguson for Christmas Ham.

My family, as always, are priceless to me, and big thanks to my wonderful readers—to whom this book is dedicated.

Most of all, thank you to my Father in Heaven for the many gifts I have received at His hand. I am blessed.

About the Author

Josi S. Kilpack is an accomplished and prolific author of nearly two dozen novels including the Sadie Hoffmiller Culinary Mystery Series. She has won multiple Whitney Awards for Mystery/Suspense, Romance, and Novel of the Year as well as the Utah Best of State Fiction Winner. She lives with her family in Utah.

It'd be a crime to miss
the rest of the series . . .

ISBN 978-1-60641-050-9

ISBN 978-1-60641-121-6

ISBN 978-1-60641-232-9

ISBN 978-1-60908-903-0

ISBN 978-1-60907-170-7

ISBN 978-1-60907-328-2

by Josi S. Kilpack

ISBN 978-1-60641-813-0

ISBN 978-1-60641-941-0

ISBN 978-1-60908-745-6

ISBN 978-1-60907-593-4

ISBN 978-1-60907-787-7

ISBN 978-1-60908-745-6

Available online and at a bookstore near you.
www.shadowmountain.com • www.josiskilpack.com
Available on audio.

SHADOW
MOUNTAIN

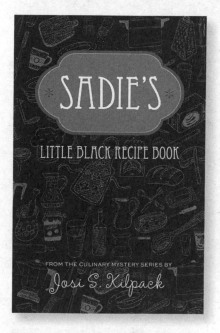